MISSING
PERSONS
And Other Essays

BOOKS BY HEINRICH BÖLL

Acquainted with the Night
Adam, Where Art Thou?
The Train Was on Time
Tomorrow and Yesterday
Billiards at Half-past Nine
The Clown
Absent Without Leave
18 Stories
Irish Journal
End of a Mission
Children Are Civilians Too
Adam and The Train
Group Portrait with Lady
The Lost Honor of Katharina Blum
The Bread of Those Early Years
Missing Persons and Other Essays

MISSING PERSONS
And Other Essays

HEINRICH BÖLL

Translated from the German by

LEILA VENNEWITZ

McGRAW-HILL BOOK COMPANY

New York   St. Louis   San Francisco

Düsseldorf   Mexico   Toronto

Book design by Stanley Drate.

1 2 3 4 5 6 7 8 9 0   BPBP   7 8 3 2 1 0 9 8 7

Library of Congress Cataloging in Publication Data

Böll, Heinrich, 1917–
        Missing persons and other essays.
        I.   Title.
PT2603.0394A28   833′.9′14   77-9351
ISBN 0-07-006424-5

TRANSLATOR'S
ACKNOWLEDGMENT

The selection of these works from among the whole of Heinrich Böll's nonfiction oeuvre was made by the translator in collaboration with the author.

My thanks are due to Professor Bogdan Czaykowski, Head of the Department of Slavonic Studies at the University of British Columbia, for so generously providing his own English translations of certain passages in *Cancer Ward* directly from Russian-language editions of Alexander Solzhenitsyn's novel.

I also wish to express my deep gratitude to my husband, William Vennewitz, for the unstinting help and advice he has given me throughout the work of this translation.

LEILA VENNEWITZ

Contents

REVIEWS

MISCELLANY

ESSAYS

MISSING PERSONS

(1971)

I am looking for a girl, ten years old, probably pale, with dark hair and very large, rather melancholy dark eyes. I have reason to suppose that she is beautiful. I know her date of birth, her place of birth, the places of her childhood and youth: Düren, Heinsberg, probably Palenberg, Aachen. I am looking for the girl in a certain year, the year 1887. She is walking along the road between Düren and Golzheim, whether toward Golzheim or coming from Golzheim I don't know. If she is walking toward Golzheim she is carrying an empty washbasin; if she is coming from Golzheim she is carrying a washbasin full of turnip tops. The distance between Düren and Golzheim is four and a half miles, which means the little girl will be covering a total distance of nine miles. I don't know how long it takes a ten-year-old girl to walk that far, on a road which may or may not already have been treeless. Shall we allow her a minimum of three, a maximum of six hours? Shall we also allow her now and again to put down the empty basin or the full one to rest her arms? I don't know how many pounds of turnip tops she was fetching from relatives or friends, or whether the turnip tops were a gift or merely a bargain. Three hours? Four or six? Eight pounds, ten or seven? I don't know. Nor do I know how much money was saved by this exercise. Ten pfennigs? Thirty, or only seven? I don't know. The girl is walking along, and I am looking for her. Her name is Maria and a few decades later she became my mother. That doesn't interest me, I know some things about my mother, about the girl I know nothing.

Eighty-five years later I drive fairly often through Golzheim, approaching Golzheim fast, through Golzheim sometimes faster than permitted, beyond Golzheim again comparatively fast. In my car. Let us assume I am driving at sixty miles an hour. For the four and a half miles I need four or at most six minutes, depending on how many farm vehicles happen to be on the road, on how easily I can pass them, the state of oncoming traffic. But in any event I never need more than six minutes. Were I to keep driving the whole time the girl is walking along the road, in three hours I would be somewhere near Darmstadt, in six somewhere between Augsburg and Munich, while the girl is still walking. And how often did the little girl do this walk? Once? Several times, year after year? What were the people called from whom she fetched the turnip tops so as to save seven or thirty pfennigs?

These are all things I don't know. Does the girl, eighty-five years later, see cars driving along this same road, and in one of these cars one of her sons? Does she see me? I don't see her, although I keep looking out for her. I know nothing about her, not much anyway. She has a strict mother, five sisters, two brothers, an—to put it mildly— irresponsible father who—to put it mildly—likes his drink. How much is a glass of beer, how much a brandy? Certainly more than the ten-year-old girl saves by walking from three to six hours with the empty basin and the full one. I would love to talk to her, try to question her, find out what she is thinking. From two or three photos I know the bitter, sour face of the girl's mother. I know a few stories about her. She was the classic cheated ward of the penny dreadful, cheated out of land, houses and, according to another version, a brewery. One can still tell from the bitter face that she used to be beautiful. The classic ward with the classic face. Catholic with a strong streak of Jansenism. Joyless, puritanical, zealous churchgoer, embittered.

I would love to talk to the little girl walking along the road. Not to my mother, I have often talked to her, but never to the ten-year-old girl. What is she thinking about, what is she feeling, what does she know, what does she admit to herself, what does she hide from herself and from others? What does she think about her—to put it mildly—irresponsible father, who in the space of two minutes drinks up more money than she "earns" or merely saves by walking those three or six hours? Eighty-five years later I would like to take the chronology apart, mix it up, so as to talk to the girl. I would give her a ride, but perhaps she would rather stay on the road than return to her bitter, sour mother, who has to scrimp and save because of someone who wastes money? There would be plenty to talk about, the five sisters and the two brothers, the—to put it mildly—irresponsible, indulged father, appearances that are kept up, appearances that are breaking down. That doesn't interest me. I am looking for the little girl who many years later will be my mother.

What I might think, imagine, conclude, even research doesn't interest me because I know how it is done. Well. Badly. Not so badly. Not so well. With a fair, a certain, a positive degree of likelihood. With a few interpolations, of this kind or that. Literature. That's not what I am looking for, I am looking for a ten-year-old girl of whom I know nothing. Eighty-five years later I drive along the same road, and I don't see her, don't hear her, know nothing about her. I can imagine a lot of things, almost everything, but—as I have said—that doesn't interest me. I am looking for a ten-year-old girl, pale, with dark, rather melancholy eyes which, surprisingly enough, are full of humor.

I am not looking for her memory, the memory of her, I am looking for the girl herself.

I am looking for a thin, freckled, ten-year-old boy, probably red-haired, who in the year 1880 was walking from Schwanenkamp Street in Essen on his way to school. His name is Victor, and many years later he will be my father. I know some things about my father, about this ten-year-old boy I know nothing. I know a few stories, I know a few of his memories and the memories of other people about him, but the boy himself I don't know. I would love to destroy the chronology, have him in front of me, alive, for a few minutes before his conventional and unconventional memories get caught up in the wheels of anecdotal convention. I would like to see his slate or his copybooks, his sandwiches, his handkerchief, would like to see whether he was already wearing glasses. Some things have been handed down, authenticated in a few variations, much could be researched, construed, interpreted, imagined, and with a fair, a certain, or even a positive degree of likelihood a genre picture could be created of the thin, probably red-haired boy walking along by the wall of the Krupp factory on his way to school. The surroundings are familiar to me, and enough of the details, but I am not after the memories of the boy or the memories of other people about him, I want the boy himself, want to look him in the eye, see his handkerchief, his sandwiches, his copybooks or his slate. The boy's name is Victor, in 1880 he is ten years old, and one day he will be my father.

I am looking for myself, aged ten, riding to school on my bicycle. Not my memory, not what others think they remember. I am looking for my wife, aged ten, my children, friends, brothers and sisters. I would like to destroy that damned chronology, see one of them in 1923, the other in 1935 or 1917, on the way to school, playing on the street, in church, in the confessional. I would like to listen in on the confessions of all these ten-year-olds; I can imagine many things, almost everything: one of those ten-year-old boys on a rubble site in 1957, the other aged ten in the yard of a boys' school in 1958, another aged ten in a park in 1960. Many stories are told, many people remember many things, there are snapshots, various perspectives, interpretations, details of surroundings, it is all there, school reports, service records, prayer books, children's drawings, letters, even diary pages; it could all be used, fleshed out, imagined with a fair, an approximate, a virtually positive degree of likelihood. I would like more: I would like to see the moisture in their eyes, hold my hand to their mouths to feel their breath, see the bread bitten into by one, the apple bitten into by another, in 1930 or 1935; the ball in the hand, the chalk line on the paving; the pattern on the washbasin used by Maria to carry the turnip tops, and the shoes of the thin, ten-year-old freckled boy, probably red-haired, whose name was Victor.

It is not the permanent I am after but the present that has become the past. Not what is told, not even what is true, and certainly not what is eternal. I want the present of those who belong to the past. To get on and off, wherever I like; the skipping rope of Leipzig Square, and the sandwiches eaten in the schoolyard on Machabäer Street; chalk lines on the sidewalk of Teutoburg Street, sawdust in the courtyard of the building on Schwanenkamp Street; the beer spilled on the paving of Pletzer Lane, brought home in a pitcher to persuade the old man to stay home for a change; the marbles from Kreuznach Street. The apple bitten into by one girl in 1940 or the other apple picked by another girl in 1935. Not as a souvenir, not as a vehicle for an anecdote, not as a fetish to keep behind glass: no, because it was there, no longer exists, and will never exist again. I want the one hair of the head that has fallen to the ground.

NUMBER SEVEN,
HÜLCHRATHER STREET

(1971)

Many people, of course, may wonder why anyone would move back to these city canyons after living for twenty-five years in a green and pleasant suburb with nothing to prevent him from continuing to do so. Perhaps our only reason for moving was to get rid of the irksome demands of a lawn forever crying out for attention and to escape the noise of the motor mowers, the dream of an English lawn—as unattainable as the dream of Swiss-style democracy.

Here, here it is quiet, quieter than in the remotest village where a tractor is sure to be droning, youths are trying out their mopeds, where city folk are tirelessly cutting their weekend lawns; here it is not necessary—as we found so often out there—to cut back every rambling shrub and cut it back again until it has been reduced to a mere stump.

Here the front yards plainly reveal their true nature: poor little strips squeezed between cars and house fronts, not even available to the children as a playground.

Most of this part of town was built in the period following 1890, the years of the first land speculation; art nouveau façades, street names recalling victories of the

Franco-Prussian War of only twenty years earlier and still ringing in the ear: Sedan, Wörth, Belfort, Weissenburg; an era of self-confidence that boldly adopted the fledgling art nouveau style in any of its forms that could be vulgarized, a period that developed a notable addiction to long-haired women smiling wistfully from over front doors or propping up balconies with melancholy expertise. It is on such streets, in such apartments, that we both grew up, both played; it is from such houses that we went to school —until the Fatherland called one of us to faraway places while the other stayed behind, in the same kind of house, the same kind of apartment. It is the return to the city, to urban life, to a more than rural quiet that lies hidden behind the façades in vast courtyards broken up by walls and roof gardens; the return from an illusory individuality, from what is in fact the standardized weekend activity of the garden-suburb, to anonymity, or should one say: urbanity?

True, here we have to share the scanty sidewalks—half of them preempted by parked cars—with the dogs, which perforce, or by force of circumstance, do little (and that unconcernedly), to improve the amenities; they are *allowed* to, they are allowed to do it where kids play and baby buggies are parked; they are *allowed* to—in fact they *have* to. But should a dog be *allowed* to *have* to do it everywhere? The results are appalling—when will town planners finally be inspired to erect dog toilets? Or should dog-owners be obliged to remove what dogs *have* to do?

And then, hardly more than a stone's throw away, to be viewed free, gratis and for nothing, is yet another, possibly the decisive, reason for moving: the Rhine. For by this almost fifteen years we lived too far away from it, the Rhine being no more than an excursion point. In its permanent impermanence, it says nothing, yet speaks for itself; it is more soothing than the lawnmower concert; and since its water has become too dirty to wash the car with, it remains completely untouched by weekend mechanical chores, no longer disturbed by bucket, hose, and sponge in its polluted majesty. Of course it is old, yet it undergoes, constantly, daily, a total renewal, in contrast to the institutions that dominate its banks.

The kids are on the street at a different time from the dogs; every day they enter upon their inheritance, so to speak, and play in their legacy. There is not much room, what with cars parked on both sides and the ban on entering the front yards, although this still can be done. So they are left with the narrow sidewalks between parked cars and front yards, with the doorways, and not even the gutters, where there might be room for a game of marbles, are available. Here many an "In our day ... !" is warranted, and many a "When our kids were little ... !" When all is said and done, our children did still have such irreplaceable playgrounds as the postwar bomb-sites, hard as these might be to reproduce artificially. There was scarcely a car on the streets, very occasionally a dog, and the rubble sites allowed the free flowering of such contradictory (or complementary) play instincts as destruction and construction. Around 1950 at least, the sites were densely overgrown—rubble parks, in fact, yet in those days many people felt sorry for the rubble children, who were in fact not all that pitiable. Children at play, even in villages, are always in danger, and some of us have long been aware that in the dark, when the children are asleep, those famous sandboxes, of which there may be one for every few thousand children, serve as handy toilets for several hundred dogs. Not only the street—half the sidewalk is owned by the cars, but of course the whole problem will solve itself in the course of time by a declining birth rate. Then at last cars, grown-ups, and dogs will have the place to themselves. Then there will be no more trouble over the front yards, they will all look like stage sets for Beckett plays.

Is it any wonder that the children's favorite pastime is shooting—the imitated or mechanically reproduced rattling and sawing of machine pistols? Banging, howling—would it be any wonder if their aggressiveness were one day to turn against their rivals, the cars, which deprive them of their play space and block their gutters? When will full-scale scraping and scrawling begin? They are good children, in spite of their yelling and shooting: they rarely damage that great taboo, the automobile, and when they do, it is not deliberate.

The dominating feature of the area is the great palace with its long façade, an attraction for many visitors since it is the residence of the great blindfolded lady. She it is who adjudges marriages, divorces, settles quarrels with landlord or neighbors, libel suits, property disputes. It would be unfair to say that the lady in her palace was unproductive; one thing we *know* is produced in her realm: dust, that special dust that collects in and on files. The lady assigns numbers and dates, examines witnesses, plaintiffs, defendants; her clients, those petitioning for their rights and seeking justice, quaking with impatience at approaching deadlines, circle city blocks trying to find a space, and when they can't they simply park in a No Parking zone, or even park in a No Stopping zone; harassed attorneys, hastily pulling on their gowns, entering the palace with briefs and briefcases for their hearings—the scene of many a swift transformation, the visible doorkeepers smile a welcome, the invisible doorkeepers, I assume, smile not in disdain but in sadness, perhaps be-

cause they suspect that this is the domain of eternal misunderstanding: misunderstanding of the various kinds of
wording that are forever in collision: the wording of those
in the know and those in agreement colliding with that of
those others who cannot and will not grasp that written,
spoken law has a wording that is foreign to their efforts
to obtain justice. There in that labyrinth, what had seemed
clear becomes unclear; written, spoken, interpreted, defined law has a different dimension from that desire for
justice which assumes things to be self-evident that apparently are not self-evident. Where the law had seemed
so clear, now, in a different wording, it becomes unclear,
there is friction, even ruction; a seemingly inevitable up-
heaval of words inexorably precipitated into files, attrac-
ting dust that is carried from archives into corridors, from
corridors into courtroom and, augmented by many words,
from courtroom into corridors, from corridors back into
archives.

The school in the neighboring courtyard saves us the
need for an alarm clock, provided we don't want to get
up before seven thirty; the slow, steady swell of children's
voices, not yet with the high spirits of recess, still subdued:
not an unpleasant alarm clock. The ten o'clock break saves
us looking at the clock, and anyone not yet awake must
surely be so now. The vehemence of short-lived liberation
fills the courtyard; a half-time din that increases in the
midday break because the end is in sight. The distance
from our bedroom window to the nearest classroom may be
ten or twelve feet; when here and there the windows are
open, in summer or on warm autumn days, it is possible to
lie in bed and join in the lesson, to brush up on our social
science, mathematics, singing. Visiting youngsters insist
on calling across suggestions from the bedroom window,

prompting of course, interfering in the lesson, sometimes joining in the singing. By one fifteen at the latest silence falls, broken not even by radios, transistors, or TV.

Since we no longer have any school-age children, we sometimes oversleep if the alarm doesn't function between seven thirty and seven forty-five, and we realize that vacation has begun, or it's a holiday. Then the silence becomes almost cathedral-like, the empty schoolyard with its tall tree invites meditation: how many children have moved through, moved on from here?

Ever here and gone every instant, Germany's river; a few miles to the north it enters upon its dirtiest, most poisonous stage—and what is the good of reciting the history we are so proud of and which is to be found here in every square yard of turned-up earth: pre-Roman, Roman, Franconian, Merovingian shards and stones? Here —as any child knows—a lot of money is made which elsewhere is despised yet gladly accepted. Strange that in this land, in this city on the Rhine, the weight of history has not impeded progress but rather furthered it. Where the most ancient churches stand, the most modern are being built; where the oldest bridge crossed the Rhine, the most modern one was built. This is not the place to clear up all the misunderstandings about "Rhine" and "Rhenish." At Lake Tegern in Bavaria they may well deride the money that is being earned up here because they are not constantly breathing the air produced by this kind of money-making, are not constantly forced to look at the water made undrinkable by this kind of money-making.

It is very easy for people in Fulda or Rott-on-the-Inn to talk about a "sound world," meaning a sound hegemony, if they are not constantly confronted with the harm done by this hegemony. A river in which people can no longer swim is no longer a river, it is a sewage canal, and even in the mid-fifties it was no longer possible to swim in the Rhine: on the few occasions when we did let our children go in the water, they came out with their shorts yellow with oil.

Such residential areas, where dogs enjoy greater freedom than children, are known as high-density areas. That is a lovely expression. Here the inexorable garbage, more recently known as "consumer garbage," is also of high density; woe to those who don't know when garbage is collected: on Mondays, and when Monday is a holiday it may be Wednesday or Thursday because the schedule has to be adjusted. Needless to say, the garbage cans are also the children's constant playmates; open or modestly covered, they stand where a bit of space has been left for children to play in, in doorways. And of course the garbage men are the longed-for liberators. On Sunday evening the race to the garbage cans begins, paper bags are hastily filled and brought downstairs before the arrival of the garbage truck that promptly causes the inevitable traffic jam. It is wide enough to block the one-way street, to cause those wishing to turn right or left to seethe with impatience, wide enough to plug the intersection, and if, in addition to all this—as sometimes happens—a delivery truck blocks the next one-way street, then the honking starts up, as cheerful as it is senseless. In this way we can, looking down from above, observe these absurdities, and if we go down, the increased pollution of the air in which at this hour pre-school-age children are playing. With their dolls, cars, and pistols, they sit among the containers for the affluence garbage that is removed by cheerful foreigners.

It is Italians, Turks, Greeks, Moroccans who, with care and dignity, deliver the street from the nightmare of a steadily growing avalanche of garbage; seated on extra cartons of garbage, sometimes also on the garbage cans or on doorsteps beneath the wistful art nouveau ladies, they eat their lunch, oblivious to the honking. Where would we be without them? Lost. There is no need to extol their energy and circumspection, the elegance with which they roll the garbage cans past the closely parked cars without ever causing the slightest dent. Most of them come from sunny countries to this fogbound city of the north, to the country through which Siegfried rode on his way to Burgundy, to Worms. Rarely is much money to be made where the sun shines, and there can hardly be much affluence garbage there—most money is made under gray skies, where people probably work out of fear or desperation.

In the evenings, just before eight, just before the news comes on, they are often to be seen at the kiosk, where cigarettes and the local tabloid are available; they are joined by many others from the neighborhood who, just before the TV screens light up, hurriedly need cigarettes, beer, or lemonade. Usually they send their children, who don't understand German too well yet, hold out money, mangle the name of a cigarette brand or murmur "beer" in a variety of Mediterranean or Oriental articulations. Now and again, quite often in fact, some Lonelyheart (man or woman), comes to buy the solace of a bottle of schnapps.

The kiosk is our salvation when we've run out of coffee or cigarettes, or when we have a sudden urge for a thriller. There are candies and chocolates too, of course, and jelly beans and wafers—all the trivia to remind us of our childhood, even a little of village fairs and fairgrounds.

The street has a history, including a social one. I assume that when it was built some seventy years ago judges of the supreme and district courts lived here—no doubt it was considered high class, a good address. Then things changed after 1918 and again after 1945, and there is a new mix. This is what makes the street so pleasant, makes it less isolated than a garden suburb. Now and again we recognize someone coming for the second or third time out of a certain house—and we know: that's where she or he lives, and then when that person gets into the green Volkswagen or the white Renault, we know that's the driver of the green Volkswagen or the white Renault. The cars include luxury models as well as medium-priced and modest ones, the calling cards of the street. Most people, of course, walk or ride streetcars, perhaps bicycles. Anyway it requires less effort and time to take the streetcar into the center of town, or to walk—with the result that many cars, including ours, occupy the gutter for days on end simply because the moment a space opens up the next driver fills it again.

The evening strollers tend to be mostly foreign workers, alone, with their wives, with their wives and children— probably to escape their cramped living quarters at least for an hour or two. To save the cost of a cup of coffee, they stroll about, well scrubbed, with their solemn peasant faces under the cloudy skies, feeling like strangers—so far away from the skies of Portugal or Morocco, so far away from the cafés where a man can play dominoes or billiards. The majority emerge from the rear buildings of the neighboring streets, where they live by the hundreds, and look about them in astonishment in this country where it will take a long time to find out whether it is really unfriendly or just so very foreign; whether the foreignness seems like hostility or the hostility is merely a manifesta-

tion of the foreignness. Our city is no more anti-foreigner
or pro-foreigner than others, and the so-called lack of contact applies not only to foreigners but also to one's own
countrymen.

One day, I imagine, pedestrians will have to be allowed
to walk along the roofs of the creeping cars and thus, step
by step, to overtake the cars. In any event, if we are going
to continue to pump more and more and more cars into
our cities, someone should invent a kind of rugged floor
covering for cartops, and satirists among the cartoonists
might take up the theme, for it would be healthier for
pedestrians to walk on top of the cars rather than beside
them. Perhaps this would even lead to cartops being
adapted as portable children's playgrounds, a sort of moving sidewalk for children, conveyer belts, one into town,
one returning, enabling both children and grown-ups to
move safely and, of course, free of charge, into and out
of town across the roofs of cars. Portable mini swimming
pools, Ping-Pong tables—there is no limit to the imagination; drivers might also be required to carry folding chairs
or benches on their roofs.

Then there would be no more need for this everlasting
urge to burrow that has persisted since 1945, finding and
inventing ever new objects, an urge that will never, ever,
leave us any peace because in 1970 they will build what
should have been built in 1960, and in 1980 will probably be
building what should have been built in 1970—because
now they are building everything that should have been
built back in 1945. The malaise emanating from these
continual and continuous construction sites may arise
from the fact that no one—no matter how progressive he
makes himself out to be or in fact is—actually seems to

believe in the future. Thus all we are doing is catching up with the omissions of the past, and what was omitted in 1960 cannot be caught up with in 1970—the least we should do is build for 1980, and even that, when completed, would be obsolete again by 1982. It is one steady, absurd process of catching up. People who park their cars on streets in heavily populated areas, those neatly dubbed "high-density areas," are familiar with this situation, this dearth of parking space which makes us so inventive that in the long run we realize: at certain hours it is cheaper to leave the car at a car wash than to park yet again in a No Stopping zone. When I need to drive to my filling station I must—since I live at the end of a one-way street which leads into complicated dead ends due to some rather impenetrable subway construction—I must drive around two or three blocks, making a figure-of-eight at least a mile and a half long; but as I usually miss the connection into the second loop of the figure-of-eight and, because of daily changes in detours and new dead ends, end up in relatively far-off suburbs or founder in the dense traffic of the freeway-type bypass which, if I cross it, diverts me into remote one-way streets rendering the way home nostalgically irretrievable—for these reasons I leave it to one of my sons to get gas or have the oil changed.

The desired urbanity has been achieved when, within a radius of two to three minutes, one is within reach of all the stores and all the services: hairdresser and shoe repairs, dry cleaning (essential under these skies with their perpetual rain of dirt), baker, butcher, and grocery store, cigarettes and newspapers, flowers, laundry, pressing, Turkish and Italian food stores—and of course the chrome giant that has everything, displays everything, supplies everything, that great, wide-open, inviting miracle of sales psychology. He, that great chrome giant, is the Lord of Hosts, clean, convenient, smiling—there it all lies, as if it were a gift. Will he swallow all the others? One day repair our shoes, wash and iron our laundry, dry-clean our suits? I hope not, and I believe not, because the shining giant does not match the surrounding architecture. These streets with their inner courtyards and annexes will continue for a while to defy the prescribed structural changes. The great giant is modern, and being modern is meaningless—even villages and small towns are modern, more modern than the cities. The claim that cities are more anti-traditional than rural areas is not true and never has been. The bigger a city, the more old-fashioned aspects, the more backwaters, it retains—as witness Berlin, London, and New York. Cities have more patience, more hiding places—and more need for services, also more tolerance toward the other than brand-new. Urbanity consists in tolerating phenomena that in terms of statistics have long been written off—there can be no urbanity in a rural area.

In our neighborhood the wrecking ball is already wreaking havoc. It is knocking down large, intact apartment houses and private homes, at the behest of that inexorable divinity that is called Profit and demands its sacrifices— and when the wrecking ball has triumphed, they will be building the kind of house that should perhaps have been built in 1951. They will no longer tolerate the shoe repairman, whom the children can still watch, nor the presser— maybe it would have been better to live in 1907, when the ruling class openly displayed itself and its generosity: the family that had then already acquired wealth from real estate, from which other people have since enriched themselves two or three times over, donated a whole church with the dimensions of a cathedral—completely equipped.

And in the year 1951 built in 1972 there will no longer be room for the old-fashioned, for backwaters, for patience and tolerance. Profit and urbanity are mutually incompatible.

WHICH COLOGNE?

(1965)

People probably feel at home only in places where they find shelter and work, acquire friends and neighbors. The history of the place where a person lives is a given quantity; the history of the person is the sum of countless details and experiences that are both indescribable and irretrievable.

I don't think my mouth will ever forget the bitter odor of raw cocoa that enveloped the city block formed by Alteburg Street—Severinswall—Bottmühle—Ubier Ring first thing in the morning when I was on my way to school from the Ubier Ring; and whenever I come upon a Stoll-werck chocolate-bar vending machine in the most remote corner of Germany, it is to me as redolent of home as the lettering "Theodor Kotthoff Paint Co., Cologne-Raderthal," which I noticed on almost every boxcar during the war. As boys we used to play Indians on the slope behind Kotthoff's paint factory. Such childhood associations are inextinguishable; I need not live in my childhood sur-roundings to reencounter them. On the contrary, their intensity is magnified by distance; as the gap narrows we are dismayed by the discrepancy between memory and sentimentality. Seen at close quarters, everything seems stale and embarrassing, as if a painter were to hoard and preserve the apples and pears that had once served as his models for a still life. Obviously we all lose our childhood and youth when we set out to make our way in the world, and the moment we take that step things are no longer "what they used to be."

There are two Colognes that evoke in me memories of "home" in this sense. The first is the prewar Cologne between Raderthal and Chlodwig Square, between Vorgebirg Street and the Rhine, plus the South Bridge and the Poller Meadows. The second is quite different: the destroyed Cologne to which we returned in 1945. Both of these Colognes are the subject of memory—and, of course, of sentimentality.

Neither exists today, and one is left with the anguish that is the lot of every author who tries, sometimes in vain, to retain his footing on the slippery ground between Proust and whatever Ostermann coffee-table book happens to confront him. The fact that the book consists of photographs will save it from being mistaken for a collection of fairy tales, and it is a relief to note that the photographer has abstained from "artistic" gimmicks. The camera has preserved—revived in the memory—that which the eyes of those who were there have forgotten: that second Cologne.

What cannot be made visible but may become palpable is the dust and the silence. Dust, the powder of destruction, penetrated every nook and cranny, settled in books, manuscripts, on diapers, bread, and in the soup; it was wedded to the air, they were united in body and soul; for years, that torment of combating—in defiance of all reason, all hope, like Sisyphus or Hercules—the horrendous quantities of dust produced by a ruined city of the size of Cologne. It clung to eyelashes and eyebrows, stuck between the teeth, in gums and nostrils, in wounds—years and years of struggling against the atomization of immeasurable quantities of stone and mortar. The other was the silence, which was as limitless as the dust; only the fact that it was not total made it credible and bearable. Somewhere in those immeasurably silent nights loose stones would crumble or a gable collapse. The destruction proceeded according to the law of reversed statics, with the dynamics of structures shattered in their very core. It seems that even the static nuclear heart of a building can be fissioned. It was often possible to look on in broad daylight as a gable slowly, almost ritually, collapsed, mortar seams breaking apart, expanding like a net—and a shower of stones came rattling down. The destruction of a great city is never a cut-and-dried process like an operation; it advances like a paralysis, a general crumbling followed by collapse. The spontaneous collapse of a high façade caused neither by blasting nor any other acute force is an unforgettable sight; at some unpredictable, much less calculable, moment this beautifully ordered structure, put together in cheerful confidence and pleasure, gives way. With an almost audible ticking, creaking, it counts down from the date of its creation to zero—like the countdown to zero when a rocket is fired—and gives up the ghost.

It seems strange that the phrase "displaced persons" should always be applied to the eastern part of Germany only. Of course no one in Germany remembers the very first persons to have been "displaced": the émigrés. No doubt the fact that the destruction of the great cities in western Germany resulted in a displacement does not fit the vocabulary of political propaganda. The words "old home" are redolent of melancholy nostalgia, the words "new home" of optimistic nostalgia. The words "migration of

peoples" sound misleading, ambiguous, because the word
"migration" has such an innocent sound. The truth is that
the migration of peoples always meant the ousting of peoples, never once did it take place without force; people
were carried off, taken along, left behind; many who, tech-
nically speaking, became "displaced" have managed to
cope better here than others who, in the same technical
sense, never lost their home.

The Cologne that was destroyed was not the "old
home," it was a second home that has since been lost again.
Cologne seemed to us the proper place to live. I broke out
in a cold sweat when, after World War II, I saw my first
undestroyed city: Heidelberg. In a dual sense, esthetically
and morally, it seemed to me improper, a particularly deplorable form of disaster for the city to have escaped
disaster in this way; I could not get rid of the suspicion
that it had been spared not because it served as a military
hospital town—Dresden was also a hospital town—and
not for a reason that would make any human settlement
worth sparing: because human beings were living there.
The horrible suspicion was that this German dream was
also a tourist dream that owed its world renown mainly to
an operetta.

What was most striking—something to which theologians, philosophers, and psychologists should give more
thought—is that in the air-raid shelters and bunkers of the
large cities there was hardly any expression of anti-
American or anti-British feelings, and that in the destroyed
cities (with the exception of Dresden perhaps, whose fate,
in the very suddenness, the unexpectedness, of the destruction, seems exceptionally senseless) no resentment
against the bomber general staffs remains. This is an extraordinary fact, still neither fully grasped nor explained,
a fact for which there is no natural or rational accounting.

The Germans have not yet revealed the secret of why they so docilely accepted punishment from the West while refusing to submit to a single blow from the East.

In the first few years after the war there was, besides dust and silence, something else, which now, in this third home called the Federal Republic, would be regarded as a deliberate provocation: total lack of possessions. Each of us possessed his bare life plus whatever he could lay his hands on: coal, wood, books, building materials. Each of us would have been justified in accusing everyone else of theft. Anyone who did not freeze to death in a destroyed city could only have stolen his wood or his coal; and anyone who did not starve to death must have acquired his food, or had someone else acquire it in some illegal fashion. No doubt all that criminality of the emergency situation that was dynamic in the second home has become static again in the third, transgressing merely unwritten laws instead of written ones, and all those early participants would now probably be the first to shout: "Stop thief!"

Present-day Cologne is as far removed from the first and the second as Frankfurt or Stuttgart. Granted there are still a few distinguishing marks around, a few points of reference, and Cologne's history is a given quantity. For many whose personal history is just beginning, it is their first home. Perhaps one day for them even the actual photographs will become part of a fairy tale. What such photos depict is true, although unbelievable. Perhaps they will be reluctant to believe what is written there, white on black on a chalkboard and photographed black on white: Meals for the Children of Cologne Donated by Irish Relief. And will the father who received one of these meals confess that at home *his* father was on tenterhooks to see whether there was still a bit left in the pot? In Ireland every child knows about the Great Famine, which occurred precisely one hundred years before ours. Research has proved that whatever legends have come down to us about it were under- rather than overstated. Human imagination and delight in storytelling are evidently no match for documents. These photographs prove irrefutably that the origins of this third home were destruction and a great famine.

It sometimes happens that author-parents tell their children a story, but if they are then supposed to write down what they have told it becomes disquieting, painful. It immediately sounds like children's books, smells of galley proofs (oh, that blessed printer's ink of earlier days!—in the linofilm process there is no longer any smell at all!), smacks of publisher's contracts and percentages.

"D'you mean to say you tell your kids about money?"

Of course we do, why not? Some time or other they will have to earn money in order to make a living, and they must give some thought early in life as to what their share of the "gross national product" is going to amount to. Isn't money imprinted with signs and symbols? Neither dirty nor clean, but both; neither rational nor irrational, but both: money is never merely money. It is love, hatred, freedom, slavery, dirt, blood, weapons, bread—so, I tell my children about it.

What do children expect of a story? That it be true and become real in the telling. (Interjection by the literary devotee: "What is true, what is real?" Reply: "True and real is the fact that a farm laborer in Portugal earns about twenty-five cents a day.") It's a terrible thing, a regular curse, and will cause anguish to the moralist: even in the oral telling of a story, the question of reality and truth is one of style. If we say of someone that he is a good storyteller, what we usually mean is that he *writes* pretty good stories. And if you were then to meet this story-teller, it might well turn out that you would find him dry, inarticulate, not to say boring and sterile (as James Joyce is said to have been).

Humanity has not yet learned, or has already forgotten, how to distinguish between telling and writing, listening and reading. Writing is as far removed from telling as is the Heaven in which marriages are made from the Earth on which they have to last.

There is absolutely no sense in offering an author material, whether personally experienced or invented: if he is an author, he will make more out of a thimbleful of dust than out of a whole warehouse of material from which he may perhaps pluck a single little thread to wind around the thimble.

The best story I have ever heard told was by a poacher who had been caught by the forester with a deer over his shoulder and a gun under his arm, and who explained this rather obvious situation to the judge as follows: "Your Honor, there I was, going for a walk in the forest, and there was this deer lying on the ground; I walked on a bit, and there was this gun lying on the ground. I picked up the gun and the deer, intending to take them along to the forester, but suddenly there was the forester walking to-ward me." Less than six lines, and everyone can see the narrator's face, can see the judge, the clerk, the spectators, he has foreground, background, a stroll through an enchanted forest where deer and guns happen to be lying around; and these less than six lines are told in fifteen seconds.

In my experience, however, the mark of the *listener* to

a story is insatiability (also when someone reads aloud, which means "giving voice" again to the written word). Three hours of storytelling is nothing, four or five hours are the minimum, and a five-hour story (the writer's courage sinks while every publisher's heart begins to beat faster) would, believe it or not, amount to a hundred and fifty pages of manuscript; eight hours would be two hundred and forty pages of manuscript or about three hundred printed pages. No, no, the author will laugh and the publisher hope in vain, for it is time now to proclaim that divine wisdom, a wisdom known to all but ignored by all: what matters is the How, and the How in oral storytelling has no truck with printer's ink, unless an author were to write something for his children and read it out loud to them (something I still owe my children, a debt I will probably only pay off to my grandchildren).

In the written story, this How, this fragile little word from which all heavenly wisdom dangles, is given in black and white: so let soothsayers and haruspeces, the literary hacks of German weeklies, shakers of fingers, nice people or less nice ones, intelligent people or merely smart ones (smartness is always being fished out of the garbage pails of intelligence!):—let them all tear it to pieces. The How of oral narration is irretrievable, it cannot be captured in print; tape and movie camera cannot retrieve the irretrievable, at most they offer an artificial nonartificiality. No indeed, eye and ear, the nose, and two additional senses if possible, even a sixth and seventh sense, must be present: all this cannot be reproduced. When the air suddenly feels cooler and the dawn relentlessly approaches, when that monster called day, meaning workday, lets reason filter through the cracks in the shutters, when the milk trucks brutally rattle their confounded crates, the baker's boy deposits the bag of rolls almost soundlessly outside the door as if he were delivering a giant butterfly; when the age-old, terrible question is asked: "Is it worth going to bed, or shall we just stay up?"; when every word begins to sound stale, when one is left with half-empty, half-full, full bottles, cups, dishes, plates, ashtrays, when candlesticks wait in vain for fresh candles, when a shy voice tries to hold back workday and reason by suggesting: "Tell us again about Otto the Window-Jumper!" In vain. It's over, finished, and we decide it is still worth going to bed. Irretrievable—and the tales told can never be repeated, can never be duplicated, there is no picking up the threads, we must wait until it "happens" again.

Yes, material and opportunity, the How and the What must "happen." Of course such material does not happen at the first try, if it did it would not be material but a soap bubble. It has to be surrounded, outwitted, coaxed, sneaked up on. When it has been "brought to bay" you have to point your pistol at it, but never, never, must you kill it. No, there must always be enough left for it to form again in an entirely new guise: a story that cannot be told at least fifty times is not a story. Repetition is not only permitted, repetition is the true How. And best of all is when a true, actual event is told when at least one further witness or participant is present (which does not apply to the story of Otto the Window-Jumper, for which we have only one witness in the family). One of the witnesses or participants must definitely play the part of the "wet blanket" or "cold shower," in other words, throw dust or acid when grim experiences of a military, political, or social nature are suddenly recounted with a voluptuous smack of the lips, when the narrator begins to enjoy them.

This provides us with a further important element of oral narration: there is no such thing as authority! There is only the credibility of the How and the What; inter-

jections, doubts, are permitted, must be replied to and
dealt with, and this brings us almost (almost, I say) to the
end, to the most important point of all: true oral narration
is the only genuine form of democracy. There can be
heckling and questions that require two hours of explanation; indeed, they can lead to years of discussion and tape-
worms of definition. Very often long-winded and complex
attempts at differentiation have to be made (it is grossly
mistaken to assume that long-windedness and suspense
are contradictory, the opposite being true: a storyteller
who is not long-winded cannot build up suspense)—as,
for example, when (unavoidably) the word "Nazi" occasionally occurs. Others words crop up too, words re-
quiring the most involved and interesting sociological
explanations, words like "subsistence minimum," or "municipal tax abatement," which signal a complete history
of the middle class.

The storyteller must have a talent for definition and
improvisation, he must also be able, when he does run out
of breath, to hand the story on to someone else, someone
who does not relegate it to the dreadful three-liner death,
the anecdote death, someone who may, should, must stray,
wander from the point. In a favorable storytelling situation you don't have to look around or beat your brains
out for long, usually there is someone waiting for you to
draw breath so he can plunge in, amend, give his own
version. And in such a storytelling situation the question of
who is to fetch beer, wine, schnapps, or make tea or coffee,
can almost never be solved without a firm understanding
that meanwhile nothing, nothing whatever, not even the
slightest nuance, not the tiniest detail, may be told, otherwise an injured voice will be heard from kitchen or cellar:
"But you promised!"

No, let's not pretend: so far we have written nothing

for our children, but we have told them a lot, usually
one- or two-liners that take three to five hours to tell. "Otto
the Window-Jumper," a half-liner, takes about three hours.
In that one, for instance, there is an unemployed young
schoolteacher, and merely to explain how there could be
unemployed young schoolteachers takes at least an hour.
A two-liner, "Why we took our wedding rings to the pawnbroker's, what we got for them, and what we did with the
money"—that takes about three hours. And this is not
literature, for even if it were, so to speak, good enough to
publish, I would not release it because I could not supply
the How, the sand and the acid, the wet blanket and the
cold shower. How could the empty and the full ashtrays
be included, the smell of freshly made coffee, of bacon
fried in the middle of the night with scrambled eggs? Also
lacking would be the voice of reason, a role to be assumed
by one of those present, preferably the wet blanket because there is not much fun in being unreasonable if the
voice of reason is not present.

No doubt our children will have long ceased to be
children by the time I—God willing—am wise and mature
enough as an author to write a children's book—that is to
say, a book that "happens" for grown-ups and children
alike. That is not merely an ambitious, it is *the* most
ambitious goal an author can set himself if, like me, he
has a weakness for the protection of adults. The protection
of children I leave to those who edit *Gulliver's Travels*
for the young and remove the sting by, among other
things, deleting the passage where the giant Gulliver is
accused of committing adultery with the thimble-sized
beauty to whom he is granting an audience as she stands
on the palm of his hand. This is just the kind of passage I
would leave in, especially for children, because the com-
mandment "Thou shalt not covet thy neighbor's wife" can

be no better expressed than by the example of a giant and a thimble-sized beauty whom he is receiving on the palm of his hand. So when you are telling this part of the story, raise one hand, extend it, and with the other place on it a Halma figure and gaze at it with desire. And that's supposed to be unsuitable for the young? The only thing the young must be protected from is those grown-ups who can tell you so precisely what freedom is. When they do, you can always hear the rattle of the chains that bind them.

One final piece of advice for storytellers: don't try to gloss over discrepancies resulting from the How and the What: attentive and critical listeners, especially when they have heard the story for the forty-eighth time, are the best. A little sand in the works when the flow of the narration becomes too smooth, too eloquent; a little acid when the oil of braggadocio flows too abundantly; now and again a stone in the path, a spoke in the wheel, perhaps no more than a mocking "Aha!" or a "Come, come now!" But whatever happens, no ritual. I repeat: true oral narration is the only genuine form of democracy. It is a production without a director, without a star, it must be improvised, otherwise it will fail, become good enough to publish, become literature. So the three-hour-long "Otto the Window-Jumper" will never be published, nor will the seven-hour-long tale "How Cologne was in flames and how we fled the burning city."

And now I must end, and inescapably my ending turns out to be literary: the milk truck has long ago rattled its metal crates, the baker's boy has long since deposited the paper bag outside the door as if he were delivering a giant cabbage white, and for a long time now there has been a glimmer through the cracks of the shutters: it is day, workday, reason.

THE PLACE
WAS INCIDENTAL
(1969)

On leafing through my notes for 1966, day by day, I feel I am following the movements and activities of a motorized lunatic who is a stranger to me. Countless short trips, three long ones, a move, a remodeling, a book written somewhere along the line and praised for its "serenity" —to me, a strange and incongruous comment on a book written, though not without care, more or less on the run. This motorized, lunatic stranger who is praised for his serenity can only shake his head over the record of his innumerable movements and activities, which he compiled —and which even he finds hard to decipher—to keep track of "time wasted." The record reveals no internal movement, only external ones: drove to X, on to Y, again to X; here and there read such and such—mainly Dostoevski, all his diaries, novels, short stories and letters that are available in translation; pages torn from paperback editions, passages marked, page numbers noted. In West Germany, Ireland, France, in East Germany, Holland, Belgium, in a village in the Eifel Mountains, in Cologne, in the Soviet Union and the Georgian Republic.

I pick a place at random: while driving back from Metz to Cologne, on the highway between Metz and Saarbrücken, I am brought up short by a road sign, the name of a place that at first seemed merely familiar but then, when I stopped and thought about it, set off a whole spate of memories. I could bypass neither the place nor the memories, I had to go into and through it all.

I remembered the place as dirty and milling with people, most of them German soldiers: twenty-two years later, around noon, it turned out to be very clean and almost empty. Somewhere on a street going up the hill there must be a large barracks; here on the square, where I parked, a hotel, a restaurant, and the church. The restaurant was there, and the hotel—a few steps away, the church; the topography of my memory did not match the present one: I would have placed the church, the hotel, and the restaurant somewhat differently. This topographical distortion persisted—the place seemed smaller than before, and now, twenty-two years later, I couldn't have found my way back to the barracks.

Twenty-two years ago I knew almost every building in the little town from having asked everywhere for lodging for my wife, who used to come up for the weekends. Now I couldn't recognize a single building, and the events that I remember found no place and no home; memory had become independent, the place no longer mattered, it had become irrelevant, arbitrary, interchangeable. On one of the side streets there had been a sleazy hotel whose owner had always been annoyed when married couples asked for a room; the surcharge for an illicit rendezvous was substantial, rates for a conjugal rendezvous were set by tariff and less profitable. The bedsheets of this dingy place usually bore distinct traces of the black boot-polish issued by the German Wehrmacht to its infantry. There was no quarter given in that trade: cash in advance, if you please, and don't be squeamish, it's wartime, ladies and gentlemen—parting and death, so closely related in war-time, are always waiting at the door. Later, whenever I booked a room, I would mollify the proprietor by volun-tarily paying the surcharge though legally married. Noth-ing is more embarrassing than a sense of being an unwelcome guest.

When large-scale troop movements were imminent into those areas melodramatically referred to as "the front," the little town became flooded with mothers, girls, and wives; if its population had already been doubled by the soldiers, now it almost tripled, and the squeamish ones lost out. Couples married and otherwise could be seen long after midnight trailing from door to door begging to be allowed to spend the night even if it meant in the living room or kitchen on chairs or sofas. In February and March the nights are cold outdoors. Civilians may perhaps imag-ine that soldiers bound for the front are treated with special consideration and kindness, since they are going where, it is alleged, their country needs them to do great things. Far from it; the final honor accorded a living soldier is to be bawled out, bullied, suspected, and humiliated up to the very last moment. All the more embarrassing, then, are the solemn honors accorded dead soldiers. Who will ever write the story of those countless last embraces, kisses, final good-byes destined to occur in those little towns where, before leaving for the front, soldiers for the last time met their girls, wives, and fiancées, their mothers and fathers, brothers and sisters? How human is the sleaziest of all those sleazy hotels compared to the stable, armory, guardroom, or barracks dormitory where soldiers are quar-tered? Anyone lucky enough to have a friend in the guard-room, or merely someone he could bribe, was allowed, when the sergeant on duty was asleep, to take his partner into an empty prison cell, the door then being bolted behind the couple. The moral standards of even the most squeamish lady decline considerably when at two in the morning, shivering with the cold, she and her lover or husband find themselves still roaming the deserted streets of some godforsaken little town in search of a room, and she is prepared to let herself be smuggled past the guard and to sleep in a feed trough, wrapped in a horse blanket, either in company or alone. Regulations, let us not forget, are for but one purpose—in fact, they have but one destiny: to be circumvented, for after all two categories of men are sent to their death in a despicable manner: prisoners and soldiers. Not, of course, that this is to be found in soldiers' manuals. It borders on the obscene; and military ardor will not be enhanced if I go on to reveal that, in this quiet, sleepy little town in Lorraine, the chicanery inherent in both the system and in war was multipled many times over by those charming characters, the superior ranks who deliberately canceled the leave of any man known to be expecting a visitor. In any army, every arbitrary act can be legally anchored within the system: a man can be assigned to fire-watching or aircraft-spotting, a defect can be found in his uniform, he can be provoked till he becomes abusive; if all else fails, he can be kept waiting—simply kept waiting for a signature while his superior dallies in his quarters with a female visitor, listening to a record of "Brave Little Army Wife." The absurdity of time wasted in war, of sensibility injured to the point of lunacy, can be prolonged while the women are waiting outside the gate: whores, mothers, girl friends, wives.

Twenty-two years later the little town yielded no relics, no fetish to which memory could sensorily attach itself: façades, paving, street names, bars: nothing. Nothing. The place was incidental, of no account. What emerged was the long suppressed or merely deferred memory of a system of forced communality, a system all the more in-human because it also had honor and honors to hand out and which still enjoys honor, and presumes to honor with monuments those whom, up to the very last moment of their lives, it has bullied, humiliated, and treated like dirt.

I didn't stay long, hardly long enough to light and finish a cigarette. I looked into a few store windows and saw what you see everywhere: transistors, electric shavers, washing machines. Memory grew no warmer, it stayed cold. After all, I had been in so many barracks and experi-enced the same thing in all of them: that pre-departure mood, those prolonged good-byes, each of which seemed to be the last till in the end the very last and then the very, very last approached, and then one more—till the soldiers were almost glad to board the freight cars designed for eight horses or forty men. No doubt that was the intention behind the ultimate refinement of those cruel tricks: not to ease the final parting but to make it seem like a relief. Any-one who has ever seen someone off by train and spent the last quarter of an hour standing at the lowered window exchanging banalities knows that cruel kind of relief, has sensed the cruel poetry of that banal dialogue carried on under the pressure of imminent departure while glancing at the station clock.

I threw my cigarette butt into the gutter, got into the car, and drove on. Even the station, as I drove past, seemed unfamiliar, not even its clock brought warmth or color into the cold hatred of my memories, yet how often had my eyes gone to the hands of that clock when a train was due to leave or to arrive. As I drove on, a few details did take on warmth, even a few flowers rose to the surface; there had been some in the room the canteen operator fixed up as a bedroom in the canteen barracks area and which he offered free of charge to men whose leave had been canceled and who had a visitor. In the grayness, in the dirt, and in the dirty grayness of my hate-fixated memory, there was no room for flowers. They didn't suit it, and they didn't suit me: I rolled down the car window and tossed out the flowers.

After the publication of one of my books, a critic gave me an approving pat on the shoulder and remarked that I had abandoned the milieu of the poor and that my books were now free of the smell of washtubs and devoid of social protest. This praise was bestowed upon me at a time when it was first coming to light that two thirds of the human race are starving, that in Brazil children are dying who have never known the taste of milk: in a world stinking of exploitation, a world in which poverty is no longer either a stage in the class struggle or some mystical habitat but has become merely a kind of leprosy which one must be at pains to avoid and which an author can be censured for choosing as his subject, without the reader having to bother whether a congruence of form and content has been established.

For myself, I scarcely feel affected by the reproach. Of more significance in my eyes is the muddled thinking expressed in such a choice of words, for if a "washtub" and its surroundings are not a worthy literary locale, where are the locales worthy of literature, where should literature establish itself, as the nice vague saying goes? Let those who wish to do so, establish themselves—with the aid of a building loan and recourse to all the tax dodges.

The specter dreaded by this muddled thinking bears an ugly name: lower middle class. What meaning can this term still have in an age when the deportment of kings is more lower middle class than our grandfathers' ever was, when field marshals knot their ties to suit the taste of the man in the street, when everyone, even the most rabid nonconformist, keeps a nervous eye on his public? Why get so indignant about washtubs when retired generals become publicity managers for laundries?

Strangely enough, I cannot recall ever having described or even mentioned a washtub in any of my short stories or novels. I almost feel obliged to mention one in a forthcoming book; perhaps I shall write a washtub novel, but in that case I would lay the scene in China or the Near East. This would mean, of course, that I could not make use of the details I know so well from my wife's tales.

For my wife can tell you that, in the little town her grandmother came from (it so happens that my own grandmother came from the same little town, so I too would be able to give a wonderfully incisive description of everything), wash day was a special feast day. In our grandmothers' time, wash day was still celebrated in that little town—called Düren—as a feast day. In an age of well-stocked linen closets, the laundry was done only once a month; mountains of laundry were washed, then the wet linen was taken by cart to the meadows beside the River Rur where it was spread out to bleach, while kegs of beer, hams, loaves of bread, and little tubs of butter were unloaded from the carts. The laundry maids were joined by the teenage loafers of that era; there was dancing, drinking, fun and games—and in the evening the bleached laundry, the empty kegs and baskets, were loaded back onto the carts, and everyone drove home. Wash day was a gay affair, and I regret having hitherto allowed these episodes to pass me by.

Of course my mother did the washing too (what a humiliating state of affairs!); she stood at the washtubs, usually on Monday mornings. All over the world, the latter part of Monday mornings saw shirts and sheets, handkerchiefs and unmentionables, fluttering on clotheslines, a sight which, far from depressing me, has consoled me, signaling as it does the tireless energy of the human race to rid itself of dirt; and the Rhine barges, as I recall them from my childhood and as they are to this day, invariably display a bunting of laundry as they ply up and down the river. I have nothing against wash day and nothing against washtubs; it is just that, in an age of washing machines, they are becoming increasingly rare, and perhaps the day will come when washtubs will be exhibited in folklore museums: Washtub, Lower Middle Class, Early 20th Century.

I could imagine a drama taking place beside a washtub; after all, so many dramas are set in mansions, dramas in which the dialogue consists of a four-hour exchange of banalities. It is with a light heart that I defend the washtub I have never described. In the days when I used to carry kindling and briquets to my mother at the washtubs and try vainly—just as in later years, as an army drudge, I tried countless times, equally vainly—to light the fire under the washtubs, the wisdom I learned and the stories I was told were not the least important: the number of oxen slaughtered at the annual country fair; how on Saturday nights the money was taken home from the taverns by the apronful; how certain people took the morning express to Cologne—as people said—to read the *Kölnische Zeitung* there; and how one of my forefathers devoted himself to drink with such consistency that—"I saw it with my own eyes"—he ended up trading his last shirt for a few glasses of beer.

As far as the milieu of the poor is concerned, I have been wondering for a long time what other milieus there are: the milieu of the upper classes, the milieu of the lower classes (poor but honest, as they say), the milieu of the great; the skill of modern advertising has spared me the trouble of defining the latter: the great of this world wear Rolex watches. What more is there to say? The lower classes? I am dimension-blind, the way some people are color-blind, I am milieu-blind, and I try not to prejudge, which is only too often confused with failure to judge. Greatness is a word that does not depend on place in society, just as pain and joy have no social relevance; interminable exchanges of banalities take place beside washtubs too, and among the great of this world there may actually be greatness; let us give them the benefit of the doubt. Some of Dostoevski's novels have horribly unpleasant titles—*Poor People* and *The Insulted and the Injured*—and if we look at the world in which a certain Rodion Raskolnikov moves, or even a prince by the name of Mishkin, we are indeed appalled; they should all have been presented with Rolex watches in order to feel genuinely great, and Dostoevski should have been told it was high time he sought better-class circles; he should be posthumously asked whether in his day, too, more than two thirds of the human race were starving.

There was a time when everything not aristocratic was deemed hopelessly unfit for literature; to regard a businessman as worthy of a poet's pen was considered revolutionary, and in fact, it was; then came those criminals who made even the worker fit for literature, fit for art; meanwhile we have art theories that declare everything which is *not* working-class to be unworthy of literature. Is our blessed society going to produce a countertheory to this? That would be interesting, enlightening, and worthy of extended analysis.

"YOU ARE NOW
ENTERING GERMANY"

(1967)

Twenty air kilometers to Nörvenich, the same to Jülich. Jülich is working away without a sound, the Nörvenich Starfighters are chopping and sawing up the innocent sky above Hürtgen Forest; these sharks of the air are fulfilling not only their "mission" (what mission, one may ask?) but also a function: they see to it that no one starts trusting the peace, see to it that no one forgets to distinguish between peaceful and uncanny silence.

It is the uncanny silence of a gigantic cemetery. Within a radius of twenty kilometers around the village of Vossenack, many more people were killed than live in the city of Aachen today; the gigantic cemetery to right and left of a line drawn between Gey—Grosshau—Kleinhau —Hürtgen—Vossenack—Kommerscheidt—Schmidt—has been planted with young trees: every postwar age group, the whole of "young Germany," is represented here, right down to the infants of 1967. Pleasant paths winding between each of the villages, silence; to this day the once tree-stripped landscape looks intimidated, reddish fields to the south of the main road, dark ones to the north,

where the red Wehe and the white, the little rivers with
the name meaning "woe," were ready with a word for
what was in store.

The dense young forest does a better job of camouflage
than older trees ever could. You have to leave the path,
creep right in among the thickly planted young trees, to
find the old charred tree stumps, rotten now, of the winter
of 1944/45, the foxholes, the network of trenches, the em-
placements, the sagging, overgrown pillboxes, of the
"Siegfried Line." On these trim paths it is not unusual,
it is quite common in fact, for a foot to strike against a
reddish-brown object that would have passed for a piece of
bark had not the impact betrayed its metallic nature: a
shell splinter that still, after twenty-two years, has not
crumbled away. A cartridge, a steel helmet, a canister with
the American stencil "Careful." For miles and miles around
each of the villages, the peaceful reforested clear-cutting,
silent—with the sawn and chopped-up sky overhead,
Jülich working away without a sound in the distance. It
is good to know that twenty-two years ago, only a few
kilometers to the west, the predecessors of the sector-
boundary markers bore the memorable legend: YOU ARE
NOW ENTERING GERMANY: BE ON YOUR GUARD!

O dead and living friends, do not forget. Be on your
guard, you are in Germany! The young forest is thriving, it
offers so many advantages: it provides distant views, a
wealth of game, in spring and summer a profusion of
flowers such as the classic dark forest of Hänsel and Gretel
could never offer; in summertime whole slopes, the ones
still stripped of trees, are a mass of foxgloves, a solemn
purple looking from a distance like a gigantic pall spread
out. What a lousy thing to be, a soldier: don't you forget
it, you young heroes up there, flying so boldly over the

graves of your fathers and brothers—and so fast, so fast!
Naturally when a person is strolling along here, out for a
walk, he can't help thinking (how can he?) of debates on
defense, of embarrassing ministerial chatter, and he avoids
the official "heroes'" cemetery, done in such impeccable
taste. (Why, he wonders, do the Germans do so much for
their dead and so little for the living?) Surely the right,
the only thing would have been not to practice personal-
ized treatment of the dead in tasteful military cemeteries,
as is done in a nice civilian cemetery, besides providing a
platform for loudmouthed survivors from this regiment or
that. If anything, then why not a gigantic somber monument bearing a cynical soldier's word or two, or better still
a dirty one; why shouldn't the dead for once have the last
word, which never, never was "Fatherland" or "Nation,"
let alone "Führer"? A German soldier's word and an American one, a girl's name or a whore's, framed in some pertinent last word such as "fuckin' war," "verdammter Scheiss-
krieg." Why this heathery illusion of a civilian "memorial
park" when only a few kilometers to the west stood those
attractive markers with the pertinent words: BE ON YOUR
GUARD: YOU ARE NOW ENTERING GERMANY!

More than twenty-eight times the villages of Vossenack,
Schmidt, Simonskall, and Kommerscheidt changed military
masters; in Vossenack the "front" ran straight through the
parish church, with the American soldiers firing down from
the organ loft, the Germans up from the sacristy. In
Monschau the *German* Army fired on women picking
vegetables in their gardens; the truth of what was true
was unacceptable: the war was definitely lost and coming
to an end. And it was unacceptable that a German woman
should actually be determined to *stay alive* in a small
town occupied by Americans. (And naturally, a person

strolling along through peaceful woods under an unpeaceful sky is bound to think that this pattern of thought continues to determine German political thinking to this day: the truth of what is true is unacceptable: that a war—and what a war!—was lost twenty-two years ago.)

Here and there a veteran of the forests, a giant oak, a giant beech. Somewhere in a village between Gey and Vossenack, at a crossroads or in the forest, Hemingway wrote a love poem for his wife in which the almost prophetic lines occur:

> In the next war we shall bury the dead in cellophane
> The Host shall come packaged in every K ration. . . .
> Every man shall be provided with a small but perfect
> Archbishop Spellman, which shall be self-inflatable

It would be a good idea for those young fellows up there to tape these words onto their instrument panels; for Archbishop Spellman they could substitute—according to denomination—Bishop Hengstbach or Bishop Kunst. It's a lousy thing to be, a soldier!

Strange thought while walking over these pleasant, peaceful heights, through these silent valleys: this part of the country is known to have had the fewest Nazis in Germany, and it was punished by the German divisions more severely than any other, punished "unto the second generation." How many children hereabouts, long after the war was over, stepped onto mines, were injured or killed by grenades? Hardly a house remained standing, hardly a tree was spared, not a field, not a path that was not mined, not a stream that was harmless. This intimidated countryside knows it is true: a war—and what a war!—was lost; this countryside, still intimidated, even after twenty-two years, by the senseless martial noises of "the truth is unacceptable" heroism, this countryside knows the truth of what the politicians are not yet prepared to admit.

The significance of the first sight depends upon the last, and I have yet to look my last on Rome. Innumerable first sights: suddenly looking down from the Via Trionfale upon that vast city in the sun, a city whose basic color seems to be yellow—yellow Rome spread out over its hills. A first sight. Past long, long walls promising cool shade and sheltering wealth, gardens and palazzi—palazzi and gardens: a first sight of that rich Rome whose rich youth chases callously around in luxury cars—rich Rome, and poor Rome in tenements where the apartments are scarcely larger than a motorcar; the Rome of cats whose ancestry seems to go back two thousand years: in the ruins of the Forum, in the walls of the Colosseum; the Rome of lovers who have more hideaways in this city than in any other in the world. The Rome known to me from my Latin books: so there really is a Tarpeian Rock, a Capitol, and a Via Appia, and the Roman emperors perpetuated their names in mountains of ruins: Caracalla and Nero. The Rome of the wealthy Church: those cold jewel-box lids, those gigantic marble angels holding up holy-water stoups as big as bathtubs, the Holy See's coat of arms on so many gateways that form entrances to limitless gardens containing priceless palaces—and the beggar-monks in their grubby cowls going from café to café with their collection boxes, all one and the same Church. A lot of first sights of things that are Roman and only Roman. Rome is the home of a most misleading adjective, and everything seen there at first sight is Roman; the waiters are Roman, and so are the children; the Church is, and so are the ruins of Imperial Rome; the monument to Victor Emmanuel, as well as St. Frances of Rome, holy sister to innumerable Roman women.

Often the first sight will also be the last, as in the case of the random incident: the waiter in a trattoria outside Rome who told us how to get to our pension—three times he went all the way from the farthest end of the terrace to the inside of the building, the first time to get a map, the second to get a pencil, and then, with a smile, the third time to get his glasses—and I knew at once that he would have been deeply offended by a tip. The plumber's apprentice in a barber's shop who dropped the glass cabinet that he and his boss were about to install on the wall: bottles shattered and tubes burst as the cabinet crashed to the ground, perfumes and hair tonic pouring across the floor, and I dreaded the blasting that must now descend upon the weeping lad; but his boss remained quite calm, said something to the effect that "These things happen," and began to comfort the boy as the latter stood sobbing in the corner, while the barbers quietly went on wielding their shaving brushes, snipping with their scissors, and a woman with a dustpan and broom swept up the remains, soaking her cleaning rag in precious essences. A first sight of Rome.

The apparent haphazardness of the motorists, who obey the unwritten laws more than the written ones—surprising in a city that is the home of *lex* to see sleeping cats and playing children breaking the law that we could never invoke even if we were within our rights in disturbing a cat's sleep or a child's game, or were tempted to teach a lesson to women who are "violating traffic regulations." The streets of Rome, while available to automobiles, do not belong to them—not yet; the "knight at the wheel," that puritanical abomination, is only a knight, we must remember, because he deigns to renounce his rights—for the moment; in Rome the cars seem—at first sight—to ignore traffic regulations, not because they are breaking the rules but because by nature cars are brutal and anti-social. No wonder that in Rome there are many more policemen than traffic lights: the law has not yet been automated.

First impression at first sight: the many different nuns, almost as varied as butterfly species—fluttering back and forth across St. Peter's Square, wearing simple coifs and elaborate ones, colored veils or plain ones, or none at all. Some look like medieval matrons, others like Spanish señoritas or Sardinian peasant women, and the modern ones with their berets and white blouses almost like the sister one might take along on a trip. And within all this variety, the differences in skin color: yellow, white, black, and copper.

All these first sights on the first day; at every sight something Roman—and how many sights does the eye take in every day?

At the Zoo railway station in Berlin it has long been possible to buy cans labeled "Berlin Air," a sentimental reminder, no doubt, for the benefit of those about to leave Berlin or those having already left. This witty inspiration on the part of the souvenir industry might soon become a genuine best-seller, with labels reading not even "Berlin Air" but simply "Air." Not oxygen, not the stuff dispensed by iron lungs: just plain ordinary breathing air. Your children could carry a few cans to school in the morning, you yourself might take some along to the factory or the office and take a few drafts of fresh air during coffee break or with your lunch sandwiches, milk, or coffee. Since it is already possible to buy water (not mineral water, just plain ordinary spring water), I find the notion of canned air far from a satirical exaggeration. In a world as productive and effective as ours, as geared to profit- and sales-growth, there will be (at least for us Europeans) a sufficient supply of bread, wine, and liquor, even milk, butter, and beer, but we are going to run out of water and air. Sometimes when I leave my car in a parking garage or on a parking lot I wouldn't mind having a can of fresh air with me. If we—efficient, up-to-the-minute inhabitants of industrial society that we are—if we search for a new myth we find there is really only one: the legend of King Midas, at whose touch everything turned to gold. Replace gold with productivity, efficiency, profit, earnings, growth —and this myth might fit very nicely.

Plain ordinary breathing air will be traded as a precious commodity, and we shall be driving miles out into the country to any place where real, plain and simple drinking water is rumored to be had, and we shall be carrying it home from weekend outings in bottles, canisters, or plastic bags, having discovered that it tastes better than the stuff our water-seller supplies us with by the day or by the week. All the fruits, all the delights of this earth will be available to us—only water will be short and air will be scarce. In the midst of our splendid super-cities, where we are now building more subways to make room for more cars, we may well see the reemergence of that ancient, quasi-Oriental figure, the water-seller; and beside him will stand an entirely new breed of peddler, the air-seller. He too will have a great tank-truck and for a coin or two will briefly hold his air hose to our lips. Hasn't the elimination of fire hazards in our modern homes and buildings already created a new branch of industry: paper-shredders or burners? Now that we can no longer burn anything, anything at all, in our homes, we hesitate to yield up our entire correspondence or our private papers to the garbage collectors.

The exploitation of man by man has been the object of speculation since mankind began; the exploitation of the environment for not quite so long. In blind, profit-hungry optimism, industrialization has been pursued for more than a century and a half. Full steam ahead, as long as the money comes rolling in. And the money has kept on rolling in, yet now it turns out that not only have man and the environment been exploited but even the elements have been poisoned or driven away. Enough architects and sociologists, psychologists and even a few theologians, have raised their voices to warn and scold, but so far nothing much has happened; and if we wonder why that hard-to-define section of mankind that we call youth is so apathetic, so pessimistic even, we should ask ourselves: what kind of future have we prepared for them or do we have in store for them? What quality of life? Even the sellers of water and air will not reconcile them to this suicidal civilization.

By 1985, so the Secretariat of the United Nations has told us, nine thousand billion marks will have been spent on armaments. In stark figures: 9,000,000,000,000 marks— an almost mystical cypher; it is almost impossiblé to keep track of the zeros and translate the figures into words. Furthermore, in order to prevent a catastrophic water shortage, it will be necessary by the year 2000 to raise 234 billion marks, the equivalent of ten budgets for the West German armed forces. Thus in order to prevent all potential disasters, which I cannot list here, there must be regional planning, urban planning, traffic planning, health services, educational reforms, environmental protection. We must work toward developing a brand-new set of values which will inevitably conflict with the existing ones of profit, productivity, growth; and the most important consideration in plans to solve all these complex problems is time, for it is high time now, and time is flying. And any politician who thinks that all this can be planned without raising taxes is deluding himself or the public.

In the light of these problems it already seems no longer sheer nonsense but suicidal cynicism for "planning" to be denounced by West German's coalition party of the Right, with its offers to solve our domestic and foreign problems.

How are these problems to be solved *without* planning? The antithesis of planning is not necessarily freedom: it can also be planlessness, and the results of planless, ruthless industrialization are there for all to see.

Air to breathe, water to drink, must not become the property of a privileged class that can afford to drive out to its weekend cottage in the country, where it also has at its disposal two further elements that have become rarities for city dwellers: fire in the fireplace and earth in the garden. The new expression "quality of life" is more than a fine phrase; it stands for something very ancient—the materials of life that have always been taken for granted: air, water, fire, earth. And there is something else, something that does not but should figure in the list of classic elements, that is becoming the property of the privileged: peace and quiet. The number of people driven away by noise is growing daily, as is the number of those to whom escape from unbearable noise means risk of losing a job.

The legend of the air-seller may soon become as true as the legend of the seller of peace and quiet: someone who devises a method of holding a small quantity of peace and quiet to the ear of those poor miserable, crazy, hounded heirs to Midas. But of course these sellers of water, air, and quiet will be merely peddlers; before long there will emerge wholesalers, giant concerns that buy up water, air, and quiet to hoard and resell to the peddlers at a profit. It is quite incredible, in view of the trend now no longer imminent but already here, that concepts such as "planning" should be denounced, for planning is going on all the time: surely advertising campaigns are planned too; they are actually *called* campaigns, their terminology being lifted from that of war.

Nations and communities are not alone in having a budget; the earth has one too, among others it has an oxygen and a nitrogen budget, and for a long time now we have been living on credit. In the blind postwar reconstruction phase of West Germany, exploitation and sell-out have been pursued in a ruthless, profit-oriented euphoria observed by the rest of the world and regarded by it as some kind of miracle. This miracle was wrought not only by a capacity for hard work but also by a blindness shared by each participant. Full steam ahead. The money has kept rolling in, in pay envelopes and in dividends. Glorious times. Yes indeed. The second miracle will be harder to perform: national planning alone is not enough, for the problems have long since become international, as Sakharov, the Soviet scientist, prophesied many years ago when he wrote about ecological problems—that is, about the budget of the earth.

In reading a novel that was published over a hundred years ago, we may easily forget that at the time it appeared it was already classified as a "historical novel." *War and Peace* was written between 1863 and 1869; the material of the novel is drawn from Russian history of the years 1805 to 1813, the epilogue from about 1820. The thirty-six-year-old Tolstoi started out on this long march nearly sixty years after 1805; in other words, he was in the situation of an author who might embark in 1973 on a novel that begins in 1914.

So when readers and critics complain from time to time that authors are still preoccupied with the Second World War twenty-five years after it ended in 1945, this means they still have not grasped the fact that it is not the material that makes the author but the author who makes the material. Every novel, unless it is Utopian, is historical, even the so-called "contemporary novel." The inevitable time lag between writing and publishing is in itself enough to turn the thematic material into history. Distance in time is a relative factor, especially since even historians do not arrive at "obejective" results: everything remains controversial, is constantly being corrected, as soon as fresh archives open up, some correspondence is unearthed, or someone discovers a new "aspect." Against the background of controversial dates in German history—January 30, 1933; June 30, 1944; July 20, 1944—whole libraries of research and analysis have piled up, and still many things remain obscure, inexplicable. Thus history, psychology, and literature, each on its separate path, attempt to close the gap. I do not believe in competition between any of the sciences and, say, literature; literature tries to close the gap in its own way, by superimposing on historical material characters who "have not made history."

The distances may become less; the desire of the contemporary reader to "cope" with history, to be allowed to regard it as "over and done with," is understandable and corresponds to the steady increase in the number of historical events whose onslaught we have been required to suffer. The urge for the "now," for "contemporary relevance," is great, the aversion to history is growing in the same way as the aversion to theology and the urge toward myth and religion, although often it is hard to discern and sometimes "perversely" disguised. This surfeit of history probably accounts for the desire for new forms of expression, for the permanent work of art that changes with every tick of the second hand and yet remains, the ephemeral sublimated into the imperishable. Every day there are half a dozen historical moments: treaties signed, treaties broken, no war, no civil war, just permanently broken truces; interventions, military aid, invasions, dollar strategy, but no war. That we don't have. We are living in a state of profound peace. Demonstrations, students being shot, striking workers being locked up, and from time to time a movie director, a writer, painter, or composer, lifts the lid off whole continents that are condemned to silence—South America, Central America, Africa—and we are told a little about the hidden, arcane history of whole continents whose official history is being determined and written elsewhere. We are told too much and too little, and the very moment it is printed it has already happened: it is history.

All the things that have "made history"! Suddenly something is there in front of us, a tangible, terrible sign: a wall clear across Berlin. Isn't that wall, from the point of view of a writer obsessed with material, a writer who wants to do more than supply captions for the illustrated weeklies, a reply to present and past simultaneously, to accumulated history that may have begun with the Order of the German Knights (if not earlier), and that consists of centuries of mistrust, of wooing, of simultaneous fear and admiration, of unsuccessful attempts by Eastern Europe to close the gap to Western Europe and vice versa, of attempts at subjugation in both directions? We need only remember that Russian and German history—in the days when it could still to some extent be "made" by both countries—rested on two people, cousins, who addressed each other as "Dear Willy" and "Dear Nicky," two extremely pathetic and absurd "pillars of European history," and that then came a First and a Second World War and still no peace; that history was made by people for whom Europe stopped at the Rhine or, at best, at the Elbe: constant giving of offense, enticements, all in the tweed jacket of freedom—and suddenly there is a wall there, a wall that locks in and locks out; close the bulkheads, turn your backs! Dear Willy! Dear Nicky! One of them was in some crazy way too "German" and the other in some crazy way too "Russian," and both had "English" features. An insane "family deal," and Western Europe's ancient fear that these two giants, one of whom was entirely Eastern European and the other half-Eastern European, might fall into each other's arms. Fear of Germany and hopes of Germany, later transformed into permanent misunderstanding of the desires and the political strength of that oft-betrayed "German working class."

And then there is, and was, not only Russia and the Soviet Union: there is Poland and Lithuania, Latvia, Estonia, and there is a state called Czechoslovakia in which an invisible and terrible wall has been erected. And on some of those maps that are used at conferences there are strangely vague pencil-scribblings, confused squiggles: the misunderstood history of Eastern Europe. One thing is certain: *someone* at that conference table understood the history of Eastern Europe. And suddenly, many years later, after so much misunderstanding, there was a wall there, jamming the flow of history, because there is still no peace. No war and no peace. And at the temporary end of an almost immeasurably long history, skyscrapers rear up beside a wall, a hotel from which one can "look down," clothed in human dignity, onto those one is so shamelessly observing; even state visitors don't hesitate to walk up the steps and, shaking their heads, indignant, moved, to glance swiftly across, behaving as if there had never been a First or a Second World War, neither Hitler nor Napoleon, nor the permanent arrogance of the West toward the East, nor inhuman and subhuman ideology, nor conferences at Yalta and Potsdam, nor the naïve notion of history-making generals that Berlin isn't really all that important. Thus East and West have reduced themselves to a sightseeing value.

Only a total poet can strive for the unhistorical, or adopt it simply as a pose—also, apparently, the politicians and history-making generals who attempt to dissolve these violable and often violated frontiers, this jumble of European frontiers, in the Alexandrian manner without being Alexander. What I do not understand is the unhistorical attitude of those who reject poetry anyway (in their search for a new poetry that will be called something else) and at the same time wax indignant over the clumsy political and military attempts that reflect a similar disregard for history. Personally I find that the reading of *War and Peace* (among other things, of course) does more to explain the Berlin Wall to me than the hollow-sounding slogans of both sides, and I will admit: such a defense of a doubly historical novel is farfetched. But it is possible that something close at hand can at times be quite convincingly explained by something farfetched.

What kind of country is this in which Germans have always pretended to be more "Russian" than the Russians? We do have some means of looking at this country: the entire literature of Russia, gigantic walks through Russia, one of these and one of the most important being *War and Peace*. A doubly historical novel of such enormous dimensions! This book has "contemporary relevance" throughout and on various levels. There are many reasons for its continuing and continuous popularity. The first of these may be the quite legitimate desire for information, a reason that has to do with the second one, and this one I prefer to express negatively because of our warped relationship to what is sometimes called "entertainment literature": the book *is not boring;* granted there are places that seem tedious, whole passages in which the author stubbornly and wilfully insists on telling us his views; I would warn the reader against skipping these passages in a desire to spare himself the stubbornness of the author Tolstoi. May every author be read word for word, may every author be allowed his tedious passages, his stubbornness.

Our attitude toward word-for-word reading is—I hope not for all time—warped by our cultural traditions. Anything that is *intelligible*, that conveys meaning, is already half-suspect of being journalistic; and as for something that goes as far as to "entertain"—isn't that, so help me, light reading? Surely the "true" German language is that pseudo-mystical jargon known to the initiated as Middle High Bohemian. A thing has to be difficult, almost unintelligible, and if it ultimately becomes "popular"—then hands off before we dirty our fingers, for doesn't popular "basically" mean vulgar? A person who reads merely in order to read, merely because he may enjoy it, surely cannot have very high standards! Or any desire for culture either, and probably he also lacks the requisite preparation and certainly the educational background. How can anyone, for instance, judge Tolstoi's depiction of Napoleon if he is historically uneducated? What kind of man is it who goes to Italy totally unprepared and finds himself confronted with, say, the stupendous city of Siena? I confess my guilt: I am one of these, also as a reader. Indeed I am. I have also, of course, acquired some "education"—because it was fun—and, it is hard to deny it: I am also an author, I write novels, all of them attempts to close the gap to all that is inexplicable in recent German history. Furthermore, I have another characteristic that has nothing to do with education or with being an author: I am inquisitive, to an extent that sometimes brings me to the very brink of indiscretion. And even after my third reading of *War and Peace* my curiosity is still not satisfied, that curiosity which sends literary critics into a frenzy, drives readers mad, but from which some authors can derive an enormous amount of pleasure—I mean the inquisitive question: where is that fellow the author in a novel such as this, how has he camouflaged himself, where is he hiding?

We are aware of him, of course, the minute he raises his finger and begins to lecture us, but what good is a finger to me? I want to have, to see, the whole fellow. According to a deeply ingrained prejudice (who was the first to bring it up, I wonder?), the author usually hides in some likable hero or heroine. I believe—yes, I believe, for there's not much that I really know—that this is not so. There might possibly be a chance of actually discovering the author in his whole *oeuvre*: add up all the characters, *all of them,* from the servant who brings a jug of water and disappears, never to appear again, to some historical personality, Napoleon or some such figure—all the characters who appear and disappear, male and female, regardless of whether the author is a man or a woman—and reduce this sum to its seventh root. I admit that I do not know how to apply this method, and that I am pinning my hopes on cybernetics, which one day will be able to spew out every desired type of author from some machine. Until that happens I, like every other reader, have no choice but to discover the author in the usual inadequate manner: by reading his entire output and watching every move, listening to every word and, where necessary, peeking under the skirt of every character that appears on the scene. Biographies are usually unsuccessful attempts at closing a gap, autobiographies are embarrassing ones; I believe (that wretched belief again!) that the autobiography of an author is concealed in his entire work. But my curiosity is concerned not only with the author: it is also directed at something else: with the thematic material offered by the Russian nobility, its frivolity and levity, its possible merits, its mania for extravagance, its mania for snobbish amusements. The question of its humanity also remains to be explored.

The novel *War and Peace* contains a great many "historical moments" in which the whole burden of history falls onto historically insignificant characters. Natasha Rostov, who makes several appearances, has her big scene in the hour when the population is fleeing from burning Moscow. The difference between flight and moving house, a highly relevant and agonizing difference for millions of people in this world, and one which most of us will never forget, is particularly agonizing for those with possessions (and this is where history takes its revenge!). While the Rostovs are preparing to flee—and we learn that there is even a special wardrobe wagon, as well as a private German dancing master with his family—the usual quarrel breaks out as to what is to be taken along and, beyond that, to the dilemma of deciding whether priority is to be given to furniture, clothing, and books, or to the wounded. To cap it all, along comes Berg, the German son-in-law, with his own ideas about furniture: someone has offered him "a charming dressing-table," a "truly delightful piece," and for a song at that (who cares—when the whole city is on fire!), the very piece he has been wanting to give his wife for so long, and who settles this quarrel, a quarrel that is building up to a thunderstorm of tension? Not the Count, nor the Countess, let alone the mediocre Berg—it is the twenty-year-old Natasha who has her historical moment; her scene requires her to decide something that should be a matter of course, and she expresses herself in no uncertain terms: "If you ask *me*," she cries, "that's contemptible, loathsome, it's . . . oh I don't know! Are we Germans or something?"

When a German is confronted with this direct hit, he will be saddened and at the same time exultant, exultant because, as a German, he is so lacking in self-appreciation. But then he will be, must be, saddened in his capacity as a specimen of that race known as human, to which, however unlikely it may sound, he does after all belong. All of us, of course, are familiar with this fetishism of possessions that has marked millions of flights, that has clung to canning jars, pillows, or potted plants. Is that German? Are not Natasha's mother, even her father to some extent, the father who cannot decide something that should be a matter of course, a trifle German? Perhaps it took the Germans until World War II to learn to appreciate that strange possession known as one's bare life; they have probably never been taught to live for the sake of living— no more than they have been taught to read for the sake of reading. Their curse is also their blessing, this constant search for the "meaning" of life—even if it is to be found, perverted to a fetish, in a potted plant.

Natasha's vehement decision, however—and this is what makes her decision as human as it is "novelistic"—also entails the consequence that, together with other wounded men, her former fiancé Andrey Bolkonsky lands in the care of the Rostov family, thus being once more close to Natasha. The modern novel (or novelist) despises such contrivances, the reading author begins at this point to doubt his own gullibility, but the unprejudiced reader may confidently abandon himself to his thoughts and feelings and say to himself, "Well, imagine that!" And furthermore, without developing the slightest complex, he should take such contrived novelistic reality for a "true story" and still wait for the happy ending, not the one that actually takes place but the expected ideal happy ending in which Andrey Bolkonsky and Natasha Rostov would "find each other." The reader should also know that, in fact, Tolstoi for a while considered the most banal of all banal titles for *War and Peace:* "All's Well That Ends Well." A title liable to repel intellectuals, a title that would attract them only indirectly, if at all. There are few novels in the world's literature that are so well suited to teach us to read as *War and Peace*. Tolstoi is forever accommodating the reader and then repelling him again, because he is forever raising a warning finger. At no point is there even the slightest suggestion of an attempt to curry favor, something that can be concealed in sheer accommodation just as easily as in sheer repulsion.

The first part of the novel, forming scarcely a tenth of the whole, already contains the grand entrance and parade of the entire cast that is later to appear according to time, history, events, and milieu, and surrounded with the minor figures; this cast, which Tolstoi sometimes blankets with whole chapters of philosophy and military history, and which then, shaking the dust from its hair, rises once more fully alive. After scarcely a hundred and fifty pages they are all there: the Kunagins, the Rostovs, the Drubetskoys, and the Bolkonskys, and that strange, gauche, stout person turns up, that eternally absentminded Pierre Bezuhov, who with the sureness of a sleepwalker always turns up at the right moment at the right place, to garner—like the simpleton in the fairy tales—the most beautiful girl, the most money, and the most history: the immense inheritance of his father of which, considering the cabal in the death-chamber and his own ineptness, he has little prospect; the battle of Borodino, the burning of Moscow, Napoleon's absurdity, as well as that experience which in such times no contemporary was supposed to miss: prison and imprisonment. And in the end he even gets Natasha.

There is an amazing similarity between Pierre Bezuhov and that fellow who, with a dead crow and a little mud in his pocket, was the only one able to cheer up the melancholy princess. In Bezuhov, Tolstoi has managed to bring off something that scarcely any other novelist has succeeded in doing: creating a hero who seems a likable fellow but with whom we wouldn't want to "identify." There are so many simpletons, and so few of them get the princess, and who wants to be a simpleton on the strength of the slim chances offered by a fairy tale? Who would want to bet, on reading the novel for the first time, that there could be a happy ending for this Pierre? This amiable, mediocre fellow, who is inclined to brood but isn't really a brooder; who, although manifestly of the male sex, is nevertheless not a "real man"; this wearer of spectacles whose very vices lack credibility—he even upstages the mighty General Kutuzov; this dilettante who is not even successful in the reforms he institutes on his estates because he is too lazy to concern himself with the proper theories or to seek out the right people; who lets himself be tricked, by the oldest and stupidest device, into marrying Ellen Kuragin; who stumbles through burning Moscow with the childish notion of killing Napoleon; a bungling millionaire who is made happy beside the camp fire with a bowl of soup and a piece of bread: this is the hero, this is the man who takes the bride home. It is to him that Natasha belongs; he finds himself, quite by chance and all unsuspecting, at the point where the battle of Borodino is being decided: this is the man who, wearing embarrassing civilian clothes and driving through the positions where the troops are drawn up, becomes a "front-line fighter." Isn't Tolstoi the first author to give war that component from which we still flinch because such concepts as "heroism" and "destiny" are still sacrosanct to us: the component of the absurdity of those who make war?

Dostoevski's *Crime and Punishment* (1866) and *The Idiot* (1868) appeared almost simultaneously with *War and Peace*. Since I can hardly assume that the two writers allowed any peeking at each other's desks, it may be a coincidence that Raskolnikov and Prince Myshkin (in *The Idiot*) have certain similarities with the stout Pierre. Needless to say, neither Raskolnikov nor Myshkin can be conceived of as even approaching stoutness; but perhaps these apparently trivial physiological details are a clue by means of which the two great contrasting figures of nineteenth-century Russian literature may be recognized in their contrasting methods of transforming their conceptions into thematic material. Be that as it may: I myself think of Raskolnikov and Myshkin as being extremely thin. The only *youthful* Dostoevski heroes to whom I might concede a certain corpulence would be the unfortunate Mihail Karamazov and that extraordinarily likable Razumikhin, Raskolnikov's friend; and it is also possible that Alyosha Karamazov might acquire a little plumpness later on.

In more than fifteen hundred pages of *War and Peace* there are only a couple of occasions on which Pierre Bezuhov finds himself in that state which, for Dostoevski's youthful heroes, is not only familiar but permanent: beside himself. During a quarrel with his furious wife Ellen, and after Natasha has been abducted by his brother-in-law Anatole. At such moments he is ripe for a duel, although fully aware of how ridiculous duels are. There is one further detail in this use of thematic material in which Dostoevski and Tolstoi differ: in the materialization of harlotry. I consider Sonya Marmeladova one of the immortal feminine figures of world literature, but one thing I don't believe of her to this day: that she was a harlot. But that Mazlova, in Tolstoi's *Resurrection*, was a harlot—that I do believe. How she got to be one is another question.

To the reader, this parade of the entire cast in the first hundred and fifty pages of a novel may not seem as audacious as it does to the reading author. All Tolstoi's great novels have been "daring"—and have won: *War and Peace, Anna Karenina*, and *Resurrection*. In the first part of *War and Peace* the inhabitants of Moscow, St. Petersburg society, the aristocracy of town and country, make their appearance in well-nigh regimental strength, entire clans, Good and Evil, garrulousness, bigotry, depravity, children, grown-ups, old men spouting French, latter-day Voltaires and Rousseaus; the world of intrigue, generosity, baseness. What is to become of them all, especially of that simpleton Bezuhov who, on top of everything else, doesn't watch his tongue? Fourteen hundred pages later the spoils are gathered in: war, peace, Russia between 1805 and 1813, her society, her fears, her uncanny stillness, her peasants, her soldiers, merchants, her cunning hesitation in the face of Napoleon, who misinterprets the evacuation of Moscow and expects to receive the homage of the Boyars at the gates of Moscow, is quite annoyed at being kept waiting so long, and then gropes his way into the silent, icily silent city, into the already smoldering, later blazing trap—Napoleon, who was insane enough to march toward that limitless horizon.

Who, when reading about the year 1812, would not think of the year 1941, when another and far more stupid arrogance and false assessment were to occur, this time Western Europe's false assessment of Eastern Europe: the invasion by the German Army, which intended to conquer Leningrad and Stalingrad and Moscow between June and November and at the same time intended to "conquer" the Russian winter in four and a half months without being even halfway equipped to do so? Needless to say, in strategic reminiscences there is much speculation as to IF, IF. The answer was clear: that winter was the severest in a hundred years, and no amount of IFs could help matters. It is always possible for those who direct battles to speculate later on the IFs; an author may never do this. Hitler's "Beresina" lasted for three winters, but the end was a semi-charred corpse at the entrance to an underground defense shelter in Berlin and a nation that had been sold down the river—and twenty-five years later, from the Springer skyscraper and the Hilton Hotel, one "looks down" across the Wall as if on apes at a zoo, still unaware that one's own apishness is already beginning to show. Oh no, people would like to be liberated all right, but what it means to be liberated by Germans is something they won't soon forget.

Since I have a tendency (a fortunate one, perhaps) to forget the contents of books, and can only keep bringing them to mind by means of the thematic material, every time I read *War and Peace* and reach the end of the first part—which may be regarded as a kind of exposition—I am filled with the same apprehension: how is he going to move this enormous parade through the years, across the spaces? I know, of course, that there are two protagonists on whom an author can more or less depend, a feminine one—peace—and a masculine one—war; and I also know by this time that things are not all going to go smoothly for Natasha: that ideal bridal pair, Natasha Rostov and

Andrey Bolkonsky, they're not going to get each other; and that wicked, skillfully outlined scheme of old Kuragin's, to rake in the two great fortunes of Bolkonsky and Bezuhov by attempts at matchmaking, of which only one succeeds, and that only for a time—this scheme, when it comes to "all's well that ends well," will be frustrated. Even financial burdens are equalized. The Rostovs, ruined by extravagance, can breathe again, Natasha marries Pierre, and Nikolay marries Marya Bolkonskaya. Isn't that a fairy tale? Hasn't Tolstoi succeeded in bringing off a superbly planned, magnificent deception with this very ordinary, mediocre Bezuhov, whom everyone thinks is so "real"? Is he not more unreal than Napoleon and Kutuzov, than that entire historically documented background and foreground, that stratified foundation, sliced like some historic prime ham, that Tolstoi needs in order to create firm ground under Pierre's feet?

Before the happy ending, eight more years and fourteen hundred pages will have passed, still to come are another fourteen parts, an epilogue, and no less than three hundred and fifty-three chapters all told. To the gentle reader, such figures may seem unimportant, indeed, a frivolous dismemberment, but for the reading author they are of exactly the same importance as the entire contents and the numerous characters with all their problems. Every novel, after all, is taken apart, bits are cut out, stuck in, altered—a process commonly known as composition; this dismemberment is part of the procedure we like to call the creative process. Such figures and numerical values bring home to us the rhythm, the breath which an author engaged on such a long journey must ration carefully. The average length of each of the fifteen parts amounts to some one hundred and five pages, the average length of each chapter is between four and five pages. Fortunately, none of the parts and only a few of the chapters achieve this "average quantity." The calculable proves to be incalculable; it goes without saying that a novel of this kind is not to be grasped in terms of mathematics; nevertheless, it has its finiteness, it has its length and even its tedious passages, it has the author's highly personal subdivision into books, chapters, paragraphs. I don't know whether there are already such things as cybernetic measurements of book-rhythms, I would imagine them to be very revealing, and if such things should exist I would like to compare *War and Peace* with *Crime and Punishment*. I would like to see these two breathing-tests side by side. Were they to be X-rayed for rhythm expressed concretely, they would probably both yield fantastic prints as by-products of literature. Reduced to a formula, a further comparison between Tolstoi and Dostoevski: Tolstoi is long-winded even in the very shortest of his tales; Dostoevski is short-winded to the point of breathlessness. In *Crime and Punishment* there is a time-condenser at work that for the nineteenth century is sensational: we don't know, nor is there any point in knowing, how long a time the novel spans, whether three or five days, whether weeks or months: in one instant the novel is over. With Tolstoi we march through centuries. At the beginning, Natasha is thirteen years old; at what is actually the end of the novel, she is twenty-one: barely eight years that seem like an eternity. If we strip the words long-winded and short-winded of their negative connotation, if we regard them simply as "technical values," perhaps we can discern the difference in rhythm. In his long novels, although they run close to a thousand pages, Dostoevski—late Dostoevski, at least—is short-winded. This also, of course, makes it possible to discern the difference in method and conditions of work.

It seems to me, in this attempt to close the gap, that nineteenth-century Russia is well taken care of and well expressed in these two so very different authors. Surprisingly enough, Tolstoi is the *younger* of the two; he seems older to us because he lived longer. I cannot include the constellations of Pushkin, Gogol, Chekov, Lermontov, and Goncharov in these deliberations, nor the many satellites of nineteenth-century Russian literature, necessary though this would be in order to provide the adjective "Russian" with even a tentative background. Is Pierre as Russian as Natasha's Germans are German; this fellow who, about halfway through the novel, thinks of himself: "And he was nothing but the wealthy husband of an unfaithful wife, a retired kammerherr who enjoyed good food and drink and doubtless grumbled a bit at the government as he sat there, waistcoat unbuttoned, after an ample dinner, a member of the Moscow English Club, and a universal favorite in Moscow society. It was a long time before he could accept the idea that from now on his own role was to be that of a retired kammerherr—a type that seven years ago he had heartily despised." Is *he* Russian, or is the flippant Dolohov, with whom he fights a duel? Is Bolkonsky; or Nikolay Rostov, who, all things considered, is a bit contemptible and none too intelligent, and who leaves Sonya in the lurch? And how about Anatole Kuragin, or that pushy and successful careerist Boris Drubetskoy? Who is the "more Russian," or even the "most Russian," of them all? Perhaps we should do something that is not permitted: modify a description of nationality by putting it in the superlative so as to discover how questionable these descriptions are.

What kind of characteristic is that which we may not and cannot modify? And where are the characters in Dostoevski, Gogol, Pushkin in all this—is Myshkin more

Russian than that nice little Petya Rostov, who has to die in the very last moments of the war and whom we can so well imagine as a peaceable, vainglorious little grandfather sitting by the fireside? Perhaps we should apply to nations the method I have suggested for detecting the author from his work as a whole: that is, add up the entire cast of characters that appear in their literatures, their politics, their economy, and their agriculture, and reduce this enormous sum to its seventh root—and then we would be justified in using an adjective such as "Russian" or "German." Needless to say, countries lay claim to their "characters," and no Russian will be willing to renounce a single one of them: neither Razumhin, who is as Russian as any other and no other, or Levin, or Vronsky, Kuragin, and Bolkonsky. Not without envy do I admit that the cosmos of men and women in Russian literature is a richly peopled one, in our own literature we are a little less generous—but what is it that even comes close to being *typically* Russian, so that we could use the adjective without hesitation? If we look closely at what is offered in *War and Peace* alone as being typically German, we find, quite apart from Natasha's direct hit, plenty of ammunition left. A proverb is quoted at some point in the novel: "The German threshes corn even on the back of his ax," and the Russian general staff is swarming with German advisers!

> Pfuhl was one of those hopelessly, unshakably, fanatically self-confident people to be found only among Germans, the reason being that only among Germans is that self-confidence based on an abstract idea, the idea, that is, of science: in other words, assuming that they possess absolute truth. The Frenchman's self-confidence is based on the belief

that he exerts an irresistible fascination, both mentally and physically, on men and women. The Englishman's self-confidence stems from the conviction that he is a citizen of the best-organized state in the world, and that—merely because he is an Englishman—he always knows what to do and that, by the same token —merely because he is an Englishman—his actions are beyond all doubt good and proper. The Italian's self-confidence arises from the fact that he is by nature excitable and easily forgets himself and others. The Russian's self-confidence is rooted in the fact that he knows nothing and wishes to know nothing, because he does not believe that one can know anything anyway. But the German's self-confidence is the worst of all, the most entrenched and the most unpleasant, precisely because he is under the illusion that he knows the truth—that is to say, the science which, although he has invented it himself, he regards as the absolute truth.

Pfuhl seems even more typical of German generals as a class than any of the others. A German theoretician of this kind, combining as he did—and so markedly at that—all the characteristics of those other men of theory, had never before crossed Prince Andrey's path.

Let the English, the French, and the Italians deal in their own way with their definition of nationality: I speak here as one who has some reason to call himself German.

Do we blush, are we ashamed, or are we merely annoyed, when we read this? Does it not seem to us somehow —unfortunately only somehow—to hit the nail on the head? Are not the ideologists of Eastern Germany somehow the General Pfuhls of the Eastern bloc, are they not know-it-alls, always knowing better, "assuming" their knowledge, their possession of "pure truth," and do not the stern pragmaticians of West Germany "pfuhl" around in the Western camp? Were not the great strategists of the war of conquest against the Soviet Union all more or less General Pfuhls who would have won if—well, if that winter had not been the grimmest, severest winter in a hundred years? But that is the kind of winter it was, and it was like that for the Red Army too.

I have no illusions about being able to solve even tentatively the problem of describing nationality, the problem of judgments and prejudices. I am only wondering whether it would not be better to withdraw such descriptions from currency for a while, until the computers, which are still to be invented and which would probably have to be a couple of miles wide, can be fed the requisite data and produce a little card giving the formula for what may be called Russian or German. As yet no nation, no people, no national literature, has begun to examine the adjectives with which we describe ourselves and others. We cannot pick out the essence of any one nation, nor can we reduce it to a handful of authors, let alone a handful of their characters. Literature in export is fraught with the danger of randomness.

Heinrich Heine would increase in importance and clarity if we could always see him in terms of his difference from Stifter. In certain parts of the world, Wagner's music is considered *the* German music, with the result that music that is less Wagnerian is no longer considered German. At what point does a German cease to be German for foreigners? Who is more Russian—Tolstoi or Dostoevski? What two authors could be farther apart from each other; is Poe more American than Jack London, is Stifter more German than Heine? And Hölderlin—who would

want to measure the distance between him and Heine? Is
not Stifter, precisely in his quality of "gentle monster," as
Arno Schmidt has called him, of an oppressive modernity,
with his restriction to objects, to stones, furniture, while
his human beings remain in some ghostly fashion "co-
cooned"—is not Stifter very nearly a nineteenth-century
specimen of the *nouveau roman,* and is not Heine's flip-
pancy and malice much more Rhinelandish than Jewish?
When is someone going to undertake the research of this
vast word "Jewish"?

Reduced to still further formulas: Tolstoi is the author
of rural life and rural economy, Dostoevski is the author of
the city. I know of scarcely another instance in which
rural life and rural economy, the people, the animals, have
been as successfully transformed into thematic material as
in the wolf hunt in *War and Peace:* surely, we think, this
is the true Russia, but then we have the other Russia:
Dostoevski's petty bourgeoisie and intellectuals in the city.
Tolstoi's secular religious feeling, Dostoevski's metaphysical one: I refuse and will always refuse to make a *choice*
between them. I accept them together, and Pushkin,
Gogol, Lermontov, and many others as well, and so, before we have installed the giant computer, I hold in my
hand something that I could for my own purposes describe as being approximately Russian.

Tolstoi and Dostoevski also differ in their significance
and relevance in the Soviet Union. Pushkin, Gogol, and
Tolstoi are probably the least controversial in terms of
ideology. Is it any wonder that, in terms of ideology,
Tolstoi was and will remain the more popular? An author
whom we may call—if one may still use the word—the
greatest realist in Russian literature; an author who as
a young man, after witnessing the death of his brother
Nikolay, conceived the idea at his brother's funeral of

writing a materialistic gospel, the "Life of Christ as a Materialist"; an author of whom no less a person than Lenin has said: "Before this Count began to write, there were no true peasants in Russian literature."

Fifty years after the Revolution, in the centennial year of Lenin's birth, there are signs that, without the era of Tolstoi, Pushkin, or Gogol having passed, Dostoevski's era is approaching. The immense gratitude and respect accorded literature in the Soviet Union does not entail one writer taking the place of another—it merely looks as if a missing link is at long last being supplied by Dostoevski. This is not always reflected in the permitted size of an edition. Some of Solzhenitsyn's manuscripts, not printed but privately mimeographed, are said to be circulating to the tune of twenty to thirty thousand copies. This means several hundred thousand readers. An author of this kind, even if he is not printed, is "present," and there is no doubt that Dostoevski is also "present" in the Soviet Union. The connection between the Dostoevski revival and a religious revival is unmistakable. Are East and West, across the Wall, switching positions? Certainly not in their administrations. In the West the administration will continue to let the banner of Christianity flutter, or at least will not lower it, and the East will officially keep the flag of atheism flying. Both flags will continue to deceive superficial observers. The social materialism that is emerging in the West will continue to be dismissed as a fad (for these social materialists, Tolstoi ought by rights to be something of a Bible—Tolstoi, who said: "The root of all evil is property"), just as the religious revival in the Soviet Union will be dismissed as a fad. Nothing is likely to change in the confrontation: Western progressives will dismiss the new trend in the Soviet Union as reactionary, and people in Eastern Europe will regard Western ideas as social illusions.

In analyzing the processes to be anticipated, a work such as *The Possessed* will be important: the murder of Shatov, taking place at the very instant he intends to begin a "new life," that senseless intellectual game-plan, as the vehicle of obedience, at the same time bringing about a magical relationship through blood-guilt—this is to be repeated over and over again. Tolstoi is by far the more earthy, the more material, the more substantial. Dostoevski is the more spiritual, also the more "uncomfortable," and this extends to such material details as the attitudes of his principal characters toward eating; expressed in modern terms, they all eat at lunch counters, hot-dog stands, snack bars, whereas Tolstoi's characters enjoy lingering over a lengthy meal.

In the Russia of the nineteenth century, such high-sounding words as liberty, equality, fraternity fell on soil that differed in every respect from the soil of Western Europe. Russia's relationship to humanism—assuming all the fragility, all the abuses, all the facets and falsifications that the term has since undergone—differs from that of Western Europe. History has presented these words and concepts in a different connotation in Russia, and to this day everything that happens there carries a different connotation. And to this day the concept of solidarity has a different history and different accepted forms of realization. In the Soviet Union, political detention has been worn—and is still being worn—as decorations are worn in Western countries; the awe felt for a prisoner has only now begun to diminish and will continue to diminish with the rise of a new class of person: the Soviet Philistine, who wants precisely what Western Philistines demand:

law and order. The political prisoners in Tolstoi's *Resurrection* clearly recognize in the unfortunate Mazlova a victim of social, that is to say political, conditions, and in the end it is they who welcome her and liberate her, accepting her as another political prisoner.

Respect for writers and intellectuals has always been great in Russia, since it was they who traditionally worked for changes in conditions of government. The *zamizdat,* the privately mimeographed and circulated manuscript that eluded censorship and still managed to become popular (as Solzhenitsyn's manuscripts, among others, have done in our time), has a tradition, and out of this tradition has grown a different attitude toward the popularity that today still appears suspect to Western intellectuals. We shall never understand it, even less shall we be able to analyze it precisely, if only because we have never quite grasped the differences, the many nuances, between Soviet Russia, the other Soviet republics, and the other Socialist states.

Taking Russian literature of the nineteenth century as a whole, I have something like an approximate idea of what is Russian, and in *War and Peace* some idea—again only an approximate one—of Tolstoi. Then, of course, we also have the immense distances concealed in an author's entire work, comparable to the scope within the term "Slavic." Is the Dostoevski of *The Gambler* different from the Dostoevski of *The Brothers Karamazov?* Where in all this is that quality, which must at least remain constant and if possible be continually intensified, that the Pfuhls among literary critics demand of an author? As novels, *Anna Karenina* and *Resurrection* are better than *War and Peace,* with its many raised fingers behind which the large cast of characters has a way of disappearing, and no doubt many clever people have already discovered the weakness of the epilogue. They are right, it is disappointing: Natasha, scarcely thirty years old, already a matron, a very average little housewife, not overly jealous but appropriately so, and Pierre—we can imagine him very well sitting by the fireside with Nikolay and that inextinguishably likable Denisov, who managed to become a general after all; in the twlight, a cap of indeterminate nature on his head, he could be both at once: Grandfather and Grandmother. The somewhat limited Nikolay at the side of that immensely good soul Marya Bolkonskaya, who might have made an excellent abbess. And one day that embarrassing fellow Berg, likewise a general for many years now, will come walking in, and, as I know him, will bemoan the loss of that "charming" dressing table that was left behind in burning Moscow, and at the same time he will rather relish that loss as a heroic sacrifice.

After so much exertion, excitement, suffering, and passion, everything ends so terribly normally. Has someone, in the final analysis, brought up the heavy artillery merely to dispatch a few sparrows? Will we, after that ample dinner, merely unbutton our waistcoats and grumble a bit at the government? Will even the feminine reader lose her desire to "identify" with *this* Natasha? Just as the masculine reader has almost stopped feeling envious of Pierre? At the very end, of course, we still have young Nikolenka Bolkonsky, who dreams of his father and idolizes Pierre and would like to do great things; new hope, a new beginning. To me, this epilogue seems like a carefully directed blow, a slap with a wet towel. Had Tolstoi been capable of producing kitsch, he would probably have written deliberate kitsch such as the intended title "All's Well That

Ends Well": yet not even the epilogue is kitsch, it is quite deliberately anti-idealistic, so it seems to me, and may correspond to the author's desire to create, at least in his work, something that he never found: ordinary everyday life. For such an unordinary person as Tolstoi, this everyday life must have been a dream, just as it may be a dream for ordinary people to lead "the life of an artist," and this ordinary everyday married life at the end of the novel is bitterly challenged in the preceding parts of the book:

> "A bad business, isn't it?"
> "What's a bad business, Papa?"
> "Women!" snapped the old Prince.
> "I don't know what you mean," replied Prince Andrey.
> "There's nothing to be done about it, my dear boy," said the old Prince. "They're all alike, and one can't get a divorce. Don't worry, I won't tell anybody. And you know it anyway."

This allusion to Andrey's relationship with his wife Liza is sarcastic and apt. And have we forgotten, in reading this happy ending, that Natasha was actually prepared, as Andrey's fiancée, to be abducted by a scoundrel like Anatole Kuragin? Enough remains to prevent us from entirely trusting this happy ending. Maybe the idea is for this happy ending to suggest that history reduces wars, both big and small, to a pathetic topic of conversation for those who participate in and survive them. The fact is that, if wars last long enough, captains do become colonels and generals, and even if the valiant Denisov, who steals food for his starving soldiers, very nearly perished miserably in a field hospital, and to our surprise becomes crabby and cantankerous—he too ends up in an atmosphere of *Gemüt-*

lichkeit. I don't find this ending all that happy, however happy it may have been intended to be.

A few years before beginning to write down *War and Peace,* Tolstoi wrote in a letter: "In order to live decently, one must exert oneself, become involved, struggle and fight, make mistakes, begin and give up, start again and give up, and constantly fight and use up one's resources. Peace and quiet are nothing more than meanness of soul." Perhaps this quotation, which could be expanded by citing many others, is the only possible comment on the happy ending of *War and Peace.*

There would be much to say about Tolstoi as a person— about his relationship to "greatness," which he explicates with Napoleon; about his attitude toward "war," which he sees as a bloody and ludicrous absurdity, again personified for him in the absurdity of Napoleon, whose activity is paralyzed in the passivity of burning Moscow; about Tolstoi and the West, Catholicism (Ellen Kuragin's ultimate depravity consists in her becoming a Catholic!). Biographical material to be noted would be Tolstoi's constant endurance of the conflicts between his life, his work, and his teachings; he was continually being torn in different directions within this triangle, and if "peace and quiet are nothing more than meanness of soul," then his soul was anything but mean. He was not an Olympian, although there were many who would have gladly placed him on a number of thrones, and he finally died like a Dostoevski figure—totally unwise, torn by the contradictions of his life—and even after death nothing was spared him: the door to his conjugal bedroom was opened wide, his sheet was lifted; there could hardly have been more misunderstandings and wretched misinterpretations, or suspicions either, than existed between him and his wife, him and the greater part of his family, him and his disciples, his supporters, The Tolstoians. Nothing, nothing was spared him. Not a trace, not even the ghost of a suggestion, of a happy ending.

Have we satisfied our curiosity, found the author, unearthed his hiding place? Where and in whom is he hiding? In Bolkonsky, in Pierre, in Anatole Kuragin perhaps, in the two Nekhlyudovs (twice—in *Memoirs of a Billiard-Marker* and in *Resurrection*—he gives his heroes this name); is he in Levin who, with his Kitty, ends up as happily as Pierre with Natasha? Has he been hiding under Kuturov's lapel or in Bagration's tobacco pouch? In Speransky, the doyen of Czarist ideologists? In Natasha's uncle, at the point where the glorious wolf hunt comes to a glorious end? Where is this author, this person of whom we know that he died in a stationmaster's bed, persecuted by fame and killed by the reflection of fame on his family? May I suggest that we leave him in peace? Allow him simply to have *existed*, not only in work, life, and teachings, which would be enough, but also *split* among Bolkonsky, Bezuhov, Levin, and Oblonsky, with "traits," possibly even of Vronsky, a "touch" of Speransky, two Nekhlyudovs, and some three hundred others.

And should we not, in all fairness, grant the possibility of his having hidden, and remained hidden, in some women? Is it not enough to know that nothing was spared him, not even public excommunication by the Russian Orthodox Church—something that he must have felt to be an honor? My curiosity, at any rate, is satisfied, and before I make a complete Pfuhl of myself I will let him have the last word. Said by Tolstoi about human beings, it might, if applied to nations, help us onward:

> It is a very common and very widespread superstition that every human being has certain inalterable

characteristics, that we are either good or bad, clever or stupid, strong-minded or passive, etc. But people are not like that. We may say that a certain person is more often good than bad, more often clever than stupid, more often strong-minded than passive, and vice versa, but it would be incorrect to say of any one person that he is simply good or clever, bad or stupid. Yet this is how we are constantly classifying people— and this is wrong. Human beings are like rivers—the water that flows in them is always the same, but every river is narrow at one point, broad at another, sometimes calm or clear or cold, sometimes murky and at other times warm again. And people are exactly the same. Every human being carries the seeds of all human characteristics within him, all come to the surface at different times, and although he will often behave in an unprincipled manner, he is still the same person. In some people, such turnabouts are very sudden. [From *Resurrection*]

Perhaps that is an attempt to close the gap to himself; perhaps not even the best attempt, and perhaps—as many a reader will think—"oversimplified." There is no doubt that Tolstoi himself was much, much more complicated than this attempt of his to close the gap to a definition of the human condition. He was inexplicable to himself.

THE ROOT OF
NORTHERN IRELAND'S
TROUBLES

(1970)

The Anglo-Irish troubles are older than Cologne Cathedral, i.e., some hundreds of years older than the Reformation. On August 23, 1970, all of Ireland would be able to celebrate an anniversary that the Northern Irish might regard as the start of the ninth century of their oppression. On August 23, 1170, Richard, Earl of Pembroke, known as "Strongbow," set foot in Ireland, and that date marks the beginning of the "troubles." In fact, inveterate Celtomanes might even consider Irish-English problems as dating from as far back as St. Patrick's century, the saint having been a Briton who tried to bring the ecclesiastical order of Rome to a deeply devout, semiclannish, patriarchal church. In one of the poems attributed to St. Brigid of Kildare, the "people of Heaven" and the "Three Maries of illustrious renown" are invited to a great drinking feast, more specifically to a drink whose barbarity and blasphemy might still horrify many Roman hearts today: namely, ale.

> I should like Jesus too to be here among them: ...
> I should like the Three Maries of illustrious renown;

I should like the people of Heaven there from all
    parts: ...
I should like a great lake of ale for the King of kings;
I should like the family of Heaven to be drinking it
    through time eternal.

Many a Roman button will surely burst at the bizarre
notion of ale being a fitting sacrament, admissible as a
drink "through time eternal." I see no place yet for the
slogan: "Have a beer with Jesus!"

This by way of indication that some kind of religious
subjugation existed in Ireland even before the Reformation. Eight hundred years after Pembroke, after "Strongbow," we now have an Ian Paisley and a seemingly help-
less government, a government that is apparently astonished to find these damnable Irish troubles not yet settled.

Be that as it may, among some 700 civil servants and
public employees in Northern Ireland there are some 70
Catholics. Among 386 medical specialists in the health
service there are all of 31 Catholics; among 61 medical
professors there are 3. Of the 3,000 members of the Royal
Ulster Constabulary the figure is 10 per cent; and in the
Ulster Special Constabulary (a body of 11,300 men, who
constitute a kind of Protestant Home Guard and are entitled to keep their weapons at home) there is, of course,
not a single Catholic, since it is recruited mainly from
among Orangemen. Were all these positions to be filled in
proportion to the Catholic percentage of the population,
the Catholic share would be one third.

Whether this will continue to be the ratio depends on
another factor; slightly more than one third of the population of Northern Ireland is Catholic, but among school-
children the proportion is more than half—for a reason

which the Primate of all Ireland, Cardinal Conway, pinpointed in words as forthright as they are plain: "The Catholics outbreed them." Needless to say, when Richard Pembroke landed eight hundred years ago he could know nothing of any distinction between Catholic and Protestant. What he wanted, and what he did know something about, was: power, something that in the twelfth century was considered in no way amoral; and naturally "Strongbow" had never heard of democracy, probably he would have taken the word for the name of some obscure and sinister disease. Nor would it be correct to call him an Englishman. He was descended from the Norman nobility that had come over from France with William the Conqueror; Pembroke came of a lineage that had already bestowed upon the Celtic population of Wales the blessings of Norman rule and order. He may have been a particularly masterful representative of the master race. The question in Ireland was and still is: who are to be the masters?

Paisley knows full well what he is warning his Protestant countrymen of: loss of power, which for them is tantamount to loss of property and of social and political privileges. And he also knows full well how this accursed "outbreeding," the Catholics' secret weapon of population increase, can be combated under police protection: by social and political discrimination to a point at which the Catholic Irish reach for their last desperate recourse: emigration, in which they are as grimly experienced as they are in social and political discrimination. Then the statistics would tally again. Paisley, the government of Northern Ireland, as well as most of the Catholic Irish in Ulster's six counties must have been astonished, in fact deeply offended, at the idea of there being another recourse: resistance, if necessary supported by violence.

It was a bad reminder of the bad year of 1916, when pa-
triots and Socialists proclaimed the Irish Republic, initia-
ting an apparently hopeless struggle.

It would be pointless to offer a condensed version of
Ireland's complex eight-hundred-year-old history from
Richard, Earl of Pembroke, down to Ian Paisley. Naturally
there was treason, there were betrayed traitors, there
were honorable and dishonorable traitors, and almost
every event in Irish history is "disputed." And naturally,
had Irish history been determined by Celts alone, it would
not have been one of everlasting peace. As it turned out,
this history is one of never entirely successful oppression.
Harsh punishments were the consequence of stubborn revolt against a superimposed rule, a rule which after the
Reformation also exploited the denominational angle and,
through still further harshness, very nearly turned the
Catholics into a "race." Between 1692 and 1829, no Irish
Catholic was allowed to sit in Parliament, no Catholic was
allowed to occupy public office or own a horse worth more
than five pounds; no armorer was allowed to take on a
Catholic apprentice, no Catholic was allowed to attend a
state school or send his children abroad to school.

That such instruments of power are not confined to
one denomination is proved by the fate of Protestants in
Spain and France. We have only to read of the dangers
that threatened Protestants in France up to 1782 and the
delightful experiences that Protestants in Spain and Bap-
tists in the Soviet Union are still undergoing today. There
are counter-examples: the handsome fairness with which
Protestants have always been treated in the Irish Republic.
The first President of this more than 90–per cent Catholic
state was a Protestant, and the Anglican Church of Ireland
has not, as far as I know, been deprived of any of its rights,
nor would any politician in the Irish Republic dream of

reviving the grim specter of denominationalism. In this respect at least, the young Irish Republic has remained true to the spirit of the first Irish Republican, Theobald Wolfe Tone, who was of Protestant descent. Hence the embarrassment of any Northern Irish or English politician at such an anachronism as Ian Paisley must be intensified by the fact of his many supporters.

And yet Paisley can have all those supporters only because this tiny corner of Europe has never been aired and because the injustice entrenched there has not been perceived. The cry of clericalism, purported to be in control of the Irish Republic, is as misleading as any "truth" of which it can be said that there is "something to it." Throughout the centuries of oppression, the Catholic clergy loyally stuck by the oppressed, many a priest even incurring death by rope or firing squad. Whether this credit—acquired not only honestly but also with courage and compassion—is still fully valid today, whether it was not already impaired in the nineteenth century, is something for the young Irish of Miss Bernadette Devlin's generation to decide for themselves. This strong-minded young woman, whose career bears ample witness to Irish Catholicism, claims that among Ireland's greatest traitors, "Mother Church," a massive obstacle on the road to equality and freedom, ranks uppermost.

Indeed, every Irish liberation movement since the French Revolution has had an unmistakably republican cast that may have been highly palatable to the poor Irish rural clergy. There is one thing the Irish have never been afraid of: excommunication. Many of them have accepted it: it is quite possible that, if this senseless religious penalty had existed in those days, even St. Brigid would have been excommunicated for inviting Jesus to drink beer through time eternal. Bernadette Devlin's judgment on the Catholic Church agrees word for word—not only in Ireland but almost everywhere in the world—with what young Catholic priests are realizing and expressing today: that the failure of the Church in Ireland is not unique, it is in line with the Church's universal failure to recognize the Industrial Age and its consequences until too late, and the resultant loss of the workers by the Church's aligning itself with the masters. In two European countries—and in each case for similar reasons, i.e., because the clergy supported the people against foreign rule with the result that Orthodox Russians and Protestant Prussians alike despised Catholicism—in two countries there is still a Catholic working class: in Ireland and in Poland.

The way power can be exerted even within a parliamentary system is shown by numerous examples in Frank Gallagher's book *The Indivisible Island.*[1] One of these is Gallagher's description of the infamous process of gerrymandering, the manipulation of electoral wards. He cites the town of Derry as a typical example. In Derry City, he says, there are 31,620 (Irish) Nationalists and 18,479 Tories. "It would seem from these figures," Gallagher goes on to say, "to be beyond the wit of man to give Derry a Tory City Council." Not at all. The city, with the active assistance of the regime, is divided into three unequal wards, as follows:

> North Ward: 13,896 inhabitants who elect 8 representatives
> South Ward: 24,768　　　″　　　　″　　″ ″　　″
> Waterside Ward: 11,435 ″　　　　″　　″ ″　　″

Thus a minority elects the majority of twelve representatives, and the majority elects the minority of eight. The wards are so arranged that there are more Nationalist votes in a single ward than there are Tories in the whole town.

Was it coincidence that the demonstrations in Londonderry exploded into riots, that it was there that violence began, in the town where, due to sudden layoffs by an electrical manufacturing company, the unemployment figure was 12.7 per cent of the working Catholic population, the ratio—of female to male unemployed—being 4.3 : 17.5 per cent? In our industrial age, sudden layoffs, however justifiable in terms of the economy, are also an indication of who wields the power. They reflect *dependence*, and anyone so clearly in a state of subjugation and forced to live from hand to mouth is dependent.

The historical road from Pembroke to Bernadette Devlin and Ian Paisley is a long one, yet the last two would not be where they are without the first. There is no cause for us Central Europeans to pretend that such ancient indications of power did not influence our present history: as if there were no ghostly Knights of the Teutonic Order haunting the Oder/Neisse Line, and as if it were not high time to accept the failure of our eastward colonization and take back the colonists; and as if, until the De Gaulle-Adenauer embrace (and possibly even after), Germany "left-of-the-Rhine" had not been plagued by the spirit of Charlemagne with its legacy of a luckless empire without natural borders, called Lotharingia. To this day French journalists unthinkingly apply the term *L'Outre-Rhin* to Germany, and a considerable section of the Rhine is not "Germany's river" but Germany's border.

In all Marxist-governed countries, Ireland's history is fairly well known, if only because at the time of Ireland's struggle for liberation it was the classic country of partisans; because Friedrich Engels found so many object lessons for his theories among the Irish industrial workers in and around Manchester; because the great Irish famine, which almost ruined that already humiliated and enfeebled country, is regarded as a classic (and conclusive) example of capitalist free trade's inability to solve crises of supply. Cecil Woodham-Smith has written an impressive study of this famine, *The Great Hunger,* which, in view of the frequent famines being experienced by the world, should be required reading for all concerned citizens; in my view, Mrs. Woodham-Smith's well-documented historical analysis is becoming increasingly relevant and is applicable to India, Biafra, and South America.

Among other things, it proves that Ireland was one of many Biafras. It is hardly a subject for disagreement that political and social conditions in Northern Ireland are an embarrassing relic in a small corner of Europe whose tidying-up has been overlooked. For eight hundred years Ireland has been a wound in England's side, its sore spot, and there can be few Englishmen who do not feel uneasy when Ian Paisley—in his clerical collar, moreover—persists in opening up the wound, preaching anti-Popery at a time when hardly a cardinal is a Papist and perhaps not even the Pope.

Yet this demagogic pseudo-preacher has his followers: it is a matter of power to be surrendered, of privileges to be relinquished. Irish history teaches us that there will be no peace until what should be obvious becomes reality. Paisley's main argument, that this would usher in rule by Rome, sounds absurd, but to the ears of Orangemen it has a familiar ring. Actually it is probably the other way around: the manifest socialist undercurrent of the new civil rights movement in Northern Ireland most certainly finds no sympathy in Rome and very little in the hierarchy of the Irish Republic. Bernadette Devlin wrote in her autobiography that, on taking a closer look at the Ireland she wished to unite, she found that what had to be done was not to liberate the Six Counties but to start the national revolution all over again from the very beginning: there were, according to her, no free counties anywhere in Ireland; in twenty-six counties the Irish had taken the place of the English but had done nothing to change the system. In 1897, she pointed out, James Connolly (the only true socialist of the 1916 rebellion) had said that, were his countrymen to kick out the English and next day hoist the tricolor over Dublin Castle, Ireland's problems, being economic and social, would remain. And that, according to Miss Devlin, still holds true.

No doubt this is music to the ears of many young people in the Irish Republic. No doubt those whom Ian Paisley sees as "Papists" take no pleasure in hearing it. Once before there was an ugly conspiracy against an Irish politician who, as early as the nineteenth century, was on the verge of inflicting grievous harm on the Empire: Charles Stewart Parnell, probably one of the most gifted and successful politicians of the entire nineteenth century, an Irishman and a Protestant, a landowner even, a born "secret king" and popular leader: an Irish David before whom Goliath had every reason to tremble. His career was destroyed not politically but "morally," because of a love affair with Kitty O'Shea which everyone knew about but which, when he began to represent a political threat, became the noose around his neck; and here "Papists" and "anti-Papists" were united, with momentous results. Parnell was voted out of his position as leader of his party, he resigned and died soon after at the early age of forty-five.

What is new about the civil rights movement in Northern Ireland is its rediscovery of republican and socialist traditions, and there is every reason for progressive young Irish people in both parts of Ireland to pray to the "most blessed Mother" that Catholics and Protestants will not perceive their *common* enemy in this new socialism or uncover any "love affairs" among its protagonists. There were times during Ireland's history when Rome allied itself more or less overtly with England in order to prevent social progress in Ireland. May the "most blessed Mother" also bless Mr. Paisley's follies and grant that once again it can be said, as it was in the nineteenth century, that "as a basis for their politics the Irish take Ireland, but their religion they take from Rome."

[1] *The Indivisible Island,* by Frank Gallagher; Gollancz, London, 1957.

Had he been born in Germany, the clichés prefabricated
by centuries of misconceptions would already have been to
hand: Leftist Catholic, worker-poet, anarchist. Not one
of those clichés would have covered even a portion of the
man. He was a Dubliner and a Republican; his resemblance to Danton was more than external, and in the end
he died for the same reason as Danton: out of boredom.

The part of Dublin in which he grew up is proletarian,
warm-hearted, and pervaded by a Catholic-proletarian
melancholy, just like Cologne used to be around the Eigelstein and Severin Gates. For eleven years my wife's route to
school took her through the Eigelstein quarter; for nine
years mine took me through the Severin quarter. These are
the only sections of any German city where Behan might
have felt anything like at home—also, perhaps, in Würz-
burg as described by Leonhardt Frank and in a few streets
around Mainz Cathedral.

This brings me to a crucial and knotty point which I
have to approach in a roundabout way: Behan's Catholicism" or "Catholicity." "-isms" and "-icities" are dreadful
appendages, horrible mutilations of something that, alas,
has virtually no other name to offer for itself. Behan has

written that, as far as religion is concerned, his family
was always Catholic and extremely anticlerical; that,
strangely enough, he knew of no priest in any of the generations of his family (indeed a miracle for Ireland!), and that
he knew of no member of his family who had died without a
priest. *Deo Gratias.* His father, he wrote, was excommunicated in 1922 for being a Republican, as was Brendan himself in 1939, but in Catholic countries no one worries about
this—least of all the priest—when it comes to getting
married or buried.

To the ears of "German Catholics" (ghastly label, sound-
ing almost like "German Christians"), this seems either
very amusing or very provocative, yet it is neither. For an
Irishman it is only "natural," but then a "natural" German
is always taken for a foreigner, not to mention a "natural
German Catholic"—good God, the Humanistic Union
would probably join forces with the Central Committee of
German Catholics to burn him (or her) at the stake outside the Federal Parliament building in Bonn! In Germany
not even the Youth Movement has brought or signified
freedom to Catholics, never having had either understanding of or attraction for the proletariat. What it did
achieve was to turn proletarians into ambitious petty
bourgeois with well-defined tastes, superior types who
make a beeline for the very best arty-crafty establishments
and whose stomachs are never without that sour taste of
social ambition, a striving for "something better." There
has never been the slightest chance of understanding the
warmth of "Catholic vulgus," let alone of accepting it as
one way of being human. Fear of excommunication has
always been a restraint on the best and most gifted members of the Catholic Youth Movement, which thus, gen-
erally speaking, has remained no more than a form of
snobbishness on the part of earnest high-school students

and pompous university professors: its members can be
turned into good little Fascists, good little Democrats, but
never into Republicans—that they confuse with "anar-
chism," and they find it "amusing" and "colorful" and "ever
so full of life!" but they refuse to be associated with it. The
final decline of the Catholic Youth Movement came after
World War II, when without resistance, indeed without
any noticeable opposition, it allowed its functionaries to
align the Movement with those in favor of rearmament.

I have had to approach this point in such a roundabout
way in order to rescue Behan from that terrible German
"-icity" and "-ism," for it would be a sad thing if posthumously he were to be labeled a "Catholic writer." There
is nothing sensational about his having been born in
Dublin, as were Joyce and Shaw, Swift, O'Casey, and
Beckett; what *is* sensational is that he also died in Dublin
and is buried there. I believe it is a good thing for Ireland
if her writers and poets, whether excommunicated or not,
are now once again being buried in her cemeteries.

After his death a number of obituaries appeared in Germany expressing a certain enthusiasm for his bawdiness.
Unfortunately, however, the petty bourgeois notion of
sexual immorality is as embarrassing as the petty bourgeois
notion of sexual mores, and Behan simply will not fit into
any one of the familiar clichés, neither those of the moralists nor those of the bawdy-house enthusiasts. Prostitution
in a country where it is illegal is quite different from
prostitution in a country such as ours, where it is taken as
much for granted as dealing in used cars. In our country
almost everything is the opposite of what it is in Ireland:
here in Germany sexual immorality is indulged in, pretended to, practiced reluctantly if need be, because it is
the fashion, it is expected; because young Fritz and young

Gretel, in their efforts to escape from stultifying restraint into stultifying liberty, are incapable of shaking off their petty bourgeois clichés and believe they can—they must—join the "smart set" by "sinning"—usually without really enjoying it. In Ireland it is a matter of passion, and there they know that human nature has fallen and will continue to fall, and that neither moralists nor bawdy-house enthusiasts can do it justice.

If Behan had been born in Germany—in 1923!—he would still be not only a "young writer," but one of the youngest, for in our country writers of forty and fifty are still posturing on that fragile platform labeled "young writers." Behan is dead, hence much, much older than Wilhelm Lehmann, who is young and writes beautiful poetry. When Behan was sixteen, in 1939, he was arrested in Liverpool for having explosives in a suitcase with which he meant to blow up a ship in the harbor. He was released in 1942, rearrested a few days later, this time in Dublin, for the attempted murder of two (Irish) secret policemen. Although sentenced to fourteen years, he was amnestied after four, in 1946; a year later, in 1947, he was jailed again for four months, this time in Manchester. By the time he was twenty-four he had spent the equivalent of every third day of his life in jail. At the Borstal reformatory he experienced something as unique as it is uniquely Irish: he wanted to go to mass, but the prison chaplain discovered that he had been excommunicated and banned him from the service—a seventeen-year-old boy and a convict! Later, in another young offenders' prison, he was allowed to be an altar boy; and a young fellow-prisoner, convicted of many thefts and a nonbeliever, rehearsed the responses with him.

He quickly became famous, not only as a writer but also as an eccentric and because of his fondness for the bottle.

On the subject of drinking he wrote that in Dublin, during the bad years of his youth, drinking was not considered a social disgrace. If a person managed to get enough to eat, that was considered heroic; if he managed to get drunk it was a triumph.

After Behan's death his brother Brian wrote that he was certainly afraid of nothing, not even of death, whose sting he kept reaching out for until he finally seized it; that he was bored, bored by people and by life; that he had reached the point where he despised almost everybody and accused the rest of living in his shadow or of waiting for a chance to borrow money from him: that he moved restlessly around and around and returned to nothing. Why, his brother wondered, didn't he write a great novel? He was too much of a personality. He expressed himself in what he said and did much more than in what he wrote. His own skin was too tight for him—and what was worse (according to Brian) was that the press began to praise his stuff even when it was garbage. Cut off from his main source, from real people, he couldn't write much about the society of double-tongued swindlers who praised each of his belches as a token of divine inspiration. But, his brother concludes, nothing and nobody can take away *The Quare Fellow* and *The Hostage*.

In many respects Behan was the opposite of James Joyce, who was hardly a "personality" at all but almost solely a writer, yet they both are inconceivable without and indissoluble from that unique city called Dublin.

On the Occasion of Ernst Bloch's
85th Birthday

THE MOSCOW
SHOESHINERS

(1970)

Moscow shoeshiners, women and men, take their time, of which they have plenty. Their booths, barely six feet high, provided with a door plus a floor area no larger than a narrow cot, are miniature temples of dignity. This dignity, were we to call it "human dignity," would merely define the first prerequisite of dignity. In these hallowed halls they have advanced beyond this. These people who pursue what is ostensibly a humble occupation all show a family resemblance, as if they were mothers and sons, brothers and sisters. Those eyes, those narrow faces and long noses, those profiles, were familiar to me from reproductions of vases and frescoes. Syrian, I thought, maybe Assyrian. And from school textbooks containing brief paragraphs on the history of Asia Minor. Later I was told that no one knows for sure: they are probably Maronites from what is now Lebanon, refugees from one of the great expulsions following World War I. Shoeshining appears to be their privilege, their fief, their unwritten law, just as the Apulians appear to have the exclusive right to sell roast chestnuts in Rome.

Their booths offer the passerby more than a shoeshine: a spot remover is on hand to clean soiled clothing, needle and thread can be borrowed to sew on a torn-off button, scissors to cut frayed edges, to mend a briefcase or a shopping bag. Shoeshining, the main occupation, proceeds without haste, without even a hint of servility, with no attempt at familiarity. Customers in a hurry, who show impatience and would prefer to have the ritual curtailed, are exhorted by a grave look from dark eyes and a gentle shake of the head to submit to the ritual in full. A rite is a rite, dignity is dignity, shoes are shoes, and here we can learn the meaning of "application," the word that perhaps comes closest to an accurate translation of "sacrament." (In this sense, marriage would be the "application" of love.)

Shoelaces are tucked in with due care, socks are protected with cardboard cuffs. Left shoe on the footrest: brushes of varying degrees of stiffness are used to remove dirt and dust, liquid shoe polish from a bottle is applied; right shoe on the footrest: the same application. Left shoe: brief polish with a special cloth for the liquid shoe polish, the same procedure for the right. Left shoe on the footrest: paste polish from a can is applied; the same for the right. Left and right foot: shine with a soft brush. Shake of the head, gentle command with dark eyes. Once again both shoes, first one then the other, must be placed on the footrest: from a different bottle a special gloss is applied, which in turn—left foot, right foot—is polished to a high finish.

The ritual application is over. The time we think we have lost is returned twofold from the dark eyes. Gained, not lost.

That's all I know about the Moscow shoeshiners; they are refugees who have found a home here; they return our lost time twofold; their profiles seemed familiar from reproductions of vases and frescoes seen in a school text-book. I would like to know more about the Moscow shoe-shiners, I would like to know everything, and I shall try to find out. I envy them.

Your Excellencies, the survivors among those born in 1917 are all of an age to be bishops, generals, or cabinet ministers, yet that is not why I am addressing myself to you. My reason is purely and simply one of *form*, since the title by which you are addressed permits me to kill three birds with one stone: Church, Army, and State. I would be quite satisfied with a priest, a major, and a senior civil servant; in fact I would even be prepared, if need be, to mingle boldly with the humble and invite a monk, a sergeant, and a streetcar conductor to join in my little game. But with you three I am offered the unique opportunity of nailing you all with a single title, and I call upon your humility, since it is not the dignity of your position but the mode of address to which you are entitled that makes it easier for me to play my game.

There is one thing I must say first: I know that your positions weigh heavily upon you, that you wield your powers reluctantly, that your powers use you unkindly, and I say to you, with that frankness which should be taken for granted among those of the same age: it shows!

How listlessly you go about your business; how listlessly you chew the cud of your caution and cunning before the TV cameras or on tape. It shows: you are unhappy! Come along now, relax now and again over a drink, rejoice with the joyful, forget the trials and tribulations of power, forget your office and the white man's burden; and should it ever enter your heads to envy the writer, whose job it is to give an air of joy even to the joyless, then my message to you is: go ahead, try! In a free economy there is always room for authors with the rank of Excellency, and publishers are always ready for a little gamble. And when the publishing contract looms near, come to me for advice, for let me warn you, my hearties, when you reach for your pen *be sure and read the fine print*. I have a delightful vision of one of you giving a "freewheeling" account of all that has happened to those born in 1917. So reach for your pens, my hearties, and give me your support! How nice it would look on your income tax return if the column "Income Derived from Self-Employment" were not crossed out—or are you spared anything as vulgar as an income tax return?

Being a professional, I am reluctant to step onto the hair's breadth of fortune that has allowed me to reach the age of seven times seven. The road has been long, political and historical events have been numerous and few among them have been happy, and the chances of slipping off that hair's breadth of fortune have been countless. Do you know, for instance, that a person born in 1880 had far greater prospects of reaching the age of sixty-six than someone born in 1917 had of reaching the age of twenty-eight? In fact, comrades, the chances of surviving were one in three, and in terms of Russian roulette that would mean that out of six possibilities, four would end in death, whereas in genuine Russian roulette, which is considered a daring gamble, the ratio is one in six. In 1945 there were almost as many seventy-five-year-olds in Germany as there were people of our own age, while those aged sixty-six far outnumbered us and there were twice as many aged fifty-six. And when you think of the surplus of women, which amounted to sixty, seventy, and even eighty per cent, please remember Giraudoux, who, in his play about the Trojan War, has a surviving hero say, "We sleep with our women—and with yours," and need I say, Your Excellencies, that that is not meant *personally*, not even for the two secular Excellencies, but *symbolically*.

To the left of that hair's breadth of fortune lies the swamp of vainglory, to the right the morass of banality, and furthermore, Excellencies: this miserable hair is split (there's no getting away from splitting hairs in a German career), and I have long since become more suspicious of my innocence than of my guilt, seeing that I possess neither of them. To balance on a split hair is impossible, even for a professional, so I beg you, Messieurs, hold out your exalted hands to me. Since my production has never been, and never will be, of the "freewheeling" kind (maybe I have the wrong kind of wheels), my usual practice is as follows: I plant an evocative word or word-cluster in prose, wait for it to flower, then wither, and then I pick it—the very same method your grandmother used to fill her scrapbook. The only trouble is that these evocative words in the scrapbook start producing *mass*—invisible to the nonprofessional—a mass of memories. Again the flowers, again they must be allowed to wither, and so on and so on, and I find myself in a terrible quandary: the list of items waiting to be stuck in grows and grows, now they are overflowing onto the third folio, and I shall soon have more items than there are pieces in an extended domino game: in other words, more than fifty-five. (Since

I assume that you despise dominoes as being too "simple-minded," and I would not expect you to have your private secretary, adjutant, or personal assistant look it up or make a trip to the nearest toy store, I am glad to supply you with the figure.) And because during the past four times seven years I have had certain quantitative experiences of my own, I know that each withered word-cluster represents one little chapter, yielding a minimum of two hundred and a maximum of eight hundred chapters (think of the item *Cologne I-CCV*, which actually would represent two hundred and five little chapters) in print, and, judging by what I have seen of the business, this would yield a minimum of three hundred and a maximum of twelve hundred pages—precisely that kind of nonsensical monster of a book for which the public is licking its chops. Let it lick —not its chops, though, but me, in quite a different place.

So we must *select*, and I am asking you to lend me a helping hand. I invite you to take part in a little game: I will throw my words into a drum, like a lottery, and each of you will select one which I shall then, by means of a secret rapid process, plant, allow to flower and then wither. Naturally the Church takes precedence—not only with me, but everywhere!—so, Your Excellency, do be the first to put in your hand. One more point about the rules of the game: I am fair enough to warn you that I shall play unfairly—in other words, while *certain* items will be offered, if one of you should pick them I shall immediately, with all the skill at my command, transform them into others. Still, I am fair enough to tell you in advance which items they are: *Cologne; Catholicism; Rhine; Suicides in the Family; Economic Crisis,* and the reason I have to exclude these is that their ramifications are too great, which is another way of saying that they would put me to too much work and are unsuitable for rapid processing.

Besides: *at the moment the author's morale is low, lower than the troops' ever was.*

I have, then, the following to offer: *Hotels; Homes, parental; Homes, private (where I have lived); Homes, private (where I have not lived); Waiting Rooms; Military Hospitals; Maneuver Areas; Barracks; Girls I; Cologne I-CCV; Schools; Truancy; Girls II; Movies; Catholicism I-XXXV; Rhine I-VII; Cigarette Prices from 1930 to 1966; My Father's Workshop; My Mother's Kitchen; My Mother's Coffee Grinder in My Mother's Kitchen; My Father's Office; My First Check Forgery (1932); Nothing; nothing; Brothers and Sisters; Uncles, Aunts, Cousins (male and female), etc.; Clerical Uncle I; Clerical Uncle II; National Youth Day; Photo Albums I-X; Wedding; Document Forgeries I-VII; Night Club at the Waidmarkt; Routes to School I-V; My Mother's Nickname: Clara Zetkin; Suicides in the Family; Pawnshops; Bailiffs; Gentlemen Boarders; Cycling Tours; Flowers from Beethoven Park; "Youth Front" Distribution Center; Schoolteachers; the Favorite Word of Those Born in 1917; School Friends; End of the War; Economic Crises I-III; My Mother's Death; My Father's Death; Swiss SS-Member; Birthday; Flu Epidemic of January 1933; June 30, 1934; First Nazi Parade in Cologne, May 1, 1933, observed from Chlodwig Square; My Grandmother's "Jansenism" (battle between State and Catholic Church, as my father told it)*—and that's all, gentlemen, unless my process of condensation of these word-clusters—a process not yet quite complete—has reduced the number to below fifty-five, in which case I will dig into my reserves and throw an extra one into the drum.

Please, Your Excellency, you go first. What did you get? *The Favorite Word of Those Born in 1917;* I am aghast.

A nice panic you've put me into, and I could kick myself for not having excluded this scrap of paper too. I am, as you see, deeply embarrassed, and I protest my innocence. How can I work this thing without upsetting you, Your Excellency? Your brothers and superiors (supposing a bishop to have any) will reproach you with having once again been a "poor picker." They will say you should never have been persuaded to join in my little game, given the laity's unfailing desire to make a fool of a man of the Cloth.

Would you care to guess at the word, or do you know? I will tell you what it was not: not "Germany," or "Fatherland," or "Father," "God," "Nation," or "Führer." You really are making it very difficult for me, I shall have to squirm a bit longer. Now when I am forced to reveal the accumulated *mass* I get cold feet; when I consider that this word was in the beginning and in the end, I feel sick; indeed, Your Excellency, when I consider that we uttered it while millions were being murdered and that for hundreds of thousands of *morituri* it was the last word spoken by them on this earth—if I were to give way to a certain inclination toward the metaphysical I would have to broach very dark and dire territory. Yes, I hesitate, I would rather not pronounce it, and you, Excellency, still have no idea what it is. Perhaps *you* are the innocent one, the one who has never spoken it, and perhaps *this* is why this word fell to your lot. Why do you turn pale? No, don't be alarmed: this word has *no* sexual connotation; that much I can spare you. It is a nasty word, an ugly word, I can avoid it no longer, but sex is not its provenance. It is first cousin to ordure, tinged with obscenity, a word that has made history, has set its stamp on an entire epoch, is to certain generations more familiar than any other; it was used casually, at every opportunity: when a date failed to show up, when someone was arrested, when tête-à-têtes fell flat, when wounds were too serious or too light, when someone died, when leave was refused or came to an end, and I even recall someone, Excellency, casually uttering it after missing out on hearing Mass and receiving the sacraments; when women or girls became pregnant—or did not—that was always the word! Millions of soldiers uttered it many times a day—it hung by the billion over Europe, wherever Germans penetrated with their German boots, their German engines, aircraft, ships, trains, or parachutes. That's right, a German word, and *not* "Germany," "Fatherland," "God," "Nation," "Führer," "Mother," or "Father." They dispensed this German blessing by the billion, to themselves and others; to food, to movies and women. O Excellencies, where would all this lead? The word was in the beginning and in the end, a man's word which, strangely enough, sounded most convincing on the lips of women. What has happened to the word? Postwar literature has assured it a place and a certain historical duration, but what has happened to the spoken word? Why has this German verbal past not been overcome, why is it suppressed, why do we never hear it in Parliament? Do you think, Excellencies, that we should jointly sign a petition to Mesdames Lübke and Gerstenmaier in the hope of restoring to this word the honor that befits it?

But I can see, Your Excellency, that you are still quite in the dark. Your look of agonized speculation tells me that you are *still* afraid of a sexual connotation. But please, relax; I will give you a hint. Your two co-Excellencies tumbled to it long ago, of course, but they merely grin instead of whispering the word in your ear, discreetly, as Excellencies are wont to do. I will give you a few adjectives and epithets to serve as a kind of laxative-locomotive, perhaps the word will then slide out behind it. How about: "bloody," "damned," "blasted," "confounded," "It's a lot of ..." O Your Excellency, how constipated is your innocence! Must I really say it and write it down?

Come to think of it, the word was first taken out of circulation with the German currency reform, stifled by the growing respectability and stability of the German mark. Now that the mark is beginning to wobble, how about reintroducing the word—after a decent interval, of course? Today it would still be the most succinct of comments on books, movies, and night-club shows, it would still be the most succinct of political commentaries. Suppose, O secular Excellencies, who smile so loftily at the innocence of your clerical co-Excellency—suppose that, at the next reception given by the Papal Nuncio, you were to be asked for an opinion on the present "Starfighter" debate and you were to answer with that most succinct of all political commentaries? The word works wonders when spoken by an intelligent and pretty woman. It would shorten negotiations, drive out false sentiment, bring common sense to the domestic political hearth. The wives of diplomats and cabinet ministers should be equipped with it for use as an unfailing remedy. O women born in 1917, take up this word again, inscribe it on your ballots, send it on postcards to the Ministry of Defense; you might even hang it as a bouquet on the railings around the Palais Schaumburg! Perhaps the time has come when this German word of blessing may actually dispense a modicum of blessing. The word can do duty for an uppercut, for the flick of a wet towel, it can be spoken in low tones and sharp, long-drawn-out and loud; in chorus, or to heckle. So please, ladies, adopt it, adapt it, the word that my Lord Bishop has fished out of the drum. The word suits the present state of German politics down to the ground.

Now I don't want any jitters from you, please, General! It's your turn, and I trust you will show courage and not try to cheat. Since it is not a battle that is being fought but a *game* that is being played among men of the same age, I will give you a hint, spur you on a bit. None of the remaining items conceals in its *mass* as much obscenity as the one drawn by your clerical cohort: annoying, embarrassing, in fact highly unpleasant things are concealed within some of those that remain, but obscenities—no! So bless our mother the Church, who may happen to be your mother too; progressive and courageous as always, she has forged ahead and snapped up a word of which she does not know the meaning, although it is a *word*. The English-speaking world enjoys the advantages of conciseness by ascribing a whole continent of problems simply to The Pill. I shall linger a while in my German verbosity, still trembling as I am from the shock over our Excellency's ill-starred hand. Come along now, General—or do you wish to be guilty of cowardice in the face of the enemy? Can it be that you are afraid of evocative words? Whatever it is that's worrying you, let me reassure you, before you put your hand in and just in case you happen to be afraid of *certain* words: *Germans are human beings too!* Indeed—and my Lord Bishop will confirm this—*even Catholic Germans are human beings.*

You lucky devil, General! You've drawn a bit of poetry: *Flowers from Beethoven Park.*

This word-cluster obliges me to complete my process of condensation, relating as it does directly to *Homes, private* (*where I have not lived*). As a substitute I place in the drum: *Street Games.* For I would like to reduce the chances of you, Mr. Minister, drawing *My First Check Forgery* (*1932*); or would you prefer me to replace *Street*

Games with *Homecoming?* Think it over, while I report to
the General.

Both the wartime apartments in which I never, strictly
speaking, lived were across from parks. The first, across
from the Volksgarten, had high rooms, old-fashioned
stucco ceilings, was very nicely furnished, and—most
important of all—had a telephone. There I once—*once*—
drank some coffee, washed my hands in the bathroom, and
within a few hours found myself on a troop train that,
with stops and starts, was circling Cologne and then, much
to my relief, swung not east but west, in the direction of
Düren. So I never lived in that apartment, although I
often phoned there just to hear the voice, over forbidden
lines that I had either persuaded or bribed to open up for
me. Six weeks after my attempt to live in it, the apartment
provided me with a week's leave, and I think back to it
with certain emotion, as to a hotel where it would have
been nice to rent a room but which burned down before
the wish could be fulfilled. And the apartment provided
me with something else too, something which may be of
importance to you, General, as an example of the errors of
psychological warfare. The telegram, which read "Apartment completely destroyed, self unhurt, Annemarie," got
me a leave pass, and this pass was handed to me by my
company commander, who, I must say, was an exceptionally silly fellow. To my embarrassment he expressed
his manliness by a hand shake and his joviality by a slap
on the shoulder (I wiped, I mean shook, each like dirt
from shoulder and hand), and he went on to express the
hope that henceforth my fighting spirit against the British
would be redoubled, and that I would perform my duties
with even greater wrath, and I believe, General—this is
the supplementary information I have for you—that sel-

dom has a person been so mistaken in me as that lieutenant. In my eyes, a week's leave was an incalculable
compensation for an apartment in which no one had been
injured; I was only too happy to accept the exchange, for
a week is a week, that's to say, in wartime an eternity.

In our next apartment we were refused a telephone. I
believe we "occupied" it for three years, and I may have
slept there a couple of dozen times. After several attempts
to achieve something like "living" there, we avoided it;
each time we met there, a particularly heavy air raid
would take place, and we would sweep up the broken
glass and plaster and go as fast as we could to the hotel
in Ahrweiler, where we could truly, that's to say, tempo-
rarily, "live." Sometimes, while I was still asleep in the
morning, Annemarie would go to Beethoven Park across
the street and pick the flowers that were the property of
the City of Cologne. These flowers—so it seemed to us—
flourished quite exceptionally in wartime; maybe they did
so well merely because they were spared the regular
attention of gardeners and enjoyed a certain *freedom:*
whatever the reason, they were the most beautiful flowers
we ever had in any apartment—armfuls of luxuriant
blooms: roses, rhododendrons, marguerites, as well as
dahlias and carnations of positively staggering dimensions.
By the time I got up and went to the bathroom, the whole
apartment would be decorated, and there in vases and
flowerpots, pickling jars and milk bottles, stood those
witnesses to Annemarie's unaffected attitude toward the
concept of property which eventually, after our apartment
had been looted several times, applied equally to our own
property. Sometimes we could take our time over breakfast—and with all the luxuries afforded by the black
markets of Europe—before going to the station to take

the train to Bonn and on via Remagen to Ahrweiler. I would leave my uniform and my cumbersome pack behind with the flowers, and when we returned to Cologne, inexorably, General (by the way: in which Fatherland will I be compensated for those innumerable good-byes?), myself to get into uniform again, Annemarie to go to school (as a teacher, not as a student), we would find a few windowpanes smashed or a whole window blown out, and the petals would be lying on the floor, the bare stalks in the vases, pickling jars, and milk bottles. We would sweep them all up, and Annemarie would make another quick trip across the street to Beethoven Park to see what it still had to offer.

Sometimes, when I went on leave unexpectedly, with no chance to wire or phone ahead (see *Document Forgeries I-VII*), I would use the time between trains to take a cab to the apartment so as to shed the uniform and the cumbersome pack (in the constant hope that someone would pinch the stuff, but damn it, no one ever pinched *that*). I always had a sense of committing a kind of break-in, although of course I vaguely recognized the furniture and was quite legally carrying a house key in my pocket, apart from having probably signed the lease jointly; I recognized the books too, the pleasant pictures on the walls, the chest in the hall, but the only truly familiar things were the flowers from Beethoven Park, proof that she had been there to keep an eye on the place, tidy up, and arrange the flowers. Then, while the cab waited outside, I would quickly change, dropping my things on the floor and drive back to the station. Later we kept the apartment merely as a pretext for leave, and on several occasions it did serve this purpose, providing us—depending on the current "war situation," needless to say, General—with two to four days' leave, but there was one favor the apartment never did us, that of becoming totally destroyed, and to this day I feel slightly resentful about that, although it was a nice little apartment, in spite of having no phone.

Once, in the fall of 1943, we took the streetcar back to the station, Annemarie carrying a mass of giant dahlias, I in uniform, and on the streetcar we ran into the principal of the school from which I had graduated six years earlier. He was a courteous, pleasant man, and he began by asking where we had got the lovely flowers. When I told him he winced, making a face as much as to say, Well, that doesn't really surprise me. Then he asked me where I was on leave from, I told him the Crimea, and he immediately glanced at my sleeve to see whether I was wearing the "Crimea patch." I was not, and he turned away shaking his head. He had been our history teacher, decent, never a Nazi, but a "war veteran" to his fingertips, and I never forgot his disappointed glance at my sleeve; it explained a lot about him that I had never understood before: that curse of Hindenburg that lies so heavily on decent patriotic German professors, and the mentality for which a thing doesn't exist unless it is *documented*. In the fifth autumn of the war, on a Cologne streetcar, six months after Stalin-grad—where no doubt many of his former students had died miserable deaths—his eyes went first to my sleeve, then, shaking his head, he looked at my face.

The last *Flowers from Beethoven Park* that I saw were in January 1945 (petalless, of course, what can you expect after three or four months?—even Cologne's municipal asters and dahlias won't last that long!) The dried petals were lying on the floor, rustling in the cold January wind; the stalks still stood in their vases and milk bottles, the pulverized mortar had dusted them white, revealing their structure. They were dead, withered, and yet beautiful, and they were strangers to me, strangers ... yes, General, *strangers*. I had cycled from Siegburg to Cologne, mainly to buy cigarettes on the black market, and in fact I managed to get some, General; I was lucky enough to be recognized by a prostitute (who was acting as lookout for some black-marketeer deserters hiding in the ruins) as my father's son, as *politically safe*. The girl's father was in a concentration camp for being a Communist; but no, Mr. Minister, *my* father wasn't a Communist, *he* was a supporter of the Center Party, Catholic to the bone, but the girl had been born and brought up in a building belonging to my father, she recognized me, she remembered me, and thus I came into possession of fifty French cigarettes, eight marks apiece. So you see, my Lord Bishop, how important it is in certain extreme situations to be *politically safe*.

Needless to say, I hadn't gone to Cologne for the sole purpose of buying cigarettes. I also wanted to look in on our apartment and see whether there was anything worthwhile left in it. With this in mind, I had hung a nice straw shopping bag over the handlebars of the lady's bicycle I was riding; so there I was, cycling from the Waidmarkt (my rendezvous with the prostitute having taken place at the Hohe Pforte) to Sülz. (I will pass over what would, under *Cologne I-CCV*, Paragraph CXXVII, provide material for a tremendous chapter: my bike ride through Cologne on that January day. It's enough my having already made illegal use of the item *Cigarette Prices*.)

I found the apartment looted but not cleaned out. The pictures, for instance, didn't seem to have been quite to anyone's taste; however, I left them in place on the walls, first because they would not fit into my shopping bag, and secondly because I dislike ballast. (Only a few months later they found someone to appreciate them after all: they were very nice colored French engravings, early nineteenth century.) Furthermore, the thief, who had obviously been in a hurry, had even missed some jewelry, its presence in the sewing basket having probably gone unsuspected, although—like all the jewelry in our family— it had been put in its hiding place by chance rather than with any dialectic cunning. The thief had also missed the table silver, yes indeed, Your Excellencies, and that I did take along because (and this should actually come under the heading of *Nothing*, or *nothing*), because it struck me as being a desirable item to barter for cigarettes. I also found stockings, scarves, and gloves, a lot of dust and splintered glass, but above all, *Flowers from Beethoven Park* from our last visit: bare stalks dusted with pulverized mortar.

Just as I was leaving I ran into our neighbor, a pleasant antiaircraft lieutenant who was stationed a few miles, maybe only one mile, away and who asked me if I would lend him (meaning, in view of the "war situation," give him) our record player. I went back into the apartment, kicking open the front door, and brought out the record player for him, plus a few worn-out Beethoven records, and just imagine, General, the advice this *officer* gave me: to carry on forging documents, desertion being the motto on the flags of the troops, whose morale was low. And "Goddamn shit" were the last words I heard that nice fellow utter.

I wish you luck, Mr. Minister, and hope you don't happen to draw the item *National Youth Day*. As a cabinet minister you must be hoping to draw something more suitable for moral export than what has been drawn so far; oh dear, you plunged in your hand so swiftly and boldly, you wanted to confront Fate head-on, and now look what you've done: *Swiss SS-Member!*

At this point, Mr. Minister, since you have shown such lack of skill (why couldn't you have bloody well hooked something *nice* like *Cigarette Prices from 1930 to 1966?*) I must make a statement in defense of my own honor: *I* am merely reporting, I am not responsible for the consequences. I am not interested in blaming Switzerland, that honorable country, for those few bad, misguided lads; and, what is worse, that Swiss lad in the next bed to me in a military hospital in a Polish (now Soviet Russian) town was neither stupid nor bad; no, even in those days he was remorseful. The terrible thing is, Comrade Minister, that I gave that boy some of my blood, so—provided the young man survived the war (which I trust to God and our Holy Mother he did), survived at least as well as the Swiss manufacturers—German blood is flowing somewhere in Swiss veins, this I can prove, Excellency: my German blood. And there is something even worse: I donated that blood not *purely* from brotherly love: I did it—and for this I humbly beg forgiveness—I also did it because I was hungry and blood donors received a nice little package of goodies. And furthermore I did it because they gave you some extra cigarettes.

But let us quickly return, before I lose my way in useless moralistic details, to that Swiss lad: I felt sorry for him, not because he was Swiss, not even because he was a member of the SS, but because—it was six months after Stalingrad, General, and the morale of the troops was lousy —because he had to put up with unbearable, inhuman ridicule, in the face of which, on account of his remorse, he was powerless. Just imagine for a moment, Mr. Minister: among those German comrades there was not *one* who wanted to return to the "front," and the fact that there was someone who had *voluntarily*, at the risk of life and limb, crossed that frontier which they would have all been so glad to cross in the opposite direction—I tell you, that was something they would not, could not, understand.

But there was something even worse, Mr. Minister. There lay this innocent, pink-cheeked, fair-haired Swiss lad, after two weeks more or less recovered, remorseful, the butt of their mockery, and he actually had the nerve *to regard stealing as immoral,* for the mockers (don't tell your children this, there's nothing about it in soldiers' manuals), those mockers stole everything in sight, everything they could lay their hands on, they stole it and sold it on the black market to the Polish inhabitants of that little town, and they spent the proceeds on drink, on living it up, or in whorehouses, or they sent it back home to respectable German savings banks where it was credited to their accounts by more or less decent German girls. Of course they didn't *all* steal, but I did, for one, and that was the only point on which the Swiss lad and I failed to agree. *That* he found improper. Yes, Excellency, *that* was something I learned in the war: how to steal; but I did not frequent the haunts of bought pleasure (see item *Flowers from Beethoven Park*), truly I did not, my Lord Bishop, do please believe me for once, or weren't you paying proper attention at *Flowers from Beethoven Park?* No, what I bought with unrighteous Mammon—and this brings us almost back to the item *Cigarette Prices*—was tobacco, a commodity traded by the Polish janitor of the hospital. It was pale, aromatic, Oriental tobacco, long and curly and pressed into two-pound bricks, and with my ill-gotten Mammon I obtained three bricks of tobacco, and back home I acquired friends with the aid of unrighteous Mammon.

This would be the spot, Your Excellencies, to squeeze in the two items. *Nothing,* and *nothing,* but I confess my nerve fails me here. I find it bad enough to be responsible for German blood flowing in Swiss veins, and a thief's blood at that, although that was all a long time ago and happened "in another country" (at this late date, dear girl, in the pious city of Münster, a trial is taking place which is bringing to light what *really* happened in that little Polish town!)—and I have long since slipped off the hair's breadth of fortune and landed in the noisome swamps to my left.

In conclusion, gentlemen, I would like to give my Lord Bishop one more chance to forget the bad luck he had with his first draw, and I can do this by selecting, rather than pulling out, an item that is not particularly pleasant but at least is not obscene. A small item loaded with an exclusively documentary mass: *Birthday.*

I don't know whether on the day of my birth my mother was in the mood to read the newspaper. On Page One of the local section of its morning edition, the *Kölnische Zeitung* would have had some fine consolation for her, that very consolation to which young mothers during a fourth wartime winter are entitled:

> During a visit from representatives of the Catholic Center Party press (four publishers and four editors) at General Headquarters, Ludendorff made the following request to the press: "*Let us not talk too much of peace,* only victory leads to peace, thus it was in Eastern Europe, thus it will be everywhere. Victory and peace are sure to come, they will come all the sooner the more united we are at home and the more steadfastly we endure whatever must be endured. *In*

military terms, no one can dispute our victory. Whatever stern tasks may lie ahead of us, with God's help we will fulfill them." During the conversation with Field Marshal von Hindenburg, a note of firm *confidence* was audible throughout, the confidence of our great leader that, having conquered thus far, we shall continue to conquer. Courage at home is unbroken, he said, our people stand behind us and will conquer with us. He concluded with: "Convey my greetings to our beloved German people and tell them they need not worry, with God we shall conquer."

In that same morning edition my mother would also have found the daily exhortation, set (on official instructions, no doubt) in heavy type: GO EASY WITH THOSE STORED POTATOES! I am sure my mother would have shed tears of emotion had she read in that same issue that Lord Mayor Adenauer had announced, just before a city council session, that the Christmas packages for the fighting men of Cologne had been sent off in good time; and no doubt she was happy to know that such a capable man, although some years younger than my father, was *not* among the fighting men of Cologne. (Strange vision: Adenauer at the "front.")

The newspaper also offered recipes for making a tasty spread from turnips, not honest-to-goodness turnip preserves, which need a lot of fuel to prepare, but what must have been a sickly yellowish mush made from boiled turnips, which may have tasted remotely of sugar. The fact that the same issue published the strict official ban on feeding turnips to *cattle* gives the day and the recipe their background and place in history: it was the notorious second turnip-winter.

Just one more comment, Excellencies, a mere three lines,

and then I will let you go back to your official positions and restore to you the dignity which, for a while there during our little game, was in some danger.

Seven times seven years later I note that Ludendorff's exhortation, *Let us not talk too much of peace,* is still being dutifully obeyed by the German press.

The first literary attempts of our generation since 1945 have been described as excessively preoccupied with the bomb-ravaged cities and towns of Germany and hence dismissed as "rubble literature." We have not defended ourselves against this appellation because it was justified: it is a fact that the people we wrote about lived in and under ruins, men and women, even children, all equally war-scarred. And they were sharp-eyed: they could see. Moreover, their living conditions were far from peacetime ones, neither their surroundings nor their own state nor anything else about them could be described as idyllic, and we writers felt close enough to them to identify with them: to identify with black-market operators and black-market victims, with refugees and with all those who for one reason or another had lost their homes—but above all, of course, with our own generation, which for the most part found itself in a strange and significant situation: a generation that was "coming home," coming home from a war which scarcely a soul still believed would ever end.

So we wrote about the war, about coming home, and about what we had seen during the war and were faced with on our return: about ruins. Hence the three clichés with which this budding literature was labeled: a literature of war, of homecoming, and of rubble.

These labels, as such, are warranted: there had been a war lasting six years, we were coming home from this war, we found rubble and we wrote about it. What was odd, suspicious even, was the reproachful, almost injured tone accompanying these labels: although we were not, apparently, being held responsible for the war, for the ruins on all sides, we were obviously giving offense by having seen these things and continuing to see them. But we were not blindfolded, we did see these things: and a sharp eye is one of a writer's essential tools.

To offer our contemporaries an escape into some idyll would have been too cruel for words, the awakening too appalling—or ought we really all to have played blind man's buff?

When the French Revolution erupted, it hit the greater part of the French aristocracy like a sudden thunderstorm: they were in fact thunderstruck, they had had not the slightest inkling. For almost a century they had spent their time in idyllic seclusion: the ladies dressed up as shepherdesses, the men as shepherds, they had strutted about in a make-believe rusticity, trilling and frolicking away hours devoted to pastoral romances. Inwardly corrupted by depravity, outwardly they mimicked a rustic freshness and innocence: they were all playing blind man's buff. This fashion, whose cloying corruption today turns our stomach, was evoked and kept alive by a certain kind of literature: by pastoral novels and plays. The authors who perpetrated this had been valiantly playing blind man's buff.

But the people of France replied to these idyllic pastimes with a revolution, a revolution whose effects are still palpable after more than a hundred and fifty years, whose freedoms we are still enjoying without always being aware of their origin.

However, in the early nineteenth century there was a young man living in London with no pleasant life to look back on: his father had been declared bankrupt and thrown into a debtors' prison, and the young man himself had worked in a shoe-polish factory before he was able to resume his neglected education and become a reporter. Before long he was writing novels, and in these novels he wrote about what he saw: he had looked into prisons, into workhouses, into the English schools, and what he had seen was not particularly pleasant, but he wrote about these things, and strangely enough his books were read, and read by a great many people, and the young man enjoyed a success rarely accorded an author: the prisons underwent reform, the workhouses and schools became the objects of a thorough reappraisal: they changed.

To be sure, the name of this young man was Charles Dickens, and he had very sharp eyes, eyes that normally are not quite dry but not wet either, rather a little damp—and the Latin for dampness is *humor*. Charles Dickens had very sharp eyes and a sense of humor. And his vision was good enough to enable him to describe things that his eyes had not seen—he did not use a magnifying glass, nor did he resort to the trick of reversing a telescope, by which he could have seen accurately enough but very remotely, nor did he wear a blindfold; and although his sense of humor allowed him on occasion to play blind man's buff with his children, he did not live in a permanently blindfolded state. The latter seems to be what is demanded of today's authors; blind man's buff not as a game but as a way of life. But, as I have said, a sharp eye is one of a writer's essential tools, an eye sharp enough to allow him to see even those things that have not yet appeared within his field of vision.

Let us suppose the writer's eye is looking into a basement: a man is standing there at a table kneading dough, a man with flour on his face: the baker. The writer sees him standing there just as Homer might have seen him, just as the eyes of Balzac and Dickens could not have failed to see him—the man who bakes our bread, as old as the world, with a future stretching to the end of the world. Yet that man down there in the basement smokes cigarettes, goes to the movies; his son was killed in Russia, lies buried two thousand miles away just outside a village: but the grave has been leveled, there is no cross on it, tractors have replaced the plow that once turned over that soil. All this is part of the pale, silent man down there in the basement baking our bread—this sorrow is part of him, just as certain joys are part of him too.

And behind the dusty windows of a small factory the writer's eye sees a young working girl standing at a machine punching out buttons, buttons without which our clothes would not be garments but pieces of cloth hanging loosely on us, neither adorning us nor keeping us warm: this young working girl wears lipstick when she is not at work, she also goes to the movies, smokes cigarettes, goes walking with a young man who repairs cars or drives a bus. And it is part of this young girl that her mother lies buried somewhere beneath a pile of rubble: under a mound of dirty bricks and mortar, somewhere deep in the ground lies the mother of this girl and, like the grave of the baker's son, her grave has no cross. Very rarely—once a year—the girl goes to the spot and lays some flowers on that dirty pile of rubble under which her mother lies buried.

These two, the baker and the girl, are part of our time, they are suspended in time, dates are wrapped around them like a net. To free them from this net would mean depriving them of life—but the writer needs life, and what else could sustain the life of these two people but "rubble literature"? The blind-man's-buff writer looks inward, constructs his own world. Early in this century a young man in a prison in southern Germany wrote a great fat book: the young man was not a writer, nor did he ever become one, but he wrote a great fat book that enjoyed the protection of being unreadable yet sold millions of copies: it competed with the Bible! It was the work of a man whose eyes had seen nothing, who harbored nothing but hate and torment, loathing and much else that was repulsive—this man wrote a book, and we need only open our eyes to see all around us the destruction attributable to this man, whose name was Adolf Hitler and who had eyes to see with: his images were warped, his style was intolerable—he saw the world not with a human eye but in the distortion created by his inner self.

He who hath eyes to see, let him see! The words "to see" have a meaning transcending the optical: he who hath eyes to see, for him things become transparent, lucid, and he should be able to see through them, and by means of language we may attempt to see through them, to see into them. The writer's eye should be human and in-corruptible: there is really no need to wear a blindfold, there are rose-tinted glasses, and glasses tinted blue or black, that color reality according to need. The rosy view is handsomely rewarded, it is usually very popular, and the opportunities for corruption are manifold; even black can occasionally be popular, and when that happens black is handsomely rewarded too. But we want to see things the way they are, with a human eye that normally is not quite dry and not quite wet, but damp, for let us not forget that the Latin for dampness is *humor*—nor that our eyes can become dry or wet too, that there are some things which do not call for humor. Each day our eyes see many things: they see the baker baking our bread, they see the girl working in the factory—and our eyes remember the graveyards, and our eyes see the rubble: the cities are destroyed, the cities are graveyards, and all around them our eyes see buildings arising that remind us of stage settings, buildings where people do not live but are "bureaucratized," as insurance customers, as citizens of a state, of a city, as persons depositing money or borrowing money—the reasons are legion for a person to be "bureaucratized."

It is our task to remind the world that a human being exists for something more than to be bureaucratized—and that the destruction in our world is not merely external or so trivial that we can presume to heal it within a few years.

Throughout our Western culture the name of Homer is above suspicion: Homer is the progenitor of the European epic, yet Homer tells of the Trojan War, of the destruction of Troy, and of Ulysses' homecoming—a literature of war, rubble, and homecoming. We have no reason to be ashamed of these labels.

REVIEWS

On Stories and Prose Poems,
by Alexander Solzhenitsyn[1]

SUFFERING, WRATH,
AND SERENITY

(1970)

In many respects, the title of one of these stories, "For the Good of the Cause," could be applied to the whole of Solzhenitsyn's work, and even to the controversy about him over the question: Which cause does this author serve?

Does the postwar literature of Europe and America serve the "causes" of the countries of its origin? Of course not. Would President Nixon feel that Selby was serving the national interest, would Chancellor Kiesinger assume the same of Günter Grass? I think not. Postwar literature is frankly antinational, it is not "healthy," and I believe the opposite of healthy to be not "sick" but "suffering." Where would we find a human being so monstrous that he does not suffer?

Corresponding to the much-debated question of the "sound" (in terms of health) world is a certain form of Socialist realism that is little more than a Marxist variant of that old-fashioned literature of edification in which Good triumphs and Evil is punished or brought to reason —a literature in which no one is allowed to suffer from the questionable nature of whatever is the current doctrine of

salvation. The formula is well known. This edifying literature is also, of course, allowed to contain some criticism
(the dogmaticians aren't all that stupid), but ultimately
the criticism must serve to confirm the doctrine.

What cause does Solzhenitsyn serve? Will any Establish-
ment ever grasp that it is not all that easy to persuade a
writer with a mind of his own to serve a purpose? The fact
is that Khrushchev's accounting with Stalinism has spread
throughout the world, been printed in every newspaper:
the dikes have been breached. Can any statesman who
considers himself a realist believe that *this* breach can be
repaired? And Khrushchev's speech was not literature: it
was the harsh, rough language of a political realist. It was
under his regime that Solzhenitsyn began to publish in
the Soviet Union.

In the interest of the cause of Socialism and Socialist
realism, I could wish for nothing better than that the claim
be dropped that Socialism is the sole source of earthly
happiness, and the fact recognized that even in Socialist
countries people can suffer, above all are *allowed* to suffer
and to wonder about the meaning of that suffering:
whether the gigantic machinery of suffering has been
working for the Hades of the absurd, or if not that, for
what?

In one of his essays Georg Lukács, who can hardly be
dismissed as an agent of imperialism, has traced Solzhenitsyn's origin to Socialist realism and—I am condensing
here—has warned authors in Socialist countries against
adopting Western forms of literature. And rightly so, I
believe: any renewal of literature there can only be self-
generated, the West has nothing to offer it, nothing to sell.

Perhaps one day—who knows when?—people in the
Soviet Union may recognize the cause served by Solzhenitsyn the author; that, in *The First Circle* especially, he

has performed the miracle of making Socialist realism a living presence, not merely reestablishing a connection between it and world literature—and not merely because of his unmasking of Stalinism. Solzhenitsyn has done more than shake the West's deplorable condescension toward Soviet literature: an author such as Solzhenitsyn is only possible *in* the Soviet Union.

What amazes me most about this author is the serenity he radiates—this man who is more controversial and more menaced than any in the world. This serenity seems to be unassailable, despite the appalling abuse to which he is exposed in his own country, and despite the publicly offered exit visa—that ouster which he has refused to accept.

Solzhenitsyn's serenity is not that of an Olympian, it is the serenity of someone involved, of a contemporary, not of a living monument angling for the patina of posthumous glory. Each item in this collection, including the brief prose poems, radiates this serenity: an astounding message to the insane turbulence of our world to which all of us have more or less succumbed.

The story entitled "For the Good of the Cause" is a bitter one: the extra-shift optimism of an entire technical college, including principal and faculty, is betrayed when the finally completed new building that they had expected to occupy is at the last moment diverted to other purposes. A few hours before the students are about to complete the move with their own hands and without pay, some inspector from the Department of Industry hands over the building for a different purpose.

In these medium-length stories Solzhenitsyn shows himself to be, among other things, an author who knows that credibility is to be found in detail.

As an example: while inspecting the old technical college, a comrade from the Ministry tries to convince the Principal that there *is* no shortage of space, and upon discovering the little bit of empty space on the wall where a lab assistant has pinned up the picture of a pretty girl ("Without the caption it was impossible to make out whether this creature had been cut out of a Soviet magazine or a foreign one"), he sneers at the Principal: "You say you haven't any space here, but look what you hang on your walls, for God's sake!"

In such episodes—or perhaps when a Party functionary parries the accusation of not working in the Soviet way with the reply: "Quite the contrary. I work in the Soviet way—I consult the people" (*Soviet* = council)—we perceive the precision of Solzhenitsyn, whose serenity, far from indifference, let alone stylistic insensitivity, is a sensitivity that patiently seeks out the proper detail and that can also afford to wait for it. This is a hallmark of that new realism that refuses to be put on a leash, that is not only humane but also able to depict functionaries with discrimination.

Admittedly, Solzhenitsyn's affection and preference are for those people whom we in our simplistic way like to call "simple" or "humble": in this volume, for instance, Bobrov, the down-and-out revolutionary veteran in "The Right Hand," or Matryona, the old collective-farm worker in "Matryona's House," or the faithful in "The Easter Procession," whose side Solzhenitsyn takes against "materialistic" hooligans.

All the characters in his stories are participants in or the source of his serenity, his patience, even his wrath: they all serve the "cause," which is an international one. The note of a national sense of injury in Soviet attitudes toward Solzhenitsyn is as unmistakable as the note of envy. Now Soviet authors have even broken off relations with C.O.M.E.S., the European writers' association founded specifically as an instrument of reconciliation between the literatures of Socialist and Western countries. And all this on account of a single author who still persists in vehemently defending himself against Western use of his works for purposes of manipulation, who keeps on emphasizing that he is writing for the people of the Soviet Union!

Does it make sense to declare this single author an enemy of the nation and thereby endow him with increasing political and symbolic significance? Can any author carry such a burden?

[1] Translated by Michael Glenny; The Bodley Head, 1971.

On *The First Circle* by Alexander Solzhenitsyn[1]
Excerpts from the novel:

"Pay attention!" he rapped out. Seven prisoners
and seven warders turned towards him. "You know
the rules, I suppose? You may not give anything to
your relatives or take anything from them. Parcels may
only be handed over through me. When talking you
will not mention the following subjects: work, working conditions, living conditions, daily routine or the
location of the prison. No surnames may be mentioned. About yourselves you may only say that you
are well and need nothing."

"Then what can we talk about?" shouted a voice.
"Politics?"

The question was so patently absurd that Klimentyev did not even bother to reply.

"Talk about your crime," one of the prisoners grimly
proposed, "and how you repent."

"Judicial proceedings are secret, so you may not discuss them either," said Klimentyev imperturbably, rejecting the suggestion. "You can ask about your family

or your children. Now there is one new rule: from now on handshaking and kissing is forbidden."

The regulation did not explicitly forbid the shedding of tears, but, if one went by the spirit of the law, they clearly could not be permitted.

Unfortunately for us mortals and fortunately for the powers that be, it is in the nature of man that as long as he is alive there is always something which can be taken away from him.

Solzhenitsyn's novel *The First Circle* has a vast span, many supporting arches, and several dimensions: one prose dimension, one intellectual, one political, one social. Its vault springs from many points to many other points, a cathedral among novels, supported by precisely calculated statics; that it also has tension in the traditional sense is due not to any novelistic method but to these supporting statics, and throughout the book the reader is constantly wondering whether they will hold. In this book, both tension and arch are used more in the architectural sense. The fact that the novel also contains historical information on our times is merely incidental to the material, the building blocks, the terse content.

The story begins with a telephone call from Volodin, State Counsellor Second Class, who wishes to warn a friend of his, a professor, about certain foreign contacts; and this first breach in the awareness of a gifted diplomat, secure in the elegant trappings and privileges of his career, provides our "entry" into the cathedral. The telephone conversation occurs around Christmas 1949; the novel ends barely two days later with a description of a transfer of prisoners through Moscow. In a van inscribed М Я С О. MYASSO VIANDE FLEISCH MEAT, prisoners are being removed from the First Circle of Hell without knowing which circle they will end up in. On his way to a hockey game at the Dynamo Stadium, the correspondent for the French newspaper *Libération* reads the words on the van, pulls out his notebook, and with his dark-red fountain pen writes, "Now and again on the streets of Moscow you meet food delivery vans, clean, well-designed and hygienic. One must admit that the city's food supplies are admirably well organized."

The novel comprises eighty-seven chapters and 581 pages, and even after a second reading it is hard to keep track of its characters; it would be helpful if the German publisher[2] were to include a Dramatis Personae in a new edition, indicating age, sex, function, position, political stance—the last because there are so many stages of transition, so many entanglements, among prisoners as well as nonprisoners (there will be more to say later on the terms "free" and "unfree"). "Captive"—not, of course, in the technical criminal sense—applies to them all, their captivity has many causes, most of which are beyond the comprehension of the West. The fact that Solzhenitsyn has forbidden publication of his novels in the West is understandable only in light of the earthly *and* metaphysical aspects of this captivity. That in doing so he (and with him the Soviet government—sufficient reason, perhaps, for the latter to join the Bern Convention!) fell victim to that absence of a copyright agreement may be seen as an irony in the game of reciprocal "publishing freedom."

This "captivity" has made the Russians the least emigration-minded people in the world. It is in this sense of the word that I would describe all the characters of the novel —prisoners and nonprisoners alike—as being captive in the Soviet Union, politically speaking too. I don't mean the kind of captivity imposed by the police; I mean the kind a person imposes upon himself. Let semantics go to work and unravel all that is implicit in "to be a captive of" and "to be captive to"; "captivity," "capture," and "captivation." In my sense James Joyce, for instance, remained to the end of his days "captive to" Ireland and Catholicism.

The wholesale castigation of the stupidity of the West at the end of the book may relate to the fact that, although Western observers in Soviet Russia do occasionally perceive certain clues, the interpretation of these clues constantly eludes them, perhaps because the code changes by the day, the hour, the week, or may be conditional on the enormous mass of "chance" in such a vast empire. I have no key to this code myself, I am short on breath, Eastern Europe is long on breath; it is not only experienced in agony but sometimes even addicted to it; it is in the true sense of the word "agonized," and not only since the Revolution or merely as the result of Stalinism.

Beneath the great statically supported vault of *The First Circle*, many esteemed Western novels—indeed, the entire output of decades of literature—seem to me like decorative side chapels or niches, or, since they have been built outside this cathedral, like temporary or, at best, permanent, often elegant living quarters. Obviously the appalling dialectic represented by such a great work inheres in its summation and illumination of a vast mass of suffering and history. The form, the expression, the manner in which Solzhenitsyn composes and controls his prose, the way his composition *holds*, down to the utmost liberties taken by the author, reveal that there is not only a great writer at work here but also a mathematician, or at least someone familiar with scientific formulas. Here prose becomes formula-material, intellectual and epic lucidity meet in a parabola in the mathematical-physical sense.

The only reason I avoid the term "metaphysics" is that I know of no name for *this* type. In any event, while systems of order are neither alleged nor propounded, order is created. "Integration" in the mathematical-physical sense takes place, and it may be that a new "materialistic metaphysics" is being created here, of the kind whose existence physicists suspect. Just as Western writers reject the dogma of "soundness," Solzhenitsyn, without rejecting the future, no longer includes it as an ideal goal, comparable to Heaven in the metaphysics we have lost. What he summates is the present, and let us not forget that it is the present of 1949, four years before Stalin's death, and that this book was written between 1955 and 1964. To be captive and captured in the Soviet Union of 1969 is not equatable with being captive and captured in 1949.

Fortunately, Solzhenitsyn does not attempt to "interpret"; he notes, registers, expands out of the elements he knows, out of experiences and experience; and since he does not have to attack alleged or propounded systems of order or polemicize against them in his text, he achieves a sobriety and a dryness which prove him superior not only to traditional, optimism-geared Socialist realism but also to the aims of the *nouveau roman*. This is not only because he has personally experienced what his Western colleagues have not: Stalinism. It is also because the West has lost its sense of hidden suffering: The one and only instance of its use is as an ingredient of sexual lust—a fact which may represent an as yet unrecognized outrage. I would ascribe to Solzhenitsyn's work the nature of a revelation, a sober revelation not only in terms of the actual historical subject of the book, Stalinism, but also of the history of human suffering. In that respect, Stalinism is in this case "only" motivation, horrifying enough, yet still "only."

The prisoners in *The First Circle*, the Mavrino prison near Moscow, are required to perform various tasks all aimed at improving and developing new methods of monitoring, i.e., supplying more prisoners. They are permanently enmeshed, they are prisoners yet as researchers they are free, whereas their guards are free yet prisoners of the never-ending fear of arrest, and it is far from certain whether they will then be lucky enough to end up in the First Circle of Hell or unlucky enough to find themselves in the Seventh. In the course of improving "voice-printing" (a process permitting identification of a person by means of his taped voice) the prisoners are given five taped voices to compare with the voice of Volodin, whose phone conversation was taped and whose voice is among the five. The prisoners' sole triumph lies in their being able to eliminate three of the five suspects from suspicion, their consolation being that, of the five, only two are arrested, one of them Volodin. Volodin's transfer to Lubyanka Prison is described in detail in one of the last chapters, the subjection of the State Counsellor Second Class (whose pocket already contained his airplane ticket to Paris) to the pedantic, dull, nonsensically impenetrable initial humiliations, an emphatic reminder to the reader of what happened during the arrests of those inmates of the First Circle whom he has already met.

It is certainly no coincidence that this First Circle of Hell should be a laboratory, a well-equipped, well-functioning laboratory. If I tell myself that physicists, medical experts, technicians, and all the auxiliary personnel involved in space programs are subjected to strict surveillance, to constant control by various types of secret police, possibly even to months of strict seclusion; if I tell myself that in addition to chemical, technical, and physical laboratories there are also politico-economic and above all propaganda "laboratories" in which new methods of manipulation are being hatched, old ones analyzed and improved; if I tell myself that probably even the dreams of those working in the innermost circle of these Heavens have to be kept under surveillance so that nothing slips out—then Solzhenitsyn's *The First Circle* becomes quickly "de-Stalinized," and captivity and freedom, suspicion and nonsuspicion on the part of the "watchers" and the "free," the manipulated and the manipulators, become entirely relative. I don't know the ratio of monitors to the free in, say, a space-research center in the First Circle of Heaven, but I would imagine that ratio and conditions differ only in degree from those in the First Circle of Hell. There is an abundance of secret worlds, and there are also worlds of hidden suffering which, if revealed, would amount to more than sexual suffering. To this extent I consider, *The First Circle*, although linked to the historical material of Stalinism, to be a revelation that transcends it.

The difference between being "captive" spiritually and "captive" legally might be the key to an understanding of the Soviet Union which, regardless of how often it may be denied or whether it may hold true constitutionally, is still dominated by Russians and by Russia: that is not to say (although the threat is increasing) imperialistically, nationalistically, or, as under Stalin, once again even tsaristically. It was only in reading Solzhenitsyn that I realized the full impact of Khrushchev's exposure of Stalinism in 1956, one result of which was that Solzhenitsyn was released, able to write, permitted to publish. That he is still writing but may no longer publish, that he is living in the Soviet Union, is captive there but not yet captured, can surely mean only one thing: it is not yet certain whether the Soviet Government will grasp something that politicians all over the world never quite seem to grasp—that an author is captive enough in language; that Solzhenitsyn, as a person and as a writer, as a writer born in 1918 and shaped in every respect by the history of the Soviet Union, is not to be taken as typical or symbolic: he is present and real for the Soviet Union. Were he not disavowed and branded as a heretic, the Soviet Union could be proud of him. Politically he goes no further than Khrushchev in his famous speech: he has merely taken de-Stalinization at its word and turned it into words. He is as much a captive of the Soviet Union as one of the "heroes" of his book, the prisoner Rubin, who remains a captive of Socialism as much as of the Soviet Union, who is completely unnationalistic yet not a cosmopolite, and who as a Marxist, with clear insight into his own "captive/capture" situation, is far superior to his guards. It has always seemed to me axiomatic that those we call nest-foulers are those who are seeking to clean up their own nests.

Solzhenitsyn's book is far-reaching, high-arched, it is also a revelation for our more or less floundering Western literature; it stems from the great Russian tradition, has passed through Socialist realism, left it behind, renewed it, and in the boldness of its statically secured construction it is part of the present. It has the breath of Tolstoi and the spirit of Dostoevski, thus uniting those two minds which from the nineteenth century right through to present-day literary criticism have been considered antagonistic, and it *is* Solzhenitsyn, unmistakably so. Transcending Camus and Sartre, he resolves the age-old debate on what is "free" and what is "captive," not by imagery, not by philosophy, but in the material, which stands unembellished and in its own right. Take, for instance, the encounter between the seemingly all-powerful Minister Abakumov and the prisoner Bobynin: the trembling Minister, who is fully aware of the number of circles in Hell, and the supremely serene Bobynin, who has already passed through several of them.

In such scenes, to which many others might be compared, the unity of reality and symbol is neither invented nor contrived; it issues from the given material like the solution to a mathematical problem. It would be idle to offer further examples. If I were an artist I would try to give graphic form to *The First Circle* within some as yet undiscovered system of order, possibly resembling a giant rosette. At least I can imagine such a method of rendering literature intelligible and visible at a glance, not with any critical claim to total comprehension but as an aid. Be that as it may: this prose, rather than flowing along with the epic serenity of a great river, is like a lake fed by many sources, minor and major. I am fully aware of all my mixed metaphors: cathedral, lake, rosette; this is because the book has so many dimensions.

There is very little of the "novelistic" about this novel: on page 10 Volodin telephones; on page 194 the experts at Mavrino are directed to identify his voice, they request comparison material, which in turn leads to further telephone monitoring; on page 509 Volodin's voice is partially identified; at the end of the novel he is arrested.

It is roughly in the middle of the book that the novel comes closest to being a novel; the comparison material requested by the prisoners is taped during an evening party in the opulent old bourgeois style, a party given by State Prosecutor Makarygin at which some of the few novelistic threads are brought together. Volodin is Makarygin's son-in-law. Volodin's wife Datoma (known as Dotti—note very Western nickname—a reminder, probably not accidental, of the customs of the aristocracy described by Tolstoi) is entirely preoccupied with problems that have little to do with those of a classless society—servants and adultery—while in his apartment Volodin slowly shifts from the ranks of the unsuspecting privileged to those of the suspecting; and it is precisely this telephone conversation with his wife that is recorded on a tape at a particular central exchange of the intelligence department after "that afternoon, Rubin had asked for further records of the telephone conversations of the suspects." Not only does the prisoner intervene at this point in the life of the State Counsellor but a few more specific and ridiculous "coincidences" occur at Makarygin's party. Clara, Makarygin's unmarried daughter, who with the rank of a lieutenant in the State Security Service is a "free" co-worker and monitor in the Mavrino prison, in love with the prisoner Rostislav (and he with her!), answers the phone, having no idea that within a few hours, in that very prison, the ensuing phone conversation will lead to her brother-in-law's arrest. Thus in two chapters do some of the threads join, only to separate immediately. Moreover, the conversation at Makarygin's party is sparkling, the conversation that of the unsuspecting, the talk that of the privileged, of prelates. "Not one of the three people crowded in the cosy little carpeted hall could for a moment have imagined that the harmless-looking shiny black receiver, that casual conversation about coming to the party, concealed a mortal danger, such as may lie in wait for us even in the skull of a dead horse."

It is only in these two chapters, located exactly at the center of the novel—in the hands of a mathematician certainly no accident—that a macabre tribute is paid to the classical novel, that destinies are "brought together." All the other destinies, and they are many, are merely documented: Spiridon, Sologdin, Sinochka, and Mishin, Stalin and the prisoner Dyrsin, whose wife's letters are withheld from him and then only given him to read in Major Mishin's office: "No! You must read it here. I can't let you take a letter like this to your quarters. What would the others think about life outside prison if they see letters like this? Just read it." And Dyrsin reads:

> Dear Vanya,
>   I expect you're upset because I don't write much, but I get home from work late and nearly every day I have to go out looking for firewood, and by that time it's night and I'm so tired I just go straight to bed. . . . Life is sheer misery and there's no escape. . . . I thought I might get a bit of rest during the holiday but we have to drag ourselves out for the big parade. . . .

And Dyrsin, completely crushed, is ordered to write his wife a letter: something cheerful to "buck her up . . . something optimistic." And further: "Write her an answer. A cheerful answer. You can write four pages if you like—you have my permission. You once wrote and told her to have faith in God. Well, that's all right, let her believe in God, it's better than nothing. . . ."

The prisoner Dyrsin, whose fate is documented in a few pages, has no "novelistic" function at all; he is one among millions and, moreover, is required to trumpet forth optimism and good cheer from the camp into the "free" world. The insane absurdity of capturing captives, already magnificently documented as to single destinies in Chukovskaya's *An Empty House* and Evgeniia Ginzburg's *Into*

the Whirlwind, is deepened, expanded, and de-individual-
ized by Solzhenitsyn in a manner so far unrivaled.

Apart from whatever else it may be, our century is the
century of camps, of prisoners, and anyone who has never
been a prisoner—whether proud or ashamed of what was
good fortune or chance—has been spared or deprived of
(whichever you prefer) *the* experience of our century. For
the survivors, i.e., those of us who are reading or writing
this—all of us, in fact—there remains merely the opportunity to recognize our captivity, whether or not we have
experienced it. Those who have, know how relative luxury
is: surrounded by the wasteland of a prison camp housing
a hundred thousand men, a piece of soap and a basin of
water are a *real,* because available, luxury; and five-
twelfths of a cigarette, when a whole cigarette costs a
hundred and twenty marks and one's entire assets consist of fifty marks, *really,* not just symbolically, represents
far greater enjoyment than that of the nabob who gambles
away a fortune in one evening with no sense of satisfaction
because he doesn't *feel* it, whereas the man who spends
fifty marks on five-twelfths of a cigarette at least knows
that at home this bank note would cover a month's rent.
The idiocy of our Western luxury-oriented society—and
that of its victims, the criminals who want to share in it—
consists in taking luxury as an absolute. In order to appreciate luxury we must know, in this century, that for the
prisoner the possession of an empty can or bottle is *really*
a matter of life or death. This clandestine philosophy of
the prisoners (which contains a good measure of theology)
also weaves its invisible yet perceptible way through *The
First Circle.*

More readily perceptible is another: that of love, of
chastity and marriage. "Yes, yes, something to love!"
whispers the young prisoner Rostislav. "But not history or

theory—you can only love a woman!" And he goes on: "What have they really taken away from us, tell me? The right to go to party meetings or to buy state bonds? The one way the Big Chief could really hurt us was to deprive us of women. And that's what he's done. For twenty-five years! The bastard! Who can imagine ... what women mean to a prisoner?"

And who can have even an inkling of what it means to the prisoners' women to be presented by their men with that "freedom" for which in most cases they have no use? Who can accept "freedom" from someone condemned to a minimum of twenty-five years? This is where something emerges that might never have done so had both been free; this is where, out of the material represented by "captivity," that "something" emerges that in the West is taboo, that "something" that is not a virtue but a quality: loyalty. The sexual agony and agonized sex of Western literature are no more than the expression of an unrecognized captivity and of a grotesque interpretation of freedom.

That they—sexual agony and agonized sex—are entirely devoid of interest to either Soviet censorship or the enlightened "non-unsuspecting" Soviet citizen may well be one of those elusive clues of which we have spoken. They might interest the bored and jaded class of the privileged and unsuspecting in the Soviet Union, for whom even servants are a topic of conversation. For a whole chapter (Chapter 39) Clara Petrovna Makarygin (Lieutenant in the State Security Service, daughter of a State Prosecutor) and the prisoner Rostislav carry on a discussion in the Mavrino laboratory on Soviet society, methods of forgery, and privilege. And it is the prisoner Rostislav who at this point plants the seed of that wonderful "corruption" of

Clara. The two lovers are forever putting their heads together. And what ideas does the prisoner implant in the head of this privileged daughter of the classless bourgeoisie? "Why did we have a Revolution? To do away with inequality! What were the Russian people sick and tired of? Privilege! Some were dressed in rags and others in sable coats; some went on foot and others rode in carriages; some slaved away in factories while others ate themselves sick in restaurants. Right?"

"Of course," says the State Prosecutor's daughter, so dutiful and so much in love, who that self-same evening will attend that opulent party given by her hyperbourgeois Mama, where there will be crystal and silver, choice food and wines, sparkling conversation and even borrowed servants; and who will lift the receiver and initiate the conversation with her brother-in-law Volodin which—taped that very night in that very laboratory—will be used to unmask her brother-in-law.

"Very well, then. In that case, why are people still so keen on privilege?" And so it continues, in that wonderful "corruption" of the girl lieutenant.

All these quotations and allusions might create an impression of many novels and romances combined in *one* novel, but it is hard to refrain from quoting when one would like to quote the greater part of all 581 pages. This novel has none of that famous (or notorious) epic flow, it halts repeatedly, makes a new start, halts again, contains whole chapters of bitter soliloquies and parentheses—for example, on the subject of inspections by philanthropic bodies that are completely, totally, misled. Or the ghastly half-hour visits of wives granted some of the prisoners once a year. The halts are the halts of one who is long, not short, on breath (the latter characteristic being perhaps the particular attraction of our Western European novels). It is this very amplitude of breath that reminds us of Tolstoi, this very sarcasm plus the acuteness of the psychological examination of the material that remind us of Dostoevski. Yet they *are* Solzhenitsyn's, now unmistakably so since we have come to know more of his work.

Then there are the experts at the Mavrino prison who refuse to improve monitoring methods or who cleverly sabotage their improvements, since they alone—the experts imprisoned solely for this purpose—know how to go about improving these methods. To me these men are the true Socialist scientists. Moreover, the women working there, those young female lieutenants of the State Security Service who must have been born after Lenin's death, prove to be highly unreliable, whereas many a prisoner proves to be reliable. Despite the appalling content of suffering, this insight makes one feel almost optimistic. After all, the Soviet Union does pay pensions to the victims of Stalinism. So what was Solzhenitsyn's terrible crime? Obviously a state that is structured and governed on Marxist principles cannot afford to harbor so much that is absurd; but in the long run will it be possible for them to close their eyes to the mass arrests under Stalin if at the same time pensions are being paid to those victims of Stalinism?

A hundred years after *Crime and Punishment* and *War and Peace* comes the publication of this book—unfortunately only in the West, for which it was not written. It was written for the liberation of Socialism. We have not the slightest cause to gloat over *The First Circle* as depicting Stalinist outrages, absurdities, and entanglements. We have more reason to wonder whether a Western author could be as brilliantly successful in revealing the world of the unsuspecting and the world of the silent sufferers within our own tangled complexities.

¹ *The First Circle,* by Alexander Solzhenitsyn; Collins & Harvill Press, London 1968. Translated by Michael Guybon. English translation © 1968 Harper & Row Publishers, Inc. New York.
² The English edition cited above includes a List of Characters.

On The Gulag Archipelago,
1918–1956: An Experiment in
Literary Investigation, I–II, *by
Alexander Solzhenitsyn*[1]

THE DIVINE
BITTERNESS OF
ALEXANDER
SOLZHENITSYN

(1974)

By Page 2 of this book I had already forgotten everything I had heard about it at second, third, or fourth hand,
from advance notices and commentaries directed at the
case rather than the book; I had forgotten the Leftist and
Rightest commentaries as well as those from every possible
middle ground.

Now here at last is the book, which I hope all will read
who express an opinion about it and are interested in it
beyond the confines of the case and the incident. I also
hope that all those have read it who have commented on it
publicly in the Soviet Union: Messrs. Shukov, Chakowsky,
and Simonov. Did the State Security Service supply them
with photocopies to enable them not only to pronounce
but substantiate their devastating judgments?

All is forgotten—advance laurels, advance poison—
as soon as one gets into the book itself, hears Solzhenitsyn's
voice through the remarkable German translation by Anna
Peturgin, and slowly becomes aware of the book's orchestration and structure. (I understand that the English trans-

lation by Thomas P. Whitney, from which the quotations in this essay have been taken, is equally outstanding.) In his subtitle Solzhenitsyn calls the work an "experiment." If after finishing the book we ask ourselves, Has this experiment in trying to cope artistically with the material succeeded?, the answer can only be yes, yes, and yet again yes.

And we have not only the wrathful moralist to thank for this artistic achievement but also Solzhenitsyn the writer who, as a kind of by-product, has created a masterly example of what we call documentary literature. Nothing in this book is invented. The material—appalling as it is— is, of course, a given quantity, as it was for hundreds of thousands, for millions, of others. Of the estimated thirty million Europeans who took part in the war, no more than three or four dozen have produced war books, including documentaries and fiction, meriting discussion, although the material—and what material!—lay ready to hand for thirty million people, lay waiting at the door.

So it really means nothing when material lies ready to hand and waiting at the door, nor does it mean much if someone industriously collects and researches documents. Even though the documents "speak for themselves," they must still be discussed and "made to speak," and that is what has happened in *The Gulag Archipelago*. It is still the author who creates the material, not the material that creates the author.

Nothing in Solzhenitsyn's book has been invented, but much has been discovered. Wherever Solzhenitsyn has to rely on conjecture or approximation, this is clearly stated. And some statistical details that can only be guessed at are presented with a precision that never fails to indicate the natural scientist. And even that is not the explanation, for there are plenty of natural scientists but very few who command the language, the voice, and who are expert orchestrators.

This preamble seems to me important, for it might be asked, Where's the trick, given that subject? But it is precisely that subject that makes of the work far more than a trick. There have been harbingers of *The Gulag Archipelago* apart from Solzhenitsyn's own novels and stories. We have had Evgeniia Ginzburg's *Into the Whirlwind* (the book that, in a miniature edition, with results disastrous for the author and embarrassing for the publishers, was wafted across into the German Democratic Republic suspended from West German Army balloons). We have had Lydia Chukovskaya's *The Deserted House* and Shalanov's prison-camp story about the infamous Paragraph 58; we have had Susanne Leonhardt's *Stolen Life*, as well as many other publications.

Solzhenitsyn's *Gulag* deprives no other publication of its rank and importance. What he had in mind and succeeded in creating was a monument for the nameless mass of those who do not command this language—or who were silenced before they could raise their own voices. Forbearance toward the Soviet authorities or lack of it—both these stances as well as numerous variations upon them, become secondary in the light of this book. It is not the Soviet present that is being accused but its smoldering past.

I lack the categories to define the underlying tone of the book. Satire, sarcasm, irony—these, I feel, are not appropriate to the subject. If the word "divine" were not commonly misinterpreted as having a sybaritic connotation (divine food, divine women, divine parties, clothes, and drinks) I would tentatively speak of divine bitterness

—tentatively and provisionally. Humor? Yes, inasmuch as it includes the dimension of hope and humanity and is not confused with the pernicious malice of a Wilhelm Busch, who almost always deprives his object of dignity.

In Solzhenitsyn's book, dignity is restored, the dignity of those almost countless millions who, under the most humiliating circumstances, were declared and rendered "vermin" (Lenin) by their guards and interrogators: political prisoners who, without mercy or protection, were ultimately delivered up to the criminals. Humor also because the author shows not even a trace of self-righteousness. I repeat—not even a trace. Moreover—this in itself is masterly—there is in this lack of self-righteousness not one grain of hypocrisy to be found.

Nor does he fail to point out the murderous consequences of *any* ideological justification. I quote:

> That was how the agents of the Inquisition fortified their wills: by invoking Christianity; the conquerors of foreign lands, by extolling the grandeur of their Motherland; the colonizers, by civilization; the Nazis, by race; and the Jacobins (early and late), by equality, brotherhood, and the happiness of future generations.

These things—the lack of self-righteousness, the remainder of the murderous consequences of other ideologies—are, of course, not publicized in Moscow. Or will that splendid Alexander Chakowsky one day devote an editorial to this subject in his *Literaturnaya Gazeta?*

This explains—because an author is not only obligated but has to be crazy enough to deal with potential conflicts —this explains the great detail with which Solzhenitsyn goes into the problem of the Vlasov Army: the conflict of a general whose army was shamefully allowed to be wiped out, a general who deceived himself and others as to the nature of the Nazis; and we can be sure that Moscow overlooked, deliberately or not, the crucial passage reading:

> But fate played them an even bitterer trick, and they became more abject pawns than before. The Germans, in their shallow stupidity and self-importance, allowed them only to die for the German Reich, but denied them the right to plan an independent destiny for Russia.

Of course, these things do not exist—conflicts, destiny, fate—and the fact that Solzhenitsyn reintroduced these ideas may be interpreted as his principal crime. And then, too, there is that touchy comparison of the MGB with the Gestapo, which I see used here in one case only, that of the émigré and Orthodox preacher A. I. Divnich. I quote:

> Divnich's verdict was unfavorable to the MGB. He was tortured by both, but the Gestapo was nonetheless trying to get at the truth, and when the accusation did not hold up, Divnich was released. The MGB wasn't interested in the truth and had no intention of letting anyone out of its grip once he was arrested.

As I see it, Solzhenitsyn is not referring in this case to the Gestapo as such but only to the case of Divnich, who was after all an émigré and a Russian Orthodox preacher and hence for the interrogating Gestapo probably not entirely a subhuman. Possibly Solzhenitsyn tends in his anger

to overgeneralize here, but I am not interested in opening
two national accounts—and trying to balance them.

A few weeks ago I was reading H. G. Adler's *Der
verwaltete Mensch*, studies on the deportation of the Jews
from Germany. For the time being, this tells me all I want
to know about the Gestapo. There may have been one or
two, or even a few more, Gestapo officials who were not
quite that bad.

The Gestapo as a whole was bad enough, and Solzhenitsyn is hardly likely to deny this. Such comparisons are not
only touchy, they are unworkable because no balance can
be drawn, nor any comparison made of all the historical
differences; and then there is also the difference between
torture for ideological reasons and murder for racist principles. Moreover, this would lead to an appalling rivalry—
especially between Russians and Germans—which would
consist of one saying; "It was worse on our side," and the
other; "No no, on ours!" I don't believe in trying to balance
accounts in this way.

We can be sure—and no one can doubt it after reading
Gulag—that Solzhenitsyn did not make light of a single
Nazi atrocity:

> There is one thing, however [Solzhenitsyn writes],
> which remains with us all as an accurate, generalized
> recollection: foul rot—a space totally infected with
> putrefaction. And even when, decades later, we are
> long past fits of anger or outrage, in our own quieted
> hearts we retain this firm impression of low, malicious,
> impious, and, possibly, muddled people.

Let us leave it at this statement and the humane, con-
ciliatory "possibly" embraced by two commas, and let us
dispense in this case with a Russo-German rivalry aimed

at determining which side was worse. It is futile to play off one cruelty against another; and for the Chilean, Spaniard, Greek, or Brazilian who is being tortured today, the volume of past German or Soviet cruelties offers not even the most minimal consolation.

Disregarding this minor ambiguity, which might be due to Solzhenitsyn's having written "the Gestapo" instead of, more properly, "the Gestapo official," I cannot find a single false note in the total of some 25,000 lines in the book. The uniqueness of the book lies in the composition, the intonation, and the orchestration; in what he chose to describe in more general terms of the development of Soviet legislation, jurisdiction, and the penal system, and the selection of documented details concerning each stage of this development—details which, since they are for the most part *paraphrased* rather than quoted verbatim, represent stylistic masterpieces, not least in their brevity.

Unerringly placed, economically utilized, are some small "merely" literary passages:

> But all we could see [on the roof of the Lubyanka prison where the inmates took their exercise] was that chimney, the guard posted in a seventh-floor tower, and that segment of God's heaven whose unhappy fate it was to float over the Lubyanka.

And on Stalin: "Did he perhaps wish to save his soul? Too soon for that, it would seem." Or: "Day divided the prisoners and night drew them closer together." Referring to his suitcase, which he had brought with him into the prison and on which his fingers traced the hole torn in it: "Things have longer memories than people." It takes someone with a gift to discover and put into words that "things" can have such long memories! And in the very midst of this enumeration and explanation of horrifying events, all presented with that divine bitterness, he quotes some lines of Mayakovsky:

> And he who sings not with us today
>   is against
>   us!

As we read this book we become increasingly aware of why the Soviet Union published less about the Watergate affair than any other country. Watergate becomes a watery soup, yet for those involved and affected, Watergate is far from innocuous. Comparisons are always odious. When Mr. Shukov, the Soviet television commentator, accuses Solzhenitsyn of "stirring up the past," I would like to refer Mr. Shukov to a certain Count Lev Tolstoi, who fifty years after Borodino was "stirring up the past," and what came out of that was *War and Peace*. And when the invaluable Mr. Chakowsky says and writes, "Time is working for us," I can only hope that this cynical joke will prove wrong and that Solzhenitsyn will prove right when he says, "If the first tiny droplet of truth has exploded like a psychological bomb, what then will happen in our country when whole waterfalls of Truth burst forth? And they will burst forth. It has to happen."

No doubt about it: what happens in *Gulag* is not merely de-Stalinization but de-Leninization. Both Little Fathers are rapped over the knuckles and have their pedigrees examined. After striking up the overall theme in the opening chapters, Solzhenitsyn systematically demonstrates, chapter by chapter, the development of Soviet legislation, jurisdiction, and the penal system, both in general and in particular—elucidated by examples and footnotes. Everything is documented, cited, the sources (mainly Lenin and Krylenko, to a much lesser degree Stalin) are stated.

For instance, capital punishment is abolished, reintroduced, reabolished, and reintroduced, and even while abolished it is resorted to. Here are some of the categories of criminals: there were the "grain-ear snippers," wives who "failed to renounce their husbands," those who "failed to turn in radio receivers," the "Africans," the "generals' wave," the "guilty Muscovites," the "non-denouncers," the "repeaters"; there were also the "vengeful children," the "kulaks," the "non-returners," the "non-prejudgers" and the "artisans."

There is a dissertation on the science of arrest:

> Arrests are classified according to various criteria: nighttime and daytime; at home, at work, during a journey; first-time arrests and repeats; individual and group arrests. Arrests are distinguished by the degree of surprise required, the amount of resistance expected (even though in tens of millions of cases no resistance was expected and in fact there was none). Arrests are also differentiated by the thoroughness of the required search; by instructions either to make out or not to make out an inventory of confiscated property or seal a room or apartment; to arrest the wife after the husband and send the children to an orphanage, or to send the rest of the family into exile, or to send the old folks to a labor camp too.

Needless to say, there is no lack of absurdities which sometimes border on the comic and may well be a Soviet specialty:

When the Orientalist Nevsky was arrested, they grabbed Tangut manuscripts—and twenty-five years later the deceased victim was posthumously awarded a Lenin Prize for deciphering them.

At the conclusion of a Moscow area regional party conference, "stormy applause, rising to an ovation" for Stalin surges through the hall. The audience claps, for three, four, five minutes—no one dares to stop applauding, so that the clapping continues for eleven (!) minutes, until the director of a paper mill finally, in that eleventh minute and to the relief of all those present, stops applauding. The following night, however, the director is arrested and is given his ten years plus the interrogator's advice: "Don't ever be the first to stop applauding!"

Then we have the famous biologist Timofeyev-Ressovsky (crime: refusal to return home), whom nothing seems to shock so much as some tea that has been spilled on the floor of the Lubyanka prison.

He considered it striking evidence of the lack of professional pride on the part of the jailers, and of all of us in our chosen work. He multiplied the 27 years of Lubyanka's existence as a prison by 730 times (twice for each day of the year), and then by 111 cells—and he would seethe for a long time because it was easier to spill boiling water on the floor 2,188,000 times and then come and wipe it up with a rag the same number of times than to make pails with spouts.

And we also have the cruel and, no doubt, pertinent joke in which the chief of the convoy guard asks the prisoner what he had been given his twenty-five years for, and the latter replies, "For nothing at all," whereupon the commander says, "You're lying. The sentence for nothing at all is ten years." Nor should we forget the young social revolutionary Yekaterina Olitskaya, who in 1924 felt she was *not worthy* of prison—what had *she* done for Russia after all?

The bitterest sections are devoted to prisoners of war returning to or handed over to the Soviet Union, and indeed this is a particularly noxious chapter in West-East relations. Solzhenitsyn:

> There is war; there is death—but there is no surrender! What a discovery! What it means is: Go and die; we will go on living. And if you lose your legs, yet manage to return from captivity on crutches, we will convict you. (The Leningrader Ivanov, commander of a machine-gun platoon in the Finnish War, was subsequently thus imprisoned in Ustvymlag, for example.)

And elsewhere:

> For not wanting to die from a German bullet, the prisoner had to die from a Soviet bullet for having been a prisoner of war! Some get theirs from the enemy; we get it from our own!
>
> Incidentally, it is very naïve to say *What for?* At no time have governments been moralists. They never imprisoned people and executed them *for* having done something. They imprisoned and executed them *to keep them from* doing something. They imprisoned all those POW's, of course, not *for* treason to the Motherland, because it was absolutely clear even to a fool that only the Vlasov men could be accused of

treason. They imprisoned all of them *to keep them from* telling their fellow villagers about Europe. What the eye doesn't see, the heart doesn't grieve for.

And further:

Those prisoners who had been in Buchenwald and survived were, in fact, imprisoned for that very reason in our own camps: How could you have survived an annihilation camp? Something doesn't smell right!

Even Churchill and Roosevelt are accused of "consistent shortsightedness and stupidity," and with good reason.

I recall having looked on, from the inner cage of an American prisoner-of-war camp, while former Russian POW's had to be positively forced into rail cars and trucks, many of them screaming and resisting in vain. At the time we did not grasp the terrible significance of what was happening; we only found out later. They were being taken to the Gulag Archipelago.

Oh no, this book does not spew forth hatred for the Soviet people; it is more an offer and a challenge for that people to liberate itself at last from a deeply entrenched inner fear. Although devoted to an inhuman subject, it is a human book written in a unique style, translated into German by someone who must speak and know both languages as her native tongue.

To prevent the reader from lapsing all too quickly into compassionate, sentimental meditation, some earthy quotations from the convict jargon have been scattered about, for instance the "uncorked" women, "trash" (for clothing), or the "quarter" (meaning twenty-five years, or a quarter of a century).

And it is not only General Vlasov's conflict that has been freed from its taboo but also that of Bukharin, who refused to accept the facts yet had to accept his own death. What a drama—Stalin and Bukharin, and those unanswered letters beginning "Dear Koba"! The sinister and the absurd abound:

> The former Chekist Aleksandr Kalganov recalls that a telegram arrived in Tashkent: "Send 200!" They had just finished one clean-out, and it seemed as if there was "no one else" to take. Well, true, they had just brought in about fifty more from the districts. And then they had an idea! They would reclassify as 58's all the nonpolitical offenders being held by the police. No sooner said than done. But despite that, they had still not filled the quota. At that precise moment the police reported that a gypsy band had impudently encamped on one of the city squares and asked what to do with them. Someone had another bright idea! They surrounded the encampment and raked in all the gypsy men from seventeen to sixty as 58's! They had fulfilled the plan!

And then, of course, we also have the "humane" and the genuinely humane: Solzhenitsyn's commandant, for example, who, contrary to all regulations, says good-bye to his captain, who has been arrested, and wishes him luck. To quote Solzhenitsyn:

> Here is what is most surprising of all: one *can* be a human being despite everything! Nothing happened to Travkin. Not long ago, we met again cordially, and I really got to know him for the first time.

He is a retired general and an inspector of the Hunters' Alliance.

It could happen to anybody, or *not* happen: the arbitrariness was total. The rehabilitation of M. P. Yakubovich, for instance, was refused:

> However, for his consolation, he has been granted a *personal* pension for his revolutionary activity! What monstrosities exist in our country.

It is appalling that responsible intellectuals such as Shukov, Chakowsky, and Simonov, instead of recognizing the offer contained in this book, should try to fan the flames of that most sinister of all forces: the wrath of the people. The fact that anybody could have been a victim, or *not* a victim, must surely have provided some basis for, if not actually supporting a fellow author, at the very least refraining from joining in the hue and cry against him.

The most astonishing thing about this book, to my mind, is that, although its subject could hardly be grimmer, it is neither hopeless nor pessimistic. We should not for a moment forget that it ends in 1956, that meanwhile eighteen years have gone by. And if there should be a Part III to *The Gulag Archipelago,* we shall be on the lookout for any differences between it and Parts I and II, with which I am now concerned.

While no sensible person can wish for an overthrow in the Soviet Union, we all see a change as desirable, and where there have been cases of clemency there should surely also be mercy. Mercy toward themselves.

Since Solzhenitsyn has attached so much importance to

it, we must mention the low price of this book in the German edition—about two thirds of what a book of this caliber and size would normally be sold for. That too is a breach in our accursed system of calculation. So it is possible, and it has been achieved by a Soviet author rather than a Western one.

Since the author shows no trace of self-righteousness, this book should be no cause for self-righteousness on the part of any of its readers. We should not forget either this or the fact that it ends in 1956. And I will quote one more short passage from the last page but one of the book:

> The young people imprisoned in these cells under the political articles of the Code were never the average young people of the nation, but were always separated from them by a wide gap.

Is this true, I wonder, only of the Soviet Union?

1 Translated by Thomas P. Whitney. Harper & Row, New York, 1973.

*On Alexander Solzhenitsyn's
new novel.*

"THE OAK AND THE CALF"

(1976)

I shall start by quoting from page 606 of this book, a quotation that would require hours of study and discussion in order to do justice: justice not only to the book and its author but also to the events and trends described and interpreted in it. The quotation reads: "Now cast your votes, behind you stands the majority. Do not forget: The history of literature will one day be interested in our session today." Thus spoke Alexander Solzhenitsyn on November 4, 1969, at that session of the Ryasan Writers' Association that ended in his expulsion. I should like to reinforce this quotation by one small variation: this historic, this shameful session made not only literary history but *history*. In no other country in the world has history been so accurately reflected in literary history as in the Soviet Union and Czarist Russia. Thus *The Oak and the Calf* is also a contribution to history.

Consisting of six parts, it is more than a documentation, it is a novel of several novels, a novel about censorship, about the secret service, a novel about literary activity tangling with censorship and the secret service. Three main protagonists stand out: the author Alexander Solzhenitsyn; Alexander Tvardovski, for sixteen years editor-in-chief of the Soviet periodical *Novy Mir* and a celebrated Soviet writer; and the third—only partially visible, partially articulated—the ubiquitous, largely intangible bureaucracy, which in this case must include not only the Politbureaus, not only the secret service, but also writers' associations and editorial staffs in their multiple cross-hatchings with the other authorities.

Five parts of the book follow five stages of development, corresponding in turn to the progression of Solzhenitsyn the author to Solzhenitsyn the *case*. The first part was written between April 7 and May 7, 1967; the second (called First Postscript) in November 1967; the third part in February 1971; a further part in December 1973; and the last in June 1974, after Solzhenitsyn's expulsion from the Soviet Union. The sixth part, the Appendix, contains the principal letters, records, and statements which supplement the five main parts.

Apart from authors who for political or commercial reasons are exposed—or have succumbed—to coercion, the general reader should find this book interesting and instructive on a more than superficial level and, in my opinion, absorbing. It explains—and this is where the dating of the separate sections over a period of seven years is important: it documents the intensification—the progress of a man (in this case an author) toward and finally into that international political situation known to us from Solzhenitsyn's fate. It was only after reading this book, containing as it does the genesis of all his works and manuscripts, that I realized how he embarked upon literature in a genuine spirit of cooperation, in the passionate desire to cure *from within* the many places where Soviet society has bogged down—and how this same literature forced him *out*, where he had never wanted to go.

One forgets too quickly that, although Solzhenitsyn,

now fifty-seven, was already writing as a young man, it was not until he was forty-three—fifteen years ago—that he first attempted to publish; and it was not he but Lev Kopelev, his jail-friend as he calls him, who submitted his manuscript to the editors of *Novy Mir*. And as recently as ten years ago, in the spring of 1966, after many years of experience with the intrigues of the literary business—with threats and slurs, with courage and cowardice, with vanity of all kinds—as recently as the spring of 1966 he proceeds not in that absolute, puristic morality of his, but strategically. I quote:

> When in the spring of 1966 I realized that I had been granted a lengthy respite, it dawned on me that I now had to write an *official* [the emphasis is Solzhenitsyn's] work accessible to all, to prove first of all that I was alive and working, and to fill that space in society's consciousness into which the confiscated works could not penetrate. *Cancer Ward,* which I had begun three years earlier, was well suited for that. Now I intended to carry on with it.

He finished writing *Cancer Ward;* and it was in and around this very work—which he himself calls politically harmless—that his own fate within Soviet literature was to be to some extent decided. The back and forth over this novel, the editorial meetings, the discussions in the Writers' Association, its publication abroad in the West (over Solzhenitsyn's protests); the carping about this or that figure in the novel, about pessimism, optimism, the shuffling of the manuscript from one authority to the next and back again to the editors: all this would be enough for a novel about a novel in which the narrow-minded-ness, the touchiness, the denseness of Soviet cultural functionaries stood revealed, but in addition to that, their intelligence, their cunning, their analytical expertise, their whole battery of instruments.

It took the confrontation with all these authorities, with these real as well as contrived arguments and objections, to make Alexander Solzhenitsyn the person he was meant to be by virtue of his talent, his inflexible will, his power of expression. He becomes the lone fighter of historical dimensions who knows very well that here it is not a matter of literature *or* politics but of both; and we find that, in addition to all his other gifts, he has one that we would not expect to find in an author: a gift for strategy. He recognizes his situation, he knows what weapons he has, and he knows how much is at stake; he recognizes his international allies, the weaknesses of his opponents; and in this labyrinth of friend and foe, of part-friend and part-foe, in which he must have been given every conceivable kind of advice, advice on where and how he ought to do this or that, or should have done this or that, he decides for himself what must be done: not to give an inch. Unafraid, yet perhaps not without fear for his family and friends, he stands his ground right up to his arrest and expulsion in February 1974.

What makes this book exciting is not only the drama of the external events but, even more, the drama of the internal processes in the Soviet Union, where for a while —after the publication of *One Day in the Life of Ivan Denisovich*—it really looked as if the floodgates would be opened. The focal point of this pregnant situation, with all its ramifications, was none other than Alexander Solzhenitsyn, who had only one weapon: his work; later a second one, which he used quite deliberately: his fame. In the end, of course, he paid a high price for his victory, being expelled from a country to whose inmost heart he belongs.

The meanness of his enemies in the Soviet Union is adequately documented in the Appendix. His greatness will not suffer from the often spiteful remarks that are included, nor from the crocodile tears of hypocritical friends. Let me end with a quotation from his obituary on Alexander Tvardovski, his courageous patron, his ultimately broken friend:

> There are many ways of destroying a writer. In Tvardovski's case they decided: take away his child, his passion, in other words his periodical. It was not enough that this man be exposed for sixteen years to humiliations which he suffered patiently just so that his periodical should survive, just so that literature should not cease, just so that people would appear in print and people would read. Not enough! To that they had to add the devouring fire of liquidation, destruction, injustice.

On The Fixer, *by*
Bernard Malamud[1]

"WOE IS
ME!"
(1968)

At first sight the plot seems straightforward: Yakov Bok moves from his *shtetl* to Kiev, where he hopes to find that pitiful minimal happiness of earning his living (or better still, the money to emigrate) by manual labor as a "fixer," a sort of odd-job man.

He violates Czarist police regulations, accepts work under an assumed name, moves to a part of town where Jews are not allowed to live. He works hard, is skilled and reliable, and has almost forgotten that in the eyes of the police he is still a Jew, although he has ceased to feel like one. Because he has violated regulations, he becomes an ideal scapegoat, someone who can be saddled with a crime which not only has he not committed but which has not been committed at all: ritual murder.

Yakov Bok lands in that most sinister of all snake pits threatening a Jew at the beginning of this century: in the anti-Semitic machinery of justice of Czarist Russia. Torture, humiliation, stool pigeons, hunger, filth, vermin: for nearly two years this "little man" endures them all, without giving in, without offering this corrupt, hypocrisy-ridden machinery anything beyond his "I am innocent."

Efforts are made to tempt him, to bribe him—in vain. The only person intending to stand by him, Investigating Magistrate Bibikov, hangs himself in the prison. Bok's cell door is left open for a while so that with his own eyes he can have a good look at the end of his hopes.

In a visionary ending he leaves the prison and has a visionary dialogue with the most wretched of all wretched Czars, a man who cannot stand the sight of blood because his son is a hemophiliac, but who nevertheless operates the bloodiest machinery of justice of his time. Bok shoots the most wretched of all wretched little Czars. Happy ending.

A second look is needed to discover all the other things done by and to this Yakov Shepsovitch Bok. At the very outset, the Ukrainian boatman who ferries him across the Dnieper on his way to Kiev rants and raves against the Jews while at the same time haggling with Bok and finally taking his old nag in place of the ferry fare of one ruble, "typically Jewish."

Bok's second stupid mistake is to behave like a human being toward a member of the militantly anti-Semitic "Black Hundreds"; he pulls the pious Lebedev, drunk with wine and his own melancholy, out of the gutter. As a reward he is permitted, for a good price and under an assumed name, to fix up Lebedev's apartment: Bok is becoming so un-Jewish that he begins to trust in his good fortune.

More stupid mistakes: not only does he uncover irregularities, he even tries to prevent them. He chases some rowdy boys out of the cemetery, among them the one who later is found murdered; he takes in a Hasidic Jew whom the boys had been stoning, binds the Hasid's wounds and nurses him back to health, sends him on his way and, out of compassion, furnishes the police with the "actual" evidence: blood-soaked rags in his home. Everything, every bit of evidence, is used against him: he bakes some bread, it fails to rise, and he eats it as rusks, so they find at his place what had to be found: matzos and blood.

He is visited in prison by his wife, Raisl, who has left him, borne *him* no children, and now has a child by another man and asks Yakov to legitimize this child. He does so. He signs. Bok's crimes are his acts of humanity.

What is original about this extraordinary novel is that it has historical material as its subject yet never once affects us as historical. It is not the idea or the ideas that make it a great novel. It is the style and the architecture. (The German translation by Herta Haas does justice to both.) A dry prose which pins down its subject with inexorable certainty, never takes a false step, not even where it gives us the banal humanity of its hero, his childlike hunger for education, his wholly unsentimental assessment of love, his delight in a few little rubles honestly earned, in books and strawberry jam.

This prose is earthy where it has to be earthy, tender where it has to be tender; it is supported and held together by something that here in Germany all too easily gives the illusion of optimism, although in fact it is the life elixir of pessimists: by bitter humor.

In his earlier books, which in Germany have been too easily dismissed, Malamud has demonstrated his familiarity with the ingredients of humor: blood, gall, saliva, sperm, sweat, tears, and whatever other "fluids" man may harbor and produce. This, the only legitimate kind of humor, is what holds the great, gloomy architecture of the novel together, and this architecture, no longer merely an idea, has become language.

Shmuel would like to keep his son-in-law Yakov in the Jewish faith: "Yakov, don't forget your God!" And Yakov replies with incorrigibly dry bitterness, "Who forgets who?"

Absurd is the word for Bok's existence: he does not feel like a Jew yet is saddled with the entire burden of the Jewish fate. He whose "nose was sometimes Jewish, sometimes not," whom the boatman takes for a "goddamn Pole," or perhaps a "motherfucking Jew" who nevertheless looks "more like a German," whereupon the frightened Bok mutters that he is a "Latvian."

To become a millionaire he would sell his last shirt, because wealthy Jews are allowed to live outside their settlement area.

In prison he reluctantly begins to read the New Testament, loaned to him by one of the guards; with increasing absorption he recognizes the loneliness of the Passion as his own, cannot understand how the Christian religion could produce such hatred for the Jews.

Malamud never allows his hero Yakov Bok a single lapse. Not even in the darkest darkness of the prison is he allowed—"forgivable though it would be"—even a trace of sentimentality. The cry *"Vey iz mir!"* (Woe is me!) rings out at the very beginning of the novel. It often rings out in Malamud's works. Small New York shopkeepers threatened by bankruptcy utter it, as do lower-middle-class Jews of all kinds who suddenly realize that in the final analysis there is no trusting in one's good fortune.

It is the old cry of dismay uttered by Eastern European Jews, brought along from the Old World into the New.

Jews are persecuted because they are rich and because they are poor; because they are middle-class and because they are not middle-class; they are persecuted because they have a sense of humor and because they lack humor; because they are dirty; and they are particularly suspect if they are clean, since they are supposed to be dirty; because they have Jewish noses; they are persecuted even more if they don't have Jewish noses, and Yakov Bok is one of the really bad ones because sometimes he has a Jewish nose and sometimes he doesn't.

He is a monster because he a human being: a "goddamn Pole," a "motherfucking Jew" who nevertheless looks "more like a German" . . . .

It is absurd. Absurdity is the theme of this great novel which never for a moment relaxes its grasp of its subject.

It is not black literature, it is human literature. The fact that there is no trusting in the modest happiness of earning a few rubles, buying flour, books, strawberry jam; that there is no more trusting in this happiness than in great happiness (whatever that may consist of): this should be regarded not as depressing but as the self-evident message of great literature.

1 Farrar, Straus and Giroux, New York, 1966.

THE POETRY
OF CURSES
(1969)

The rumor that "Irish" and "Catholic" are synonymous obstinately persists, although sufficiently refuted to all the world by Yeats, Shaw, Beckett, and Synge.

The English Reformation and its Cortes—its enforcer in Ireland, Cromwell—have reduced the problematical aspects of Anglo-Irish relations emphatically, but, as I believe, only seemingly, to their religious element. Here Martin Walser would be justified in pointing to the meeting between Caesar and Vercingetorix and lamenting the triumph of Roman over Celtic civilization. Indeed, this confrontation between Roman and Gaul is not a bad model for the complex cruelties that are perpetrated when an unimaginative sense of order coupled with military superiority confronts an imaginative people whose "exoticism" is beyond the grasp of the orderly mind. Latest example: the United States, a world power with no lack of tanks, aircraft, and other material, retreating before a land of pedestrians and bicyclists.

It was the pedestrians of history, the poets, who at Easter 1916, in defiance of all reason, challenged Caesar in Dublin and unsuspectingly ushered in the end of colonialism. As the Irish saying goes, "A song outlasts the voices of the birds, a word outlasts the treasures of the world." That could have been said by Vercingetorix on entering Caesar's tent, and Caesar would have laughed aloud. Now the Czars and the Caesars no longer laugh that easily. Since Easter 1916 England the world power has had little to laugh about. It would be impossible to interpret the historical confrontations between England and Ireland as "Catholic vs. Protestant," Protestants having played a vigorous and leading role in every Irish liberation movement.

At this point I must indicate something of the complexity of Anglo-Irish and Protestant-Catholic relations if I am to do at least partial justice to the autobiography of another Irishman of Protestant descent: Sean O'Casey.

This six-volume work has biblical dimensions and biblical greatness. This fierce torrent of beatifications and curses is the Protestant counterpart to Joyce's *Ulysses*, not yet properly recognized as such and yet the necessary complement, not one iota less Irish, not one iota less "blasphemous." The enlightened intelligentsia was quick to recognize the prophet Joyce, the New Left has apparently not yet discovered its prophet O'Casey. His autobiography contains ample theory on and factual examples on the subject of repression, in schools, church, marriage, and cultural life. It would seem to me that the New Left has so far been reading too much "theology" and not enough bible. Here they will find a bible.

In all their detailed clarity, these six volumes comprise the autobiography of a writer who, more than any other, could lay claim to a title that educated society has awarded rarely and reluctantly in the form of a patronizing cliché: the "working-class writer." Would it occur to anyone, I wonder, to call Kafka a "white-collar writer" or Goethe a "civil-service writer"? . . .

Sean O'Casey was eighty when he died, disputatious and disputed till his last breath. As far as I am concerned, to be disputed is the only possible status for an author, even if the dispute is sometimes an annoyance. When O'Casey was fourteen he was earning four shillings a week as a stock boy, although a member of the privileged Protestant class which he describes as follows: "Somehow or other we protestants were a better type of person than the wretched catholics."[1] In more detail it sounds like this: "As a protestant and member of the staff he swept no farther [than the threshold] but handed the heap of rubbish over to a roman catholic messenger, who carried it on to where it would be eventually taken away by the city scavenger."[2] (O'Casey often writes of himself in the third person.)

As we see, the gulf between Sean O'Casey and Berna-dette Devlin is hardly more than a stone's throw. The religious conflict that has atrophied to a class conflict was as fraught with problems in the nonliberated Ireland of 1898 as it is today in the Ulster of 1969. Because he was wounded in the Boer War, Miss Devlin's grandfather was rewarded with a street-sweeper's job; no doubt he was then permitted to sweep the rubbish from the thresholds of Protestant warehouses.

O'Casey never availed himself for long of the meager privileges of his Protestant descent. Ignoring the moral consequences, he admits that later on, together with a Catholic vanman, he stole right and left from his hypo-critical boss as "poetic justice" for the outrageous "Christian" wages paid to him and the vanman; "and once, in a fit of recklessness, [he] said to one of the evangelical whisperers that he'd rather open a girl's bodice than open a prayer-book."[3]

Not until he was thirteen was O'Casey, who was plagued by serious eye trouble all his life, taught to read by his sister—after experiences in Protestant schools that prompted him to remark, "The curse o' God on every school that was ever built and every teacher that was ever born!"[4]

That was written not out of contempt for school and education but out of a yearning for education. The curse was directed at the denomination school *system*. O'Casey merely hated and despised the route of beatings and fawning along which education was offered him. He read and studied with a hungry, passionate intensity such as I find only in the autobiographies of Jack London and Maxim Gorki. O'Casey laboriously deciphered his deceased father's small library, each book was for him THE BOOK; every penny went on secondhand books, and he discovered Shakespeare, the poetry of the whole world.

If the patronizing term "working-class writer" (for which those who accepted it must share some of the blame) was never valid, nor was the equally patronizing term "self-taught," and neither applied to O'Casey. What writer ever learned, in the course of a standard education, the things he learned as a writer? And who when he starts to write does not discard, often at great effort, the things he has been taught, in order to start all over again as "self-taught"?

These are the condescending clichés of an educated class that so far has produced little that is creative. The greater part of modern literature has been the product of the honorable and worldwide pastures of the lower middle class and quite often of that in-between class where material standards are below those of the proletarian level.

This declining lower middle class is the one for which education is still as hard to obtain as for the working class. Knut Hamsun was, Eyvind Johnson is, a "working-class writer" in the same sense as O'Casey, who was in his forties and had experienced and actively participated in much political and social history before he became well known.

Things were never made easy for him, nor did he make things easy for himself. He not only respected the great William Butler Yeats, he admired him, yet he never gave in to Yeats when his plays aroused nonliterary, merely diplomatic arguments. It cannot have been easy for Lady Gregory and Yeats to maintain their beloved Abbey Theatre in the face of the hypocritical moralism common to both denominations. O'Casey was no help: he was stubborn, radical, uncompromising, unreasonable, whether he was discussing the Labour movement with the British Prime Minister Ramsay MacDonald or the "Irish problem" with other English politicians, or being advised by Mrs. Shaw on how to be "diplomatic."

He hated being told what to do and left Ireland, like so many others before and after him. Let us not imagine that the problem of expatriate Irish writers is attributable solely to clerical influence, of either kind. One of the reasons is that Ireland has fewer inhabitants than the two Berlins, West and East. We have only to imagine all German writers having lived or still living in Berlin: what would be the accumulation of malice and intrigue, the influence of combined clerical/socio-democratic moralism, on publications! My guess is that the telephone directory for the entire Republic of Ireland is smaller than the Berlin directory. And of course, in a small country everything collects in the capital, in this case in Dublin, a city with hardly as many inhabitants as Cologne. Imagine the entire body of German authors living in Cologne!

O'Casey left Ireland, embittered and angry—and no doubt others were embittered and angry about him. He did not stop short of the most sacred of sacred cows. As an expatriate he wrote those 1,716 pages that are filled with poetry, with verbal power and blasphemous extravagance, that are rough and tender, fair and unfair, subjective and objective, obstinate and obdurate, sometimes discursive and farfetched, devout when concerned with people and their future.

O'Casey knows no limits, he does not stop at the shrines of that saint to whom Miss Devlin owes her Christian name; he does not stop at the saintlike Matt Talbot, an Irish worker who chastized himself and despised earthly rewards—to be promptly played off against strikers, trade unionists, and "materialists" by employers of both Christian denominations. And not even those sacred cows Chesterton, Belloc, Knox, and Orwell are spared.

How is it that during the course of history theologians lowered themselves to minimize the violence of the Old Testament and the dangerous meekness of the New and render them palatable, adapt them neatly to their catechisms, to proclaim the rightness of war and again war, exploitation and again exploitation and yet again exploitation and again war in their docile Roman, German, Anglican, Czarist, etc., churches? O'Casey takes the churches' Latin and theology and flings them back at them in extravagant poetic mutilation. Are not the blasphemies of a Joyce, the biting satire of a Shaw, the "subversion" of a Beckett—all of them Irishmen—the only possible reply to the reduction of both Testaments to a duty-bound, joyless routine?

It is not my problem how Ireland copes with its "nest-fouling" O'Casey; small countries with a history of humilia-

tion have a right to be sensitive. Big countries have no
right to be spared. As it is, the nest-foulers are sitting
right in the nest; those who are called such are usually
outside. It is very difficult to foul a nest from the outside.

Unfortunately, there are a few things that O'Casey
chooses to ignore: that Stalin-Hitler pact, for instance.
And when he calls Hitler a "good Catholic," this betrays
an embarrassing lack of understanding for Central European denominational problems. I do not expect an old
cardinal publicly to recant, to "go over," to surrender his
faith, and O'Casey was an "old cardinal" of Communism.
I only see to whom he dedicated the six volumes: to his
sons, and "the young of all lands, all colours, all creeds";
to the Scottish poet McDiarmid; two volumes to the Roman Catholic theologians O'Hickey and McDonald; one
volume to a Protestant clergyman.

It is no accident that O'Casey, who piles abuse upon
the churches, dedicates three of the six volumes to men of
the church whom he admires and pays homage to in his
work. There were misunderstandings between him and
Yeats, even between him and Lady Gregory, whom he
greatly admired. I have the impression that O'Casey was
one of the most undiplomatic writers who ever lived—
and that, to me, is just as flattering as his "disputedness."
In his autobiography he also eliminates—and that is the
wonderful part about it—the stupid alternative clichés of
"committed" or "uncommitted." This cliché simply does
not apply to him. I would gladly read as much poetic
power, as much word-sense, word-play, and wordmanship
in many a declared uncommitted writer.

It would be a pity if more credit were given to *I
Knock at the Door*, the first volume of the autobiography,
than to the later ones. In all autobiographies, the childhood periods are the most successful, something that has

to do, not with the authors, but with the poetry of distances: the nearer a person approaches the coldest of all cold homes, the grave, the warmer in recollection becomes the nest from which he came. And O'Casey had a bitterly poor nest but a warm one: what he writes about his mother makes her biblical, too (O'Connor wrote in a similar lofty, biblical vein about his earthly mother; O'Casey also writes in a similar way about his wife).

When old Shaw lay dying, he wanted Eileen O'Casey-Carey near him, and he told her that it was lovely to feel the touch of a soft Irish hand and hear the sound of a soft Irish voice. That tells us a lot, more than I can express. About Ireland.

[1] Vol. II, *Pictures in the Hallway;* Macmillan, London, 1942.
[2] *Ibid.*
[3] *Ibid.*
[4] Vol. I, *I Knock at the Door;* Macmillan, New York, 1950.

LOOK BACK
IN RANCOR
(1976)

For Bonn theologians, one of the most shocking sentences in Augstein's book has been: "The Holy Ghost, provided it has any journalistic talent at all, is a bad reporter." But this is not even blasphemy; according to what we have been taught, the reportage handed down to us has passed through the scrutiny (or censorship) of the Holy Ghost. Moreover, rather than wincing piously over this particular image it would have made more sense to use it as a criterion for Augstein's point of departure. Surely Augstein cannot seriously believe that a reporter, no matter how talented, is a more faithful purveyor of the truth than any "ghost," holy or otherwise, or that "poetic force" has less communicative value than the immediacy of the reporter's word. If in the beginning was the Word, and since words are the usual vehicle of reports, it is no disgrace to be called a reporter.

It is at this starting point, in my view, that Augstein's errors begin—not his blasphemy, of which, alas, there is little to be found in this book. In his Foreword he does discuss the limitations inherent in such an immense undertaking; furthermore he does not cast doubt on the historical existence of this Jesus: he merely calls into question the staggering claim of a giant imperium founded on the existence of Jesus, that everything now regarded on this earth as "moral" is based on that "message."

I have never really been able to visualize faith as something that can be taught, inherited, or handed down by tradition, and it is precisely the reasonableness of theologians that I have found most difficult to accept: those contrived proofs of God's existence, those primitive, "scientific" explanations of miracles, those attempts to use equations of the second degree to explain incredibilities of the eighth degree.

One thing I find very difficult to imagine for myself—i.e., that faith without a mystical, personal constituent is possible—I am prepared to grant to others. I cannot even begin to give an "expert opinion" either on Augstein's theological efforts or on the more than eighty standard works he lists and the more than six hundred works from which he quotes. As far as religion, church, and so on are concerned, I am very much a part of the vulgus, and I wonder whether there is one "God of the theologians" and another for the vulgus.

I am tempted to adopt Augstein's challenging thesis: "Definition of Church: the place where the errors of the preceding generation of theologians are rectified." Except that I would like to substitute theology for church: "Definition of Theology: the place ... etc." I find it a typical theologian's error (and Augstein has without question joined the ranks of the theologians here) to equate church with theology. Isn't it one of the most amazing miracles that not only religion but faith has survived *despite* theology, and that there are still even some vestiges of "church"?

What we were expected to swallow (I probably had a similar upbringing to Rudolf Augstein's, hence the "we"), was—to put it mildly—somewhat outrageous: in addition to Giordano Bruno's fiery death at the stake, all those embarrassing and theologically unnecessary superfluous agonies of conscience to which our parents, grandparents, and great-grandparents, and we ourselves, were subjected.

We have only to open a catechism from the year 1930, a school Bible from the same year, those idiotic sterile editions with corresponding illustrations, and try to discover how much they contain of the theology of an Erich Przywara or of the early ecumenical strivings of an Arnold Rademacher.

Whenever we attempt to persuade those learned divines to get down to brass tacks, the reaction is a patronizing reference to vulgarization or popularization. But for whom is religion there, for whom is it being processed by theology, if not for vulgus or populus? Of any other science we may grant that it has theoretical and abstract areas that cannot easily be communicated. I do not expect the formulas and insights of Werner Heisenberg to be peddled on the street; but for what other purpose than to be vulgarized have theology, church, and religion ever existed? For my grandmother, the dogma of the infallibility of the Pope was, although an article of faith, a matter of total indifference like the man in the moon, because it did not concern her directly, and a "mortal sin" such as adultery probably lay beyond her scope and imagination.

What she did suffer from, with the scruples that had been dinned into her, what she did take seriously and what caused agonies of conscience to entire generations, was something theologically so absolutely trivial as the requirement that Holy Communion be taken on an empty stomach. I would ask you to try and remember how many hours of religious instruction were wasted on discussing the possibility that a drop of water might slip down your throat while you were brushing your teeth, and what a system of fear was erected around such absurdities.

Today, no doubt, the theologians laugh at this rule, which was abolished overnight with no reason given and with unparalleled insolence. I see nothing to laugh about in that. The vulgus experiences religion quite simply in a vulgarized form. In *those* days no theologian came forward to liberate the suffering and groaning Catholic part of humanity from this trivial and magically effective disciplinary rule and thus risk the ridiculous punishment of excommunication.

The point is that the vulgus always suffers in its vulgar way; and if it is so despised that "vulgar" has become a term of abuse, then they might as well do without the vulgus. This despised vulgus never suffers from the problems resulting from high-level theological discussions. Such problems invariably arrive at the lower levels in vulgarized form, more often than not as disciplinary rules; down there, where they truly become flesh, they cannot but be vulgar.

Only by looking back, in much anger and even more rancor, can one, I imagine, guess at which of *today's* rules will turn out in the future to be equally trivial: celibacy, birth control, indissolubility of marriage.

Unfortunately, Augstein's book is far from being either vulgar or popular, and once again the dispute turns into one among theologians. It is a pity that Augstein, possibly in a fashionable fear of "emotion," has published neither a religious nor antireligious book, but a theological one. There is nothing dishonorable about joining the ranks of the experts in this way. The question is merely, Will it do much more than shock a few theologians who will then do their best to refute or correct him on a pro-

fessional level? That will be all—unless, yes, unless
the theologians of both denominations can get over their
annoyance at a few digs (good God, how could it be a
scholarly work without these digs!) and themselves supply
a point that Augstein has denied himself and them: that
here is an author who has doubtless enjoyed a classic
Catholic education and who certainly has no more reason
to be "angry" or "vengeful" than countless millions of
others.

When all is said and done, here we have someone
seriously concerning himself with Jesus and the Church,
and not by any means as unfairly as his accusers would
have it; and even if the result of this study leads to the
shattering half-sentence. "... it seems that theology is
doomed to walk its bitter path of self-cancellation to the
very end," one should not again take the easy way out of
damning and denouncing the shatterer but instead ponder
whether there is not more than a spark of truth in that
half-sentence.

Hasn't classical theology reached a dead end? Isn't it
becoming more and more a game played by initiates in-
dulging in twists and turns, infatuated by and obsessed
with their own jargon, a group of illusionists who deem it
a sensation when the Vatican graciously permits them to
discuss the question of whether laymen should be allowed
to preach in church? Isn't it obvious how absurd this is,
how ridiculous and, relatively speaking, more trivial than
the empty stomach before Communion? At some time or
other there was in the beginning the Word, and the end
of classical theology might be epitomized by the sentence:
"And the Word was lost."

Augstein's errors are almost identical with those of
classical theology. When he notes that Jesus used only
words to cast out demons, I am unkind enough to ask, So

what? Words can indeed heal, as can caresses, saliva, laying on of hands, love. Similarly, it is wrong to assume that written traditions are more reliable than oral ones. Written traditions can also be edited, manipulated, falsified; and when Augstein, in an effort to cast doubt on the historical reliability of a text, says that "poets have had a hand in it," his insinuation that poetry equals untruth or inaccuracy is quite simply mistaken.

If I want to know what lies behind the word "Spain," and I read my Cervantes, am I then merely being "misinformed"? Or doesn't Cervantes convey an image of Spain which partially coincides even with that of so contrary a spirit as Andersen-Nexö?

I don't mind being accused of bias here in attacking not a contemporary and a journalist but Augstein the theologian. Poetry is not equatable with falsehood, and legends and myths are not identical with lies. Nor is poetry incompatible with history as a science. Each can complement the other by approaching the same object from very widely differing standpoints. Writers, too, practice something physicists might call "material testing." Moreover, even a reporter selects, condenses, composes, reworks; and when Augstein twice contrasts "poetic force" with reality, he falls into a typical theologian's error. I wonder if one day it may not turn out that the only theologian and religious literature to be taken seriously is that written by poets?

When Augstein says of John the Evangelist that he wanted to know exactly, more exactly than Mark, he confirms my assumption. Quite a number of writers (or poets, if you like!) want to know as exactly as possible: Augstein should read Peter Handke's *A Sorrow Beyond Dreams* (in German: *Wunschloses Unglück*) and ask himself where poetry becomes truth and truth poetry. I would even recommend that theologians study this message. They might discover how the vulgus looks upon theology: as too piddling to be taken seriously. In the scientific sense Dostoevski had not the faintest notion of psychology, yet it was he who wrote *the* psychological novels, and to this day I know of no better literary presentation of Jesus than in *The Idiot*. In Augstein's book the few lines of Rilke light up the sky like shooting stars.

To my mind, Augstein has given us much less in this book than he might have. Religion is not an emotionally neutral subject. Hence it is extremely unrealistic to treat it without emotion. It is for *this* that he can be reproached rather than for his "blasphemy," or the fact that he received help in his extensive researches.

This settling of accounts on the part of a contemporary with a Catholic background was overdue, as was his challenge to theology that is the upshot of the book. Mere annoyance or offense at Augstein's book would be a deplorable reaction on the part of his "colleagues."

This book, written by a man who probably enjoyed an upbringing roughly the same as mine, has stimulated me, and what some may stigmatize as subjective in this review in fact originates in a possibly unrecognized and entirely different objectivity and rationality. To disparage that which is poetic, with its own objectivity and its own rationality, is a gross error on the part of theologians. What else could prove to be, and remain, true of the Gospels and of Him about Whom they were written but the poetry they contain about Him? Can disdain *and* courtesy be expressed better than by remaining silent in court?

[1] Urizen Books, New York, 1977. However, Mr. Böll's article was translated before publication of the Urizen English-language edition. Hence the passages quoted have not been taken from the Urizen translation.

MISCELLANY

Nobel Lecture given by
Heinrich Böll before the
Swedish Academy in Stockholm,
May 2, 1973

AN APPROACH TO
THE RATIONALITY
OF POETRY

(1973)

I would like to begin by explaining that I have changed the subject of my lecture. I had intended to discuss the relationship between Russian and German literature, the political and historical relationships of Russia and the Soviet Union to Germany—to both Germanies. But when I came to prepare my talk I had to turn to a job which authors must occasionally face: I had to correct some proofs. Among these I encountered a number of essays which I had written in recent years, and I realized that I had already written about all these things.

Between 1966 and 1969, in the preparation of a documentary film, I became deeply involved with Dostoevski and wrote a scenario, text, and commentary for a film about him. Later, on the anniversary of his hundred-and-fiftieth birthday, I took part in a wide-ranging radio discussion; then, a year or two after that, in 1971, I composed a ninety-minute lecture that later appeared as the epilogue to a new edition of Tolstoi. It was called *Annäherungs-versuch* (*Trying to Close the Gap*), and in it is contained everything I would have had to cover here. So, in order to save you as well as myself from boredom, I have ·turned to a different subject. I hope you will understand, for I find repetition uncongenial and boring. And I have hit upon a subject that seems to me highly topical. I have tried to approach the rationality of poetry, since in conversation, discussion, and written works I have been observing a tendency to reduce literary and artistic problems to the general formula: information *or* art. That is why I have entitled my present talk "An Approach to the Rationality of Poetry."

It is said by those who should know—and disputed by others who also should know—that in an enterprise as apparently rational and calculable as the construction of a bridge, the joint product of architects, draftsmen, engineers, and workmen, a remainder of a few millimeters or centimeters will be left that defies calculation. This element beyond calculation, minute in terms of the vast quantity of material involved, may arise from the difficulty of calculating precisely not only every possible reaction of a mass of intricately related chemical and technical items but also the additional interaction of the four classic elements of air, water, fire, and earth. It would seem, therefore, that the problem lies not only in the plan, the technical-chemical-statical composition that is under constant review, but also in the embodiment (my term for it) or realization of this plan. This incalculable remainder, though it may consist merely of fractions of millimeters corresponding to unpredictable minute differences in expansion—what are we to call it? What is concealed in this gap? Is it what we used to call irony? Is it poetry, God, resistance, or, to use a more fashionable term, fiction? Someone who should know, a painter who used to be a baker, once told me that baking rolls, which was done, of course, in the very early hours of the morning, had been an extremely tricky business, that it had been necessary to stick one's nose and behind out into the predawn light to be able to decide, more or less by instinct, on the mixture of ingredients, the temperature, and the oven time, since every single day had called for its own rolls: that vital, sacramental element in the first meal for all those taking up the burdens of the day. Are we also to call this well-nigh incalculable element irony, poetry, God, resistance, or fiction? How can we dispense with it? Leaving aside love: no one will ever know how many novels, poems, analyses, confessions, sufferings, and joys have been heaped upon this continent called love without its ever having been fully explored.

Whenever I am asked how or why I have written this or that, I always feel a certain embarrassment. I would gladly give not only the questioner but also myself an exhaustive answer, but I never can. I cannot reconstruct the entire sequence, yet I wish I could if only to make at least my own literary output a less mystical process than building bridges or baking rolls. And since we know that literature as a total entity, as communication, can have a liberating effect, it would obviously be very useful if we could convey the creative process of this embodiment so that others might share in it.

What is it that even I, although it is clear that I produce it, cannot begin to explain? What is this Something which from the first line to the last I commit with my own hand to paper, constantly revise, rework, partially re-emphasize, and which nevertheless, more so as time goes on, seems to grow farther and farther away from me, like something that is past, or has passed, becoming increasingly remote to me while for others it may be acquiring importance as communication? Theoretically speaking, a total reconstruction of the process should be feasible, a kind of parallel record produced during the work which, were it complete, would probably be far lengthier than the work itself. For it would have to do justice to the dimensions not only of the intellect and the spirit but also of the senses and the material; it would have to furnish *explanations* of atmosphere, metabolism, moods, the function of the environment not only in its materialization, its embodiment as such, but also as a setting. Sometimes, for example, I watch sports events on TV with an almost empty mind in order to use this emptiness for contemplation: a somewhat mystical exercise, I admit, yet all these events would have to be included in the record, in full, for might not a kick or a jump—a gesture perhaps, a smile, a commentator's remark, a commercial—prompt something in my unthinking contemplation? Every telephone conversation, the weather, all one's correspondence, every single cigarette would have to be included; a passing car, a pneumatic drill, the clucking of a hen, breaking a sequence of thought.

The table at which I am writing this is 29¾ inches high, its top measures 27 by 43¼ inches. The legs are turned, it has one drawer, it is possibly seventy or eighty years old, it once belonged to my wife's great-aunt who, after her husband had died in a lunatic asylum and she had moved into a smaller apartment, sold the table to her brother, my wife's grandfather. So, a despised and somewhat despicable item of furniture, quite valueless, it eventually, after the death of my wife's grandfather, ended up in our home; there it stood, somewhere, no one knows just where, until as the result of a move someone noticed it and saw that it had been damaged in an air raid; at some point, at some time, during World War II its surface had been pierced by a bomb splinter. Not only would it have sentimental value, it would be entering into a dimension of some politico-socio-historical interest to use the table as a vehicle for such an entry, for then the profound contempt of the movers, who almost refused to transport it, would acquire greater importance than its present use—which is more random than the stubbornness with which we preserved it from the garbage dump, not out of sentimentality or nostalgia but almost as a matter of principle, and since by now I have done some writing at this table I may be permitted a passing affection for it (the emphasis is on passing). Let us ignore the objects lying on the table: they are loved and interchangeable, and also random, except perhaps for the portable Remington, a "Travel Writer De Luxe" model, vintage 1957, of which I am also fond—this means of production of mine that has long since lost all interest for the income tax department, although it has contributed considerably, and still does, to that department's revenue. On this instrument, which any expert would view or touch with contempt, I have written, I would say, four novels and several hundred shorter pieces. This is not the only reason I am fond of it: again, it is a matter of principle, for it still does the job and proves how few are a writer's possibilities or desires for investment.

I mention table and typewriter to bring home to myself that not even these two essential utensils are wholly explicable to me; and if I were to try to determine the origins of both, their precise material, their industrial-social evolution and orgin, the result would be an almost endless compendium of the industrial and social history of Britain and West Germany—to say nothing of the building of the room in which this table stands, of the soil on which the building is constructed, or what is more, of the people who—probably for centuries—have inhabited this building, the living and the dead; to say nothing of those who deliver the coal, wash the dishes, and bring the mail, let alone our own nearest and dearest. And yet *everything,*

from the table and the pencils that have lain on it throughout its entire history, to our own nearest and dearest,
would have to be included. Isn't there room enough here
for residue, gaps, resistance, poetry, God, fiction—even
more than in the building of bridges and the baking of
rolls?

It is true, and easy enough to say, that language is material and that in the process of writing, something ma-
terializes. But how to explain the fact that—as we sometimes discover—something like life is created, people,
destinies, actions; that an incarnation takes place on something as pale and lifeless as paper, where the author's
imagination is combined with the reader's in a still unexplained manner, a total process that defies reconstruction, where even the most discerning and sensitive interpretation can never be more than an attempt or achieve
more than a qualified success? Indeed, how would it even
be possible to describe, accurately record, the transition
from the conscious to the unconscious—on the part of
both writer and reader—and then to extend that in all its
religious or philosophical multiplicity in terms of the interplay of nations and continents? Nor must we forget the
ever-shifting relationships on the part of and between
writer and reader, and the sudden switch when one becomes the other, thus making the one no longer distin-
guishable from the other. There will always be something
left over, call it inexplicable, a mystery if you like; something that remains and will continue to remain an area,
albeit minute, which our human rationality cannot penetrate because it runs up against the still-unexplained rationality of poetry and imagination, the physical quality of
which remains as much beyond our grasp as the body of
a woman, a man, or even an animal.

Writing is—for me at least—a movement forward, the

conquest of a body still totally unknown to me, away from something toward something as yet unknown. I never know how it will turn out: not in the sense of how the action is revalued in terms of classical dramaturgy, but in the sense of a complex experiment that, given a combination of invented, spiritual, intellectual, and sensual material, is struggling for incarnation—and on paper at that! To this extent there can be no successful literature, there could be no successful music or painting, since no one can have seen the body toward which he is struggling, and to this extent everything known superficially as "modern" but better described as *art vivant* is experiment and discovery—and transient, measurable only in terms of its place in history, and to me it seems beside the point to speak of, or look for, eternal values. Where can we dispense with this gap, this remainder, which we may call irony or poetry, God, fiction, or resistance?

Nor can political entities ever do more than approach what they purport to be; there can be no state that does not leave this gap between the wording of its constitution and the embodiment, a residual space in which poetry and resistance grow—and, let us hope, thrive. Nor is there any form of literature that can exist without these gaps. Even the most accurate reporting cannot preclude mood, or the reader's imagination, even if the writer denies himself this; and even the most accurate reporting must omit something—for example, the exact and detailed description of those objects that are essential to the embodiment of an environment or way of life; any reporting has to compose, to transpose elements, nor are the interpretation and recording of these elements communicable, if only because language as material is not reducible to a universally valid communication factor. Every word is loaded with so much history—so much history of the imagination,

so much national and social history and historical relativity
—and all this would have to be conveyed too, as I have
tried to show by the example of my table. And to define
communication factors is more than a problem of translation from one language into another: it is a far greater
problem within the languages themselves, where definitions can mean world views and world views can mean
wars: we need only think of the post-Reformation wars
which, although *also* explicable in terms of power politics,
were at the same time about religious definitions. And,
incidentally, it is useless to say that we speak the same
language if we neglect to include the overtones of regional
or even local history with which every word is charged.
To my ears at least, some of the German I read and hear
sounds more foreign than Swedish, of which, I am sorry
to say, I understand very little.

Politicians, ideologists, theologians, and philosophers
are forever trying to offer us total solutions to problems,
cut-and-dried solutions with no loose ends. That is their
job, and it is our job, the job of the writers—knowing
as we do that we can explain nothing totally and un-
equivocally—to penetrate the gaps. There are too many
unexplained and inexplicable loose ends, whole areas of
shortfall. Bridge-builders, bakers, and novelists usually
manage to cope with theirs, and their loose ends are not
among the most problematical. While we continue to
argue about *littérature pure* and *littérature engagée*—one
of the false alternatives to which I shall return—we still
unconsciously worry about, or are unconsciously distracted
from the thought of, *argent pur* and *argent engagé*. We
have only to watch and listen to politicians and economists
talking about something as apparently rational as money
for the mystical, or merely mysterious, area within the
three professions I have mentioned to become less and less

interesting and surprisingly innocuous. We need only take the example of the recent reckless attack on the dollar (modestly referred to as a "dollar crisis"). My layman's mind was struck by something that nobody has put into words: the fact that the two countries most severely affected and most forcefully compelled to undertake such extraordinary measures (assuming the word "freedom" to be no mere fiction) as "support buying"—in other words to pay up—had something historically in common: each was a loser in World War II, and to each are imputed the same characteristics—efficiency and capacity for hard work. How can the man most affected by the "dollar crisis," the man turning over the coins in his pocket or proffering the paper money printed with all those impressive symbols, be made to understand why, although he works no whit less for it, this money yields him less bread, milk, coffee, or mileage? How many gaps show up in the mystique of money? In what vaults is their poetry concealed? Idealistic parents and educators have always tried to persuade us that money is dirty. I have never understood this, because the only money I ever received—apart from the great prize awarded me by the Swedish Academy—was in return for my work, and for the person who has no alternative even the dirtiest job is clean. It represents a living for his dependents as well as for himself. Money is the embodiment of his labor, and that is clean; yet it is true that between labor and product there is always an unexplained remainder that is far less easily disposed of by such vague formulas as making a "good" living or a "poor" one than is the gap left in a novel or a poem by interpretation.

Compared with the unexplained gaps in the money mystique, the unexplained loose ends in literature are remarkably innocuous, but there are still people who with criminal thoughtlessness utter the word "freedom" in cases where it is perfectly clear that what is being encouraged and implemented is subjection to a myth and that myth's claim to hegemony. Appeals are made to political reason precisely where a reasoned examination of the problems is being blocked.

On the bottom line of my checks I see four different groups of figures totaling thirty-two symbols, of which two resemble hieroglyphics. Five of these thirty-two symbols I understand: three stand for my account number, two for the branch of my bank—but what can be the meaning of the other twenty-seven, of which several are zeros? I am sure that for all these symbols there is a sensible, meaningful, plausible explanation. The trouble is that in my brain and consciousness there is no room for this plausible explanation, and what is left is the number mystique of a secret science that is more incomprehensible to me—the poetry and symbolism of which will always be more remote to me—than, say, Marcel Proust's *A la Recherche du temps perdu*. What those thirty-two figures demand of me is faith in the fact that all's right with the world, that everything is beautifully clear and, if I would only make an effort, intelligible; and yet I shall still be left with a residue of mystique—or perhaps fear, far more fear than any manifestation of poetry could ever instill in me. Almost no political process involving currency is intelligible to the man whose money is affected.

Thirteen numerals on my telephone bill, some more on each of my various policies, then taxes—my car—my telephone number: I don't even bother to count all these numerals that I should be carrying in my head or at least have noted down somewhere if I am to be able to pinpoint my place in society on demand. Let us arbitrarily multiply the thirty-two signs and symbols on my check by six, or give a discount and multiply by four, add birth dates, a few abbreviations for religion, marital status—do we then have the Western world in the sum and integration of its rationality? May not this rationality, as we understand and accept it—and not only is it made comprehensible to us but we do in fact comprehend it—be nothing but a form of Western arrogance which, by way of colonialism or sense of mission or a blend of both, we have proceeded to export all over the world as an instrument of subjection? And for those affected, would not the differences between Christian, socialist, communist, and capitalist become trivial? Even if there are times when they do comprehend the poetry of this rationality, will not the rationality of their poetry win in the end?

In what did the greatest crime of the American Indians consist when they were confronted by European rationality as it had been exported to America? They had no conception of the value of gold, of money! And they fought against something which today we are fighting as the end product of *our* rationality, against the destruction of their world and their environment, against the total subjection of their soil to profit—a notion stranger to them than their gods and spirits were to us. And how much of the Christian spirit, of the glad new tidings, could they have been expected to grasp from that insane, hypocritical complacency with which on Sunday one served God and praised Him as the Redeemer and on Monday promptly reopened the banks, where the true, the one-and-only, concept of money, property, and profit was served? For the poetry of wind and water, of the buffalo and the grass, the poetry in which their life was embodied, there was only derision: and now we of the Western civilization are beginning in our cities—the end product of our total rationality (for to be fair we must say that we have not spared ourselves)—to appreciate something of the reality of the poetry of wind and water and what is embodied in it. Is it possible that the tragedy of the churches consists not in what the Enlightenment would have called irrational, but rather in the desperate and desperately unsuccessful attempt to pursue and adopt a rationality that can never be compatible with anything as irrational as God incarnate? Rules, paragraphs, the consensus of experts, a forest of numbered regulations, and the creation of prejudices that have been hammered into us and placed on the conveyor belts of history teaching in order to intensify estrangement among human beings. Even at the outermost edge of Western Europe our rationality stands faced by quite a different one, one we simply call irrationality. Do not the appalling problems of Northern Ireland arise from the fact that here, for centuries and without hope, two kinds of rationality have been opposing one another with locked horns?

How many areas of disparagement and contempt have been left to us by history! Continents are buried beneath the victory symbol of our rationality. Population groups have remained strangers to one another although ostensibly speaking the same language. Where marriage of the Western type was prescribed as promoting order, the fact was suppressed that it was a privilege: beyond the reach, beyond the purse of, say, the farmhands and servant girls who simply did not have the money to buy even a few sheets or, if they had saved or stolen the money, would have had no beds to put the sheets on. So they were callously left to their illegitimacy—after all, they did produce offspring! To those above and those outside, everything seemed totally explained. Clear answers, clear questions, clear rules. Catechistic illusion. As long as there were no miracles and poetry was only a symbol of the unearthly, never of the earthly. And then we are surprised, we even long for the old ordered ways, when the areas that were despised and covered up show signs of rebellion, and then, needless to say, one party or the opposing party must derive some material and political profit from this rebellion.

Attempts have been made to bring order to that unexplored continent known as sexual love by dint of rules and regulations resembling those proposed for novice stamp collectors. Caresses permitted or declared taboo were defined down to the minutest detail, and suddenly theologians and ideologists discover to their horror that on this continent which we considered long since charted, cooled down, and ordered, there are still a few live volcanoes—and we cannot expect volcanoes to be quenched by the old familiar fire brigades.

And what have we not unloaded onto God, that abused and pitiable authority? Everything, all the problems bequeathed to us; all the signposts for hopeless misery of a social, economic, or sexual nature have pointed to Him, all that was contemptible has been shunted onto God, all the loose ends, while we have continued to preach Him as the incarnate, without realizing that one cannot unload man onto God or God onto man if He is to be regarded as the incarnate. And is it any wonder that He has survived in places where godlessness has been decreed and where the misery of the world and human society have been shunted into an unfulfilled and equally dogmatic catechism and an endlessly postponed future that has turned out to be a dismal present? Again, we can only react with intolerable arrogance by presuming, from where we sit, to denounce this process as reactionary; and it is arrogance of the same kind when, again from where we sit, the official administrators of God claim as their own the God Who seems to have survived in the Soviet Union, without removing the rubbish heaps under which He is buried here, and, furthermore, claim the appearance of God *there* as the justification for a social system *here*. We constantly desire, whether the convictions we boast are Christian or atheist, to profit by one or the other dogmatically held ideology. This madness of ours, this quintessential arrogance, is constantly burying both: God incarnate, Whom we call God-become-Man, and the vision of the future that has replaced Him, the vision of total humanity. We, who find it so easy to humiliate, lack something: humility, not to be confused with subordination, docility, let alone subjection. That is what we did with our colonized peoples: we turned their humility, the poetry of their humility, into their humiliation. We always want to subject and conquer: no wonder, in a civilization in which our first foreign-language school book is Julius Caesar's *Gallic Wars*, and our first exercise in complacency, in clear-cut answers and questions, was the catechism, any catechism, a primer of infallibility, of complete, cut-and-dried solutions to all our problems.

I have moved somewhat away from bridge-building, baking, and novel-writing and have indicated the gaps, ironies, fictitious regions, residues, divinities, mystifications, and resistances of other areas: to me they seemed worse, more in need of clarification, than the minor, unclarified corners that conceal—as, say, in a novel—not our traditional rationality but the rationality of poetry. The approximately two hundred numerals which, in exact sequence, group by group, and including a few code symbols, I ought to have in my head or at least noted down somewhere as proof of my existence, without knowing exactly what they mean, are the embodiment of not much more than a few abstract claims and proofs of existence within a bureaucracy that not only pretends to rationality but is in fact rational. I am obliged, and also conditioned,

to trust them blindly. May I then not expect that we trust
the rationality of poetry, indeed that we reinforce it, not
that we leave it in peace but that we adopt something of
its peace and of the pride of its humility, which is always
a humility directed downward, never upward. Respect
dwells within it, and courtesy and justice, and the wish to
recognize and be recognized.

I do not wish at this point to furnish openings or vehicles for some new literary mission, but I feel bound to
say, in the sense of poetic humility, courtesy and justice,
that I find much similarity, many possibilities of assimila-
tion, between alienation in Camus's sense, the alienation of
Kafka's characters, and God incarnate, Who has always
been an alien and—if we disregard a few temperamental
lapses—in a remarkable way both courteous and verbal.
Why then, one wonders, did the Catholic Church for so
long—just how long I don't know—bar access to the literal
texts of what was considered Holy Writ, or keep them
hidden in Latin and Greek, accessible only to the initiated?
I imagine it was in order to shut out the dangers it suspected were lurkng in the poetry of the incarnate Word,
and in order to protect the rationality of its power from
the dangerous rationality of poetry. It is no coincidence
that the most important consequence of each Reformation
was the discovery of language and its bodiliness. And what
empire has ever managed to dispense with linguistic
imperialism, that is to say, the dissemination of its own
language and the suppression of the language of the ruled?
It is in this context and no other that I see what are now
not imperialistic but apparently antiimperialistic attempts
to denounce poetry, the sensuality of language, its embodiment, and imagination—for language and imagination are
one—and to introduce the false alternative of information
—agitatory poetry as a new manifestation of *divide et*

impera. It is the brand-new arrogance, one might almost say once again international, of a neo-rationality to permit, for instance, the publication of American Indian poetry as an insurgent force while denying the classes at home which they wish to liberate the right to their own poetry.

Poetry is not a class privilege, nor has it ever been one. Over and over again, established feudalistic and bourgeois literatures have regenerated themselves from what they condescendingly called "popular speech," or to use a more modern idiom, jargon or slang. We need not hesitate to call this process linguistic exploitation, but nothing of this exploitation is changed by propagating the false alternatives of information versus poetry or literature. The disparagement, mixed with nostalgia, inherent in such terms as "popular speech," "slang," or "jargon" is no justification for now consigning poetry too to the rubbish heap, together with all other forms and expressions of art. In this there is much to remind us of the Church's bigotry; the withholding of incarnation and sensuality from others by dreaming up new catechisms for them which reduce the possibilities of expression to the "only true" and the "truly false." One cannot separate the power of communication from the power of the expression chosen by that communication; this contains the rudiments of something that reminds me of the disputes—theologically somewhat boring, but quite important as an example of withheld embodiment—regarding Holy Communion in both forms, disputes which in the Catholic world were reduced to the pallor of the Host, which was not even allowed to be called bread. Not to mention the millions of gallons of wine that were withheld! This constituted an arrogant misjudgment not only of matter but, even more, of what that matter was intended to embody.

It is impossible to liberate a class by first withholding

something from it, and whether this new school of Manichaeism represents itself as nonreligious or antireligious, either way it is adopting a model of hegemony that could end with the burning of Hus and the excommunication of Luther. It is quite all right to argue about the concept of beauty, to develop new esthetics, which are overdue, but they must not begin with instances of withholding, and one thing they must not exclude is the possibility of shifting that literature offers: literature can shift to South or North America, to Sweden, India, or Africa. It can *also* shift to another class, another time, another religion, or another race. It has never been literature's aim—even in its bourgeois form—to create alienation, but rather to abolish it. And if one regards as superannuated the class from which literature has mainly emanated, as the product of that class literature was also, in most cases, a hiding place for the resistance to that class. That internationality of resistance must be preserved which has kept or rendered the one—Alexander Solzhenitsyn—a believer, and the other—Arrabal—an embittered and bitter opponent of religion and the Church.

Nor must this resistance be interpreted merely as a mechanism or reflex prompting belief in God on the one hand and disbelief on the other; rather it is the embodiment of the historical interplay of ideas emerging from among a variety of rubbish heaps and areas of disparagements ... and also as the acknowledgment of solidarity without arrogance or claim to infallibility. For a political prisoner or merely an isolated oppositionist in the Soviet Union, for example, it may seem wrong or even insane for protests to be made in the Western world against the Vietnam war: psychologically we can understand him there in his cell or in his social isolation—and yet he should realize that the guilt of the one cannot be offset against the guilt of the other, that in demonstrating on behalf of Vietnam, people are demonstrating on his behalf too!

I realize this sounds utopian, yet to me it seems the only possibility of a new internationality, not neutrality. No author can adopt prescribed or imposed divisions or judgments, and it seems to me almost suicidal to persist in even discussing the division of literature into *engagée* or otherwise. It is not merely that if we identify ourselves with the one we must for that very reason defend the other to the uttermost: no, it is precisely with this bogus alternative that we adopt a bourgeois divisive principle that alienates us. It is a question of dividing not merely our potential strength but also our—I say this without blushing—potential incarnate beauty, for this incarnate beauty can liberate in the same way as the communicated idea; it can liberate as itself, or as the provocation it may represent. The strength of undivided literature is not the neutralization of trends but the internationality of resistance, and this resistance is made up of poetry, incarnation, sensuality, imagination, and beauty.

The new Manichaeistic iconoclasm that seeks to deprive us of poetry, to deprive us of all art, would rob not only us but also those for whom it is doing what it believes it must do. No curse, no bitterness, not even the information concerning the desperate condition of a certain class is possible without poetry, and even in order to condemn it one has first to arouse awareness of it. One has only to read Rosa Luxemburg with care and observe which were the monuments first ordered by Lenin: the first was to Count Tolstoi, of whom he said that before this Count began to write there had been no peasants in Russian literature; and the second was to Dostoevski, the "reactionary." One may wish, for one's own sake—in order to choose an ascetic path of change—to renounce art and literature. One cannot do this for others until one has aroused their awareness of the things they are to renounce. This renunciation must be voluntary, otherwise it will be no more than a bigoted ecclesiastical ruling like a new catechism, and once again a whole continent, like the continent of love, would be condemned to barrenness.

For reasons transcending frivolity or the desire to shock, art and literature have constantly changed their *forms* and, by experimenting, have discovered new ones. Moreover, in these forms they have embodied something, and scarcely ever was this the confirmation of what was already present and available. And in abolishing art and literature another possibility is forfeited: that of cunning. Art is still a good hiding place, not for dynamite but for the explosive material of the spirit and for the social time fuse. What other reason could there have been for all those Indexes of the Church? And it is precisely because of its despised and sometimes even despicable beauty and opacity that art is the best hiding place for that barbed hook that prompts the sudden jolt or the sudden enlightenment.

Here, before coming to a close, I must make a necessary qualification. The weakness of my suggestions and remarks lies inevitably in the fact that, in casting doubt on the tradition of rationality in which I have been—let us hope not entirely successfully—brought up, I am using the resources of that very rationality, and I admit that it would be more than unfair to denounce that rationality in all its dimensions. It would seem that this rationality has incidentally managed to provide us also with doubts as to its claim to totality, to what I have called its arrogance, while at the same time preserving the experience and recollection of what I have called the rationality of poetry, something I do not look upon as having the privilege of bourgeois authority. It is communicable; and precisely because it can, when verbalized and embodied, sometimes have an estranging effect, it can also prevent or do away with strangeness or estrangement. For to feel strangeness can also mean to feel astonishment, to be surprised or merely touched. And what I have said about humility—in the most cursory manner, of course—comes not from any religious upbringing or recollection, which always equated it with humiliation, but from my early and later reading of Dostoevski. Just because I regard the international movement toward a classless, or no longer class-conditioned, literature—the discovery of whole regions of the humiliated, of those alleged to be human refuse—as the most important literary trend, I wish to warn against the destruction of poetry, the barrenness of Manichaeism, the iconoclasm of what seems to me to be a blind zealotry that refuses even to fill the bathtub with water before throwing out the baby. I regard it as futile either to denounce or to glorify the young or the old. I regard it as futile to dream of old orders that can be reconstructed only in museums; I regard it as futile to construct alternatives such as conservative/progressive. The new wave of nostalgia that clings to furniture, clothing, forms of expression, and gamuts of feelings is, after all, merely proof that we are becoming more and more estranged from the new world; that the rationality on which we have built and in which we have trusted has not made the world any more familiar to us, that the alternatives rational/irrational were false too. There have been many things I have had to bypass or omit, since one idea always leads to another and it would have been impossible to chart all of these continents here. One of these things was humor, which is not a class privilege either, yet it also is ignored in its poetry and as a hiding place for resistance.

*Address given at the awarding of
the City of Cologne's Prize for
Literature to Jürgen Becker,
October 26, 1968, in the
Gürzenich Concert Hall*

ART AND
ITS OBJECTS

(1968)

H ere we are then, gathered once again in this beautiful building where the people of our city have so often paid tribute to themselves with varying degrees of grace. I shall try, with as much grace as I can muster, to honor and discuss a few of the objects with which art is concerned.

I recall one evening during the war when I was hurrying across the Quatermarkt on my way to the station and saw this beautiful building going up in flames. On the street stood a man in officer's uniform painting this burning building. Hurrying past, I saw on his canvas a lot of red for flames, gray for the Gürzenich walls, black for smoke. I am not telling this anecdote in order to introduce fragments of an autobiography, nor to confront this respectably and tastefully restored building with its scorched past and to work in an admonitory "Lest we forget!" I mention it so that, on the spot, I can approach my objects by an on-the-spot example. A painter standing in front of the burning Gürzenich with easel and canvas, holding palette and brush with the all-too-familiar artist's gesture —this was a sight I felt to be somewhat embarrassing: the artist on the front line of reality. I also felt the whole thing to be unjust, unjust toward the intended art and the reality. Moreover, I felt it to be discourteous toward both.

The problem that torments us all—the young artists and writers who are being honored here no less than myself—is the problem of transforming objects into material and transforming this material back into a new reality that does justice to both object and material. Linguistic objects also offer themselves to writers for materialization. Every painter, sculptor, and composer is faced with the same problem, except that language is fraught with particularly ticklish objects, and their materialization, the double transformation language must undergo, is burdened with conventional images, with morality, politics, history, and religion, with misunderstood and misguided ideals lying in readiness on the palette of interpretation.

It seems to me that for a painter the problem might be how to materialize light, which is the sum of all colors, that intangible object light, and that he might weary of this bane of producing art and place himself before the raw canvas with a flashlight and supply the viewer with light as the sum of all colors from a battery. The trouble is that the curse is twofold for it would not be much use or help to him to stand there all alone in his studio spotlighting his canvas. He has to exhibit himself and his work, and this is where his hand quickly fails him; and were he to supply the light by a switch—even the most cooperative museum director or gallery owner has the lights switched off at night if only for reasons of safety and insurance—and were the ingenious painter to go home with the switched-off flashlight that supplies his canvas with art, he would seem to me somewhat sentimental, holding his unexploited object, the flashlight, and having called it a day. There is no such thing as calling it a day, that's only—O thrice cursed!—for those who can afford to regard a thing as beautiful or not beautiful, or to pluck petals from the flower in their buttonhole: "I like it," "I don't like it."

Our dilemma, of course, is that while rejecting society and despising it, we simultaneously seek it. I make no distinction here between the flashlight painter, the signed soup can, and a Nolde watercolor. If someone declares art to be dead and at the same time confronts it with objects that are exhibited, selected, arranged, these invariably appear as an embarrassingly pretentious claim to art. Objects that have been withdrawn from use always become sentimental and mendacious if they do not become material and, as such, are in turn exhibited and arranged, in other words: transformed. Similarly, linguistic objects do not gain in authenticity simply because someone regards their experiential character as objective and that objective character in turn as material. Let us for these few minutes refrain from uttering the word literature, not out of modesty but out of arrogance, so that for this brief while we may avoid the ineradicable misunderstandings that prevail between those who commit something to paper and those who believe that they have to collate and collect that which has been committed to paper. From time to time I, too, join the collaters and collectors, which is to say: I, too, sometimes attempt to bridge the gap, attempts which as often as not fail. That, too, I should like to forget here.

How much farther do antiart and antiliterature take us, when they also become consumable, exhibitable, have their market value dictated to them and, by the collectors and collaters, even their rank? Their seriousness and their frivolity, their poverty and their loneliness, end up in the old cul-de-sac that has always been lying in wait for them: despising society and yet seeking it; and they become victims of the age-old illusion that they alone have joined the *correct* society.

The embarrassing part about the burning Gürzenich was that it was still burning and had not yet burned down. Flames are too much alive to be intrinsically suitable for that double transformation into object and material; that is why I considered the artist's heroic endurance in the front line of reality to be a waste of time. It is sufficient to pass by. What *is* interesting is the residue from the fire, from the flames, the ashes, including the ashes of remembrance and the ashes of the future; there is no present—what I have just said has already passed, is remembrance. The only thing that tries to remain within the present, that tries to grasp at a shred of permanence, is art, which creates something from the ashes, from the handful of dust or dirt.

What we are doing, therefore, is sheer blasphemy, we are living in a constant state of sacrilege because we do not need life for what we create but create life itself, and because we are the only ones who create the present. Society innocently participates in these widely differing examples of our sacrilege. Sometimes society feels offended, but always for the wrong reason: when we occasionally succeed in objectivizing and materializing, in our double transformation, society believes it has discovered itself, mildly protests, and demands that the transgressor be chastised. The fact that each and every creation of the present, each and every attempt to endure—and a few years already constitute permanence; we need only think of all the history, politics, tradition, and religion that in the course of a few years vanish in Hades without trace—the fact that each and every attempt is in itself sacrilegious is something that these iconoclasts may have sensed, and perhaps it is we who understand them best. So the churches and museums are filled with blasphemous works, they are hung with sacrilege, with doubly transformed, man-made life, with the present and with permanence.

The sacrilege committed by society is as undiscovered and unrecognized as our own; *society* removes madonnas and crucifixes, turns them over to trade and to the museums, and then, in never-ending weekend debates at charming convention sites, expresses surprise that—how do they put it so nicely?—religious art is in a state of crisis. Sacrilege is never recognized at the point where it is committed. The sellout of objects once declared worthy of veneration, extorted from craftsman or artist for a pittance, objects declared to be art, is far more sacrilegious than exhibiting or chronicling one's own genitals on canvas or paper; the latter is merely sentimental, an embarrassment for the very fact that it records life and object without transforming them. Furthermore, we know that any genital-sacrilege is permissible provided it yields taxes or has the blessing of Church and State, even if that blessing be only pro forma, which in most cases means: illusory.

Society does everything as if for ever: it builds for eternity, declares works of art to have eternal values, it does what we do not do: it relies on the future. We know that nothing remains, in the ashes of the past we can taste the ashes of the future, and from both we try to create the present and to awaken life. We pass by and, precisely because now and again we do awaken life, that which is called real life is so precious to us—precious because we know what society, if it wishes to remain itself for even a week or two, must not allow itself to become aware of: that transience and death are always at the door, that all will turn to ashes.

This might sound pessimistic, it is not. It is merely an

expression of a sense of reality, and perhaps we are the only ones who have a sense of reality and all the others, though with a more or less high admixture of hypocrisy or self-deception, are what we can least permit ourselves to be: idealists. We are materialists in a sense I hope I have at least suggested; we create our own material by materializing objects and even life itself. The Marxists have so much trouble understanding our materialism because they are idealists; and regardless of any other instances of enthroned infallibility, our sacrilege on yet another count will never be understood: that we are members of a species that is just coming into being—the human race. And inherent in our humanity is something else still insufficiently recognized, inexorably confused as it is with humility, modesty, servility, cowardice, conformity, and so on. It is our courtesy; we must find a new word for it, this one being derived from "court," and we have no business at court, since that is what we are least of all: subjects. Courteous transgressors is what we are, passing blasphemers, and if we do not follow the fad of displaying and recording our genitals, this is only because sentimentality, untransformed objectivization, embarrasses us: it is the antithesis of our intent.

The text of an address given by Heinrich Böll in October 1967, after receiving the Georg Büchner Prize from the German Academy for Language and Literature in the Federal Republic of Germany

GEORG BÜCHNER'S RELEVANCE TODAY

(1967)

My thanks are sincere, my words not without bitterness, nor can they be otherwise since the award bears the name of Georg Büchner. But I have this to say about whatever bitterness may show itself: it emanates not from above, from those lofty regions of a preceptor's superior knowledge, nor from below, from a brimming slop bucket; still less from the center, inert in its complacency. It comes rather from the perimeter, that unquiet perimeter of our times that makes the man of *his* time, Georg Büchner, so relevant to our own.

It seems so easy to assess Büchner's life and work. His life was so short, his work—fragmentary and inspired—comprises a single volume that slips neatly into the pocket. These facts lend themselves to a cultic simplification, an idealized motif for an epitaph fraught with poetic anguish. Premature perfection; premature death; farewell, finale; peace.

But Büchner's life and work leave no room for such peace; they are the antithesis of the cemetery, they make the handsome final plaque an impossibility. The unease that Büchner generates is astonishingly relevant today; it is here, present in this auditorium. Across five generations it leaps toward us, at us, with a wild beauty marked by a sense of impending death, with a darkly glowing fire such as our literature has seldom known. This lightning attack, this unerring choice of material, this human materialism in every object upon which he seized, and, over all, that breath of incompleteness, of impatience even, without which art can never be art but which must never be artificial: this contradiction carries its own definition—his impatience is not artfully contrived, his incompleteness is not artfully contrived. They are simply there, they exist, like those men and women of whom Lena speaks in *Leonce and Lena:* "I believe there are people who are unhappy, incurably so, simply because they *exist.*"

Büchner exists. To describe his art as living would be too biological and lead us into the shallows of dilettantism, and Büchner was no dilettante. Let us listen to what he has to say in his lectures about the cranial nerves, speaking neither as a biologist discussing living matter nor as an anatomist dealing with dissected material: "... and so for the philosophical method [which he contrasts with the theological method] the whole physical existence of the individual is not brought into play for purposes of its own self-maintenance: rather it becomes the manifestation of a primeval law of beauty that, using the simplest designs and lines, yields the highest and purest forms. In terms of this method, everything—form and material—is bound to this law."

These words, which might serve as an epigraph for Büchner's work, show him to be both natural scientist and poet. Here is another social comment he is reported to have made: "It is not hard to be an honest man when you can have soup, vegetables, and meat every day." And a still further example of his uncompromising social realism from the lips of his character Woyzeck, the first—one might even say the last—worker in German drama: "I think when we go to Heaven we must help make thunder." In one person, from the lips of one man, I give you two writers, both German, who a century later seem to be mutually exclusive: Gottfried Benn and Bertolt Brecht, both present in Büchner, who is still relevant today.

It is not difficult to perceive Büchner's present political and aesthetic relevance, to discover the link between the prison death of the student Minnigerode, Büchner's friend, and, in our own day, the shooting of Ohnesorg, the Berlin student,* and of Corsten, the soldier in the German Bundeswehr: each case a horrifying example of public murder committed by the power of the state. Nor would it be hard to translate Büchner's *The Hessian Courier* into Persian, or even to distribute it (in German) in the form of a newly annotated pamphlet rather than buried in an India paper classical edition with its political sting removed by an academic literary aura. In such a new pamphlet the allusions to aristocracy and court life would not even have to be altered: they would merely need a fresh interpretation. Our Great Coalition of Christian Democrats and Social Democrats is arrogant enough. It has nothing more to fear, not even the voter's little X with which, when we are offered no alternative, we are permitted to express our political illiteracy. For those who have eyes to see, there is ample grinning collusion and smirking arrogance: the new feudalism of the little man, who feels more secure in the great bureaucratic apparatuses of two powerful (practically all-powerful) established parties than any sycophant could have felt at any court. And for those

* Ohnesorg was shot during a student demonstration in Berlin organized to protest the visit of the Shah of Iran and social conditions in Iran.

whose conscience has been sacrificed to a political party, here is a telling quotation from Büchner's *Danton's Death:*

> Conscience is a mirror with an ape twisting and turning in front of it; each of us decks himself out as best he can before setting out after his own fashion for his own amusement. This gives us the right to defend ourselves.

Nor should a tract of this kind fail to include the description of a funeral, that paralyzing function that in the spring of this year (1967) closed a bygone era and gave expression to a new one. For the best part of a week, Chancellor Adenauer's funeral in Cologne held the Federal Republic's television screens in thrall, with its parade of legislators and heads of government from at home and abroad, from Europe and overseas: among cardinals and wearers of the Knight's Cross, flock after flock of impeccably dressed lawgivers. This was of our time, and yet—for me, at any rate—in an eerie kind of way, without relevance to our time: the numbing docility with which these obsequies were accepted without question; the expressions on people's faces, the clothes, the automobiles; modern statesmen, modern prelates, modern politicians, modern military leaders, all occupying Cologne Cathedral. It is worth reflecting that, in a society calling itself democratic, two professions are exempt from modern dress conventions, two professions that are scarcely the invention of democracy and in fact manifestly hostile to it: the clergy and the military. The attire of these two professions is always up-to-date, always *comme il faut.*

It is time for another Büchner quotation, this one from *The Hessian Courier,* written fourteen years before the publication of the *Communist Manifesto:*

The law is the property of an insignificant class of *notables* and scholars that by its own machinations has arrogated power to itself. This justice is only a means of keeping you in your place, that you may be the more readily oppressed; it is based on laws that you do not understand, on principles of which you are ignorant, and pronounces judgments that are beyond your grasp.

Another fact that should give us pause is that we all— Germans as well as the delegates of the European countries that have been decimated by the Germans—took one fashion trend for granted: the Knight's Cross is being worn again, this time an updated, doctored, democratized cross from which the little swastika has been excised. It is a cross, after all, and crosses—in art and society—are "in." Perhaps it would be better to say of this new trend, crosses are still being worn. When whole nations were being crucified, crosses were awarded as decorations. If that in its absurdity is not modern! Just as that whole week-long, awesome ceremony was modern, staged, cleverly staged, and yet in an eerie kind of way was not *there*—a piece of Occidental fiction, a clever theatrical production, turned into reality by the gigantic multiplication of the screen. I have no further comment, except to let the twenty-year-old Büchner speak to us again, in the words he wrote to his fiancée:

> I feel annihilated by the appalling fatalism of history. I find in human nature a terrible sameness, in human relations an inexorable force with which each of us and none of us is endowed. The individual nought but foam on the wave, greatness a mere coincidence, the rule of genius a puppet show, a ludicrous struggle

against an iron law that to grasp is the utmost, to control is impossible. No longer do I have the slightest intention of bowing to the strutters and gawkers of history.

Included in this revised *Hessian Courier* I would like to see a precise analysis of the fact that in this country, due to some mysterious protocol, democrats and socialists on state visits are received with labored courtesy and crowned heads and royal visitors with overwhelming cordiality. Is it any wonder that students, in the process of acquiring a new awareness, protest against this protocol in the only way open to them: by unrest and categorical rejection? Why should they feel obligated to show a courtesy that this mysterious protocol would like to force upon them with the aid of police pressure? In the Federal Republic, progress is in any case impeded by matters less of fact than of protocol. Even the discreet wording on invitations —"dark suit" or "informal"—constitutes a massive pressure. Who is to tell me what is dark or what is informal? As for massive threats such as "black tie" or "tuxedo," perhaps these are not even worthy of our sarcasm. Who dictates to us, who manipulates us, who gives us unwritten laws? Must we be surprised that our young people's protest is expressed in the way they dress and wear their hair? How else but by unrest, by unambiguous protest in the form of dress and hair, are they to express themselves, since the voter's little X, which confers responsibility and no longer offers any alternative, is not enough? Let me quote the young Büchner again, this time from a letter to his family:

What I believe is this: if anything can help in our time it is force. We know what we can expect from our princes. Every concession they have made has been wrung from them by force.... Young people are criticized for the use of force. But are we not in a perpetual state of force?

I find myself unable to separate Büchner's aesthetic relevance from his political immediacy. One might well regret the failure of history to provide for a meeting between two Germans: Büchner and Marx, only a few years his junior. In all its grassroots power, its material realism, the language of *The Hessian Courier* unquestionably has a political thrust matching that of the *Communist Manifesto*. Büchner's instinctive certainty in recognizing and depicting social realities extends seamlessly from *The Hessan Courier* to his plays, prose, and letters; and this instinctive certainty in the awareness of social realities on the part of Büchner the poet, the natural scientist, and the political writer might have made it possible to avoid many of the literary errors and detours of Marxism and to mitigate the sufferings of later Marxist writers. Perhaps this encounter that history failed to bring off could be effected posthumously by confronting the idealistic aesthetic of Marxism as practiced today with Büchner's material realism, since Büchner was a contemporary of Marx and would have been no mean ally. Büchner's work, and all he has to say about it, is dominated by neither prudishness nor its opposite, but precisely by this desire for material realism. Referring to *Danton's Death*, he writes to his evidently shocked family:

> ...but history has not been composed by the Almighty to be read by young ladies, so no one should take me to task if my play is equally unsuitable. I cannot turn a Danton and the bandits of the Revolu-

tion into virtuous heroes.... I could, of course, be censured for choosing such material. But this objection was refuted long since. Were it considered valid, the greatest poetic masterpieces would have to be condemned. The poet is not a moral preceptor: he invents and creates characters, he brings the past to life.... If one thought *thus*, one could not study history because it depicts many immoral things, one would have to walk along the street blindfold because one might see indecent things going on there, and one would have to cry out against a God Who has created a world so full of vice and profligacy. And were I to be told that the poet must show the world not as it is but as it ought to be, then I would reply that I have no wish to surpass our Heavenly Father, Who has no doubt made the world as it ought to be.

The name of Georg Büchner, ladies and gentlemen, compels me to express my gratitude in this way, from the unquiet perimeter of our time, from a point where confidence begins to crumble and self-confidence is impossible, whence criticism may be misinterpreted as annoyance—as if it did not demand the inclusion of oneself. There are some other relevancies in Büchner's life and work: the problem of emigration, discernible in his correspondence with his friends and family, notably with Gutzkow; and the medical relevance of Büchner, no less important than any other, as expressed in his *Woyzeck*.

Had I the remotest resemblance to Büchner or Danton you would not have had to listen to this address. For Lacroix said of Danton, "Sheer laziness. He would rather be guillotined than make a speech." And Büchner, in a letter to Wilhelm Büchener, writes:

I am in quite good spirits, except when we have a steady downpour or a nor'wester. I must admit that I am among those who, at such times, on retiring for the night and having taken off one stocking, are capable of hanging themselves on the bedroom door because it is too much trouble to take off the other one too.

And so, having touched on laziness, to which Büchner obviously was no stranger, we might move on to a wide field: his humor. This could be as grim as it was tender, and it was undoubtedly present even when he had lost it, as was probably the case when, after emigrating to Zurich, he received the letter from his Alsatian friend Boeckel in which one passage begins: "In Germany I am quite happy: it is not half as bad as you think...."

On August 20, 1968,
Heinrich Böll happened to arrive
in Prague at the
invitation of the Czechoslovakian
Writers' Association.
Thus for four days he was
a chance eyewitness to the
occupation of Czechoslovakia
by Soviet troops.

THE GUN
WAS AIMED
AT KAFKA

(1968)

It was audible, visible, tangible, yet impossible to grasp. Early Wednesday morning someone knocked at the door of our hotel room and shouted, "We're occupied!" For a moment I thought he wanted to cancel an appointment, although the time and method of letting us know seemed somewhat unorthodox; besides, the tone of voice was too emotional for any conventional announcement. Before we could take in what it was all about we heard the first shots, and the words "We're occupied!" acquired their true meaning. The shots were live, and numerous, and they swept us back twenty-three years and a few months. The shots declared categorically: Europe knows no peace, it exists in a state of varying armistices. Here, in Prague, an armistice was being broken.

Simultaneously with the memory of machine guns and mounted cannon firing in the streets came the instinctive actions of self-preservation: get away from the window, look for cover, in the corridor, in the bathroom. How smoothly we slipped back into it all. The hotel opened out onto Wenceslas Square, the firing sounded close. Somewhere glass shattered, for somewhere each bullet, half-spent though it may be, must hit and penetrate something.

Our son wanted to be out there, *now*, and we let him go. He wasn't looking for adventure or thrills, he just had to be there, *now*. We could understand this, and we let him go, unafraid but apprehensive. A little later we went out too, found him, and stayed together. For two days his ears hurt. Soviet soldiers had fired past his ears into the air. He might well have passed one of them in Moscow, Leningrad, or Tiflis, on the street, in a theater or movie, on the beach near Riga. Now they were firing past his ears into the air, in Prague, and not *only* into the air. No, this wasn't the movies or TV, no cameras were being turned here; these weren't extras, these were soldiers in action, shattering sentimentality, and here in Prague sympathies were being shattered by order of the Soviet Government.

The fate of Czechoslovakia was decided that Wednesday around the Wenceslas Monument, in front of the Museum. Politicians probably always think dualistically: subjection or armed revolt. They would have preferred the first, they had presumably allowed for the second, they had not expected a third: a permanent, solid front of resistance, unarmed. This third power, often imagined, was born Wednesday, August 21, 1968, in Prague, and within four days it had become a giant. It too was audible, visible, tangible, yet impossible to grasp; a new creation, and it created many new things; it was full of passion, power, and imagination, forever beyond the grasp of today's breed of Soviet politician. Might it have been possible to withdraw immediately, leaving the brutal action behind like a bad dream? It was the declaration of bankruptcy of Soviet diplomacy, of the secret service, and of

Muscovitism. Each hour that the tanks—incredibly—remained, another year of trust was lost, so that by eleven that night the level of trust had dropped to roughly that of 1953.

With staggering audacity, waving the Czechoslovak flag, the young people leaped onto the tanks and defiantly rode along on them shouting, "Dubček, Dubček, Svoboda!" When the tank crews retreated inside and closed the turret hatches, the young people opened the hatches and dragged the men out of their "ivory towers," to confront them with unsentimental reality—and to engage them in argument. Certain things they may have accepted grumblingly in the past now turned out to be useful: a knowledge of Russian and a training in dialectics; and I imagine —I hope—they sowed the seeds of doubt. This third power was a new creation, and it created many new things: at least one European flag regained meaning, and here in Prague the worn-out word "freedom" was recharged. Even monuments became acceptable again, and the gospel of democracy was proclaimed.

Now and again, in its efforts to struggle free, a tank resorted to an ugly weapon: the driver would rev up the motor to full speed, and clouds of gasoline fumes would envelop Wenceslas Square in a blue fog. Tank columns would ostentatiously drive along side streets, crushing cars against walls, reducing curbs and traffic islands to rubble. Their brutish message could have been spelled out: The stupidity of arms is triumphant.

At the hotel people carried on "as usual." The waiters were as courteous as ever, seldom showing any signs of nervousness even when the firing echoed right outside the hotel. When someone at the next table asked for white

wine, the waiter said, "All we have left is red!" and it
sounded as if for the time being he couldn't stand the
sight of red. In the overcrowded hotel the guests remained
calm. No evidence of panic. Perhaps it was the population's solid front of self-confidence that reassured them.

Journalists were "in their element." Were they really?
I thought about the difference between journalists and
authors; the two men who combined both, Hemingway
and Fontane, both war correspondents, were not much
help. It seems that one doesn't exclude the other, but even
less does one include the other. One journalist told me I
had been fortunate. I didn't think so. I would gladly have
gone without this misfortune.

It still defied one's grasp. Even three days later, when
we were crossing Wenceslas Square late one evening, a
pale, bespectacled young man led us over to the tanks
parked in front of the *Prace* publishing offices. He shook
his head, raised his fists in impotent rage, drummed them
against a gun barrel, and wept as he muttered over and
over again, "*Je suis Communiste, je suis Communiste!*" He
apologized for being a little drunk, "*un peu ivre.*" It was
obvious from his breath that he had been drinking methyl-
ated spirits.

There was no alcohol in the city. All bars, cafés, restaurants, churches, museums, movies, and theaters were
closed. Whoever decreed and enforced the strict ban on
alcohol deserves the Nobel Peace Prize: he could not bring
the Czechs and Slovaks total salvation, but he did manage
to prevent total disaster. A few hundred drunks in the
city and the permanent simmering point could not have
been maintained. The permanent confrontation would
have turned into battle fronts. So fury remained cold, a holy,
hungry, desperate soberness. During these days the leg-

endary soldier Schweijk died from want of beer. Jan Nus was present. The Czechoslovaks wanted their Communism both ways: socialist and democratic. Just as for centuries Rome had callously consigned Catholics to a diet of dry bread, so Muscovitism was now consigning the Czechoslovaks to the aridity of the one and only socialism.

It was a marathon council from which the responsible parties were absent and where only the victims confronted each other. And both sides were in fact victims: the population and the Soviet soldiers. The ugliest feature of the whole event was that two historically innocent groups were forced into mutual inhumanity. Both devout, both deeply wounded in their trust, they might conceivably pity one another but on no account might they put this pity into practice. The unthinkable—to join hands against the brutality of the undertaking—would have been the spirit of revolution, the true salvation from counterrevolution, and perhaps if there had been Dantonesque Soviet marshals...but then most of them must be Napoleonesque. It was an imperialist, hegemonic action, yet the Soviet soldiers did not seem imperialistic. I searched the faces of a great many of them: they were not at ease, not nearly as at ease as the German soldiers had been when they invaded Prague and Paris during World War II. Although they may have been raised to believe in the infallibility of the Kremlin (I have my doubts as to the "success" of this education), they have not been raised to be imperialists. Their choice was between going mad or committing suicide, and I wonder what goes on inside people who have faced this choice for three days? No one would have taken them in. A soldier who cannot choose to desert can only cling to his weapon. They were neither exultant victors nor convinced occupiers; they were in an inhuman position—just like the people of Prague, who might "theoretically" have offered them tea, bread, and water and the use of their toilets. Here there was no more "theoretically": everything was concrete. And it had to be that way. Twice I saw Soviet soldiers being offered cigarettes during a heated discussion; they accepted them, and in the acceptance there was more humanity than in the offering, which was not so much a sign of friendly feeling as an automatic gesture of debate. Besides, a cigarette is not the same as a piece of bread; it is a piece of nothing, and bread is still a symbol.

An elderly lady was walking her dog, a Soviet soldier tried to make friends with it, looking for "humanity" at least in a dog. The elderly lady whistled her pet to heel; not even the dog was to collaborate or fraternize. This was not cruelty, it was consistent realism; it was not a studied action but a natural reaction. Only the innocent can be that harsh toward one another. The guilty always find some way of making others believe that their corruption is humanity, whereas in fact it is sentimentality. Thus, when a general is taken prisoner, it is usually an action carried out among gentlemen. Innocent victims cannot afford this luxury, they turn nasty because they suffer everything at first hand. In a state of emergency no one is exempt. I believe that this has been applied for the first time to the full and with inexorable realism during these four days in Prague. Those who believe in democracy don't think in terms of privilege. The democratic principle must have been particularly alien to the Soviet soldiers; their society, including their army, is a society of the privileged—like our own which, in its V.I.P.'s, creates its new aristocracy while continuing to idolize the old.

Prague was in a state of emergency, and the population claimed no exemptions and no privileges. Nobody complained of the beer shortage, of the lineups. Friends offered us food for fear we might not be getting enough to eat at the hotel, whereas, absurdly enough, the hotel waiters apologized on the second evening because there were only four hors d'oeuvres, the third evening only one: stuffed tomatoes with smoked salmon. Any attempt to reverse the situation and take out food from the hotel would have been defeated by the people's pride. Yes, they were proud: this was another word that had been given new meaning. The madness of a privileged existence in a luxury hotel was respected without grumbling or envy, while at the same time this existence excluded the foreigners, the tourists. It would have been quite natural, and not in the least unreasonable, to commandeer the kitchen of some hotel, with the cooperation of managers, chefs, and waiters, to supply meals to the third power. But there simply was no revolution, hence no counterrevolution. Foreigners remained locked out and locked in with their privileges. It was the proud, holy, democratic, sober, solid resistance of realists, unique in Europe, unprecedented in history.

Very occasionally someone who was not a hotel guest would come in from the street, exhausted, to relax in the lobby over a drink. In the hotel there were all kinds of alcohol. A Czech poet sipped his bottle of pilsener, neither melodramatically nor voluptuously, but realistically, sacramentally, reverently. "Irony is dead," he said on leaving. His eyes had lost the gleam of Schweijk. Outside the building where Kafka was born stood a tank, its gun barrel aimed at the bust of Kafka. Here, too, symbol matched reality.

A drunken worker staggered past the hotel steps, shouting, "Communism is dead! They haven't rescued Communism, they've destroyed it!" He was surrounded and escorted to safety. There seemed to be a tacit understanding that the occasional drunk be protected with gentle force. The simmering point remained constant, the third power had triumphed. And over and over again there were the women and girls arguing with the Soviet soldiers, trying to convince them, pale, beautiful in their wrath and their courage, insistent and determined. Yes, she existed all right, the "woman of Prague," and now that monuments have reacquired meaning I hope some day one will be erected to her—in Prague. She is fair, slim, passionate, utterly unfanatical, yet fiery, and she is realistic, democratic. She wants to live, not under capitalism, not under the hegemony of dogmatic aridity and blindness; her realism is of the earth. I could wish for her eyes to have laser beams.

In the hotel lobby someone enlightened me as to the dialectic of humanity, the leniency toward criminal Stalinists with whom accounts were not to be settled until the Party Congress in September. Even the murderers among them were being handled with nothing so rough as kid gloves: they were being carefully dabbed with swabs of soft cotton to spare them even minimal pain. A pale, blonde Prague girl at the next table said quite distinctly, "They still haven't found a quisling." And the man I was talking to said, "What's more, in 1956 there were no Czechoslovakian troops in Hungary." He went on to speak about the Catholic Church in Czechoslovakia, which now, after years of suppression, was proclaiming solidarity with a Communist regime and intending to remain propertyless, with not so much as a wistful backward glance at a bygone feudalism. Counterrevolution?

In four days and much of four nights spent in the streets, on the telephone at the hotel, in private homes, I never once heard a word to warrant the pretext, "counterrevolution." Needless to say, those who believe that socialism is defined in Moscow may bow to the dogma of the infallibility of the Central Committee. The day the Cierna conference took place, Rome published the *Encyclica Humanae Vitae*. Soon there will be Catholics who no longer heed Vaticanism, and I hope that Western Communists publicly, and many Eastern Communists secretly, will no longer heed Muscovitism.

At a former partisan's home I was told the story of Heinrich, the German Communist who parachuted in to join the Czech partisans during World War II, and twenty-four years later, in March 1968, arrived in Prague wearing the uniform "of those we fought against side by side," offering his support against the counterrevolution. His offer of assistance was declined with thanks. "Now I suppose he's sitting somewhere outside the city and waiting. If he turns up here, I won't know him."

The third morning, the waiter, unasked, brought us each two eggs with our breakfast, saying something like "Take them and eat them. Who knows what there'll be this afternoon or tomorrow." This unexpected offer of eggs was further evidence of that sacramental realism which no longer distinguishes between symbol and reality. "Theoretically" the waiters would have been justified in treating us as totally superfluous parasites and spectators, but there was no more "theoretically," and hence no idealistic supersensitivity. We were human beings and entitled to breakfast. Nowhere was there any servility, merely an unquestioning courtesy.

When the younger waiters and busboys took off their tailcoats and white jackets they looked exactly like the young people outside who were leaping onto tanks, distributing leaflets and newspapers, greeting tanks with catcalls, and dashing around on their motor scooters. They *were* young people, they might just as easily have been students, workers, journalists, actors, or photographers. I believe that nowhere and never in Europe has a nation been so close to democracy.

I asked a Communist official about two vicious officials of the Writers' Association whom I had met in 1961. "Between January and June," he replied, "—and here again you have the dialect of our democratic humanity—they were kicked upstairs. Now they're sitting at home, hiding, not daring to go out, watching and waiting. Nobody will talk to them. Up to now we've gone easy on them. If one of them were to be appointed President of the Writers' Association to replace Goldstücker, he would preside over nothing but empty benches—maybe a few stooges would turn up, but even stooges have to hide more carefully nowadays than our legal secret radio transmitters."

The evening of the third day, the Soviet soldiers were faced with the worst ordeal of all: ridicule, a weapon with which they could not retaliate. On an insurance company's building, the inscription: "We regret our inability to insure Soviet soldiers against insults." Fictitious letters on posters: "Dear Ivan, come home quickly, Natasha is already sleeping with Kolya." Even more malign: "Dear Ivan, Dad has sold his felt boots for booze, your uncle has been eaten by a bear. Hurry home. Love, Mama." The first field kitchens were rumbling through the streets in the darkness. It was the evening when suddenly all street signs, all house numbers, and all nameplates were removed in Prague. It was done very quickly, word being passed from house to house and acted upon immediately. I was in someone's apartment at about seven that evening when another tenant in the building gave the word, and my host at once stepped outside his front door, unscrewed his nameplate, and tossed it onto the hall table. Next day, the only house numbers and street signs I could see were on the building where Kafka was born and in the streets near by. The tanks were parked too close.

Among intellectuals the chief topic of conversation was whether to stay or not. The word "emigration" was taboo, besides being inappropriate. Those who had emigrated from Germany in 1933 had reason to fear the "man in the street" and the neighbors. In Prague democracy was born "in the street," and one's neighbors were democracy's staunchest support. Rumors of arrest were not confirmed, and yet: How far would they go? What lay ahead? Stalinism was at the door, visible and tangible. Its methods had not been forgotten. Would Dubček, Svoboda, and Cernik stand for it? As yet no one knew what *they* had had to stand. Trust in them was unshaken, but what and how much would they be able to endure and for how long? Politics behind closed doors, with tanks at every street corner, outside every ministry, every newspaper office, every radio and television station. Both alternatives unthinkable: to demand the suicide of a whole nation, or: compromise. The situation was unprecedented, the third power—whose solidarity would surprise even those returning from abroad—was also unprecedented. How could politics behind closed doors establish contact with this third power? The question of emigration remains open and will continue to do so for a while yet, because the situation is unprecedented, because the "man in the street" stands behind the intellectuals, and it is not inconceivable that he, the man in the street, might prefer to know that his intellectuals were out of the country rather than in the country and in prison. And what about wives, children, mothers, grandmothers, and mothers-in-law? Perhaps, perhaps, perhaps an as yet invisible third power will demolish Muscovite infallibility: perhaps—but when, when? Perhaps the monument to the woman of Prague is being cast during these first three days, to be sunk for a time in the Moldau, in whose honor Brecht wrote one of his finest poems and which Soviet soldiers were using for drinking and washing, the men who, "theoretically," had not deserved to be ridiculed.

On the fourth day the Soviet soldiers would hardly talk to anyone, nor would they allow themselves to be filmed or photographed. The sun was shining, it was Saturday. Many Prague citizens were out for a walk. We were out from seven in the morning until eight at night. Lists were displayed outside the houses, signatures were being collected for the new, illusory catchword "neutrality."

We got hold of a taxi and were driven around the sights; it was like a bad documentary on Prague: Hradcin Castle, Loreta, view over Prague from the stadium, past the Belvedere (tanks blocking the entrance), to the ghetto, to the synagogue, to the Faust building; close by, St. Ignatius' Church was open, and we went in. The taxi driver was courteous, spoke German, and was well informed. He casually mentioned that the Soviet Union owed Czechoslovakia 450 billion crowns for uranium, Dubček was asking for this money now in order to restore the economy, that was why there were tanks in Prague. I felt a bit jittery when he drove through an intersection under the very nose of the evening tank patrol. We walked the rest of the way.

The Jan Hus monument on the Altstadt Ring had been blindfolded. A young man, obviously a West German and not a journalist, was caught photographing it. A Soviet soldier crossed the square from the Hus monument toward him as he stood in the colonnade. Holding his machine pistol to the young man's chest, the soldier demanded the camera. The soldier looked uncomfortable. We felt uncomfortable. I would have handed over the camera at once, even at odds of a hundred thousand to one that he wouldn't shoot. It is so easy to press the hair trigger of a machine pistol, if only through tension. I advised the young man to hand over the camera. He refused. A group quickly formed, and the Soviet soldier, surrounded, became more and more nervous. He was a nice-looking lad, sensitive, and obviously acting on orders. A handsome young gypsy woman pushed up the barrel of his machine pistol so that it no longer pointed at the young man's chest but at the door of the Týn Church. At the same time she was shouting angrily at the soldier, no doubt to the effect that this was no way to behave, to point a gun barrel directly at a person's chest.

Two more sentries were dispatched across the square as reinforcements. They looked less sensitive. A young Czech asked the young man in German, "Do you really have a camera, and did you use it?" "Yes," said the young man. "Just hand it over to him," I said. The young Czech said, "I don't think he should." My wife said, "Why don't you show him your passports?" We did. This caused delay, easing of tension, confusion. The young Czech talked, talked, talked insistently to the first soldier in Russian, while more and more gypsies gathered round with their children. In their dark eyes I saw something for which I would have given several hundred cameras: life, and the joy of living. Suddenly the sentries turned on their heels and walked back toward the Hus monument. They had failed to carry out orders, and I have no doubt they will have received at least a reprimand, probably worse. The young man had kept his camera. The gypsies were beaming. I shook hands with the young Czech. My wife and I then both found that our knees were trembling. For the first time in twenty-three years and a few months we had once again seen how senselessly someone could have died. And all because of a camera. I had no use for the young man's "courage."

We sat down on a bench, under trees, in the sunshine, on Saturday afternoon. People were sitting there peacefully, only a few paces from the tanks. A boy had come out with his pet: a little owl. He wore a broad leather armband with a chain attached to it, and the little owl jumped on his head, shoulders, and arms while the neighbors children stood around. I envied the boy—an owl is something I have always wanted. Strange: somehow, undeniably, "one" had got used to the tanks. People sat quietly on their benches, smoking and chatting in subdued voices. Children clambered around on a jungle gym, played in the sandbox. The slogans on house walls had become cruder; to put it politely, the fecal and anal elements predominated. A tank soldier replied in phallic terms: with an unmistakable gesture he sat himself astride the gun barrel and gave a coarse laugh. Only one person laughed with him, the others were too tired; or maybe they felt embarrassed.

The only people left in the hotel were journalists. They stood on the steps in front of the hotel, waiting. A group of new journalists arrived. They were tired and hungry; you could tell at once that they were old hands at "trouble" of all kinds. By the elevator two Americans recognized each other. "We've met before, haven't we?" "That's right, two years ago in Saigon." "What d'you think—is this going to be a European Vietnam?" Shrug of the shoulders.

The elevator came. The elderly operator was a living image of "better times." Gray-haired, sensitive, courteous, unobtrusive. A relic of the Hapsburg days. He might have been a cabinet minister or a cultural attaché, but in a democracy who can tell? Maybe he really was an elevator operator by profession. He accepted tips calmly, but that proves nothing: cabinet ministers sometimes accept tips too.

Sunday morning the hotel lobby was almost empty. In a baronial armchair a girl sat printing slogans on waste paper. She looked in need of sleep, her makeup a trifle smudged. It was quiet, sunny, and down here in the lobby the firing—already part of the morning ritual—sounded more remote. We had long given up moving back from the window at the sound of shots. We were reluctant to leave, but our Czech friends insisted. The correspondent of *Der Stern* took us to Smíchov station. We had no trouble getting there—driving between tanks.

Much kissing, much weeping, at Smíchov station. And for the first time since Tuesday evening there was beer. People were standing in line at the station buffet and going off with their pint mugs. From Prague to the German border there wasn't a single tank to be seen from the train. Just two soldiers at a level crossing somewhere. Was Czechoslovakia really occupied? The forests of Bohemia are deep and vast, the villages so quiet. At Pilsen many passengers rushed to the station buffet to turn their last

Czech crowns into pilsener beer and came back with six, eight, ten bottles.

Beyond Pilsen, in the lovely river valley, we looked in vain—as we had done on the way to Prague—for the little station of Malovice which had figured so prominently in my wife's family stories. Her father had been a lawyer with the state railway in Pilsen, and the family had spent much of the summer in the waiting room at Malovice, or deep in the woods, by the little river, collecting mushrooms, and their Czech grandmother would tell them stories and bring home flowers and herbs from the forest, once even a crow. There were two trains a day, and with the evening train the engine driver used to bring my father-in-law a mug of beer from Pilsen. It can't have been very far from Pilsen, for according to tradition the foam was still on the beer. It is probably on a branch line. We didn't find it on the way back either. Like a dream it remained buried in the Bohemian forests. Like a story by Božena Němcová.

In our compartment were two Czech matrons chatting in a mixture of Czech and American. They were elderly but still had that pinkly gleaming platinum hair, those crazy gingerbread glasses, too-conspicuous underwear, and embarrassing décolletés. I wished they were wearing headscarves and shawls and steel-rimmed spectacles, like the Czech grandmother in our family photos. They would have looked much prettier.

There were other Czechs on the train, too, even some emigrants. At the border not a single suitcase was opened. But every hollow space in the compartment was opened up and a flashlight shone into every last corner by a plain-clothes official. And the water tanks were tapped and all the toilets minutely searched.

HE THAT HATH
EYES TO SEE,
LET HIM SEE!

(1970)

Let me start by confessing that I am not particularly fond of coffee-table books, whether they present Danish, Soviet, American, German (West or East), or Czechoslovakian achievements: well-snapped, well-lit splendors, leave me somewhat cold. But I do have some appreciation for the fact that peoples, nations, states, communities, and business enterprises like to show off what they have wrought or what they have inherited: the astounding Kremlin or the entire city of Leningrad, Cologne Cathedral or the Roman cellar of that city; the treasures of Italian towns from Verona to Palermo that can be counted off like the beads of a rosary. Then there are the economic achievements: stud bulls, automatic rolling mills, fist-sized potatoes, spanking new buildings, subway tunnels, and the mandatory look at the flourishing night life. There is much that is childish about this pride in showing off, like a boy proudly bringing home an A from school and placing this documentary evidence of his achievement on the table, as much as to say, "Aren't I smart!" Backs are patted and prizes distributed, faces beam with pride and pleasure, and the whole thing—whether a city elder or a factory manager has a decoration hung around his neck, or the boy with the A is given some money for an ice cream—has something touching about it. Don't politicians and industrialists also bask in a kind word of recognition?

We could meditate endlessly here on the meaning of "representation" in the sense of presenting the typical and the prestigious, and supply a detailed appendix on the points system, but I will spare myself and the potential reader. The prominent, i.e., the conspicuous, is often prestigious but seldom typical, regardless of whether the prominence is literary or political. Since I have already made one confession, let me add another: I find the Kremlin magnificent, Leningrad exquisitely beautiful, the Hermitage indescribable (both as a building and a museum), and from time to time I enjoy going down into the Roman cellar of Cologne. For when we go sightseeing we can do what we should indulge in to the full when we are away from home: we should walk around, and everywhere we go we will meet people, so that the sights, while being "seen," remain secondary. A coffee-table book such as this one is bound to consist of straight A's, like the model student's report card. However, model students are as problematical as their A's, as the entire system of achievement and grading. If, for instance, I were obliged to hand out grades I would give an A to a boy who had only 56 mistakes in his dictation instead of 110, although no doubt with 56 mistakes he would, "objectively speaking," deserve an F.

So much for my confessions and preambles. I have a hunch that many painters, authors, and filmmakers feel the same way and that this leads to a great mass of misunderstanding, hurt feelings, denials, slander, and smear campaigns. Privately, of course, an author or a painter is entitled occasionally to feel sentimental—to the point of tears even—but what he creates must never prompt sentimentality. It may move people, may even move them inwardly in the sense of that much-maligned word "emotion," but make them feel sentimental? No, never! There are certain artists who do evoke feelings of sentimentality, the school of genre painters, for example. Emotion is something else. Nothing in and about Moscow is sentimental, nor in and about Cologne, that much-maligned city blessed by the dirt of millennia, but there is much that is moving.

Given the time and the opportunity, plus a good, highly sensitive cameraman and plenty of good color-sensitive film, I would like to make two movies. The first would show the crowds on the streets of Moscow, a movie with some two million stars and no tourist attractions to "show off" the city in the traditional sense. I might, inconsistently enough, permit the Kremlin occasionally to peek over the shoulders of the crowds on Moscow's streets and squares; in my movie you would not see a single car, you would see only pedestrians, that ever-flowing, ever-moving multitude of human beings which to me is not a "mass." It might even be enough to drive along very slowly with a camera, with one's back to the Kremlin, past the mile-long lineup of people waiting on Red Square for a look at the embalmed body of Lenin: first just the faces, then just the legs, the hands, finally the torsos; then again the faces. To most audiences a movie like this would be boring in the extreme because, although they have become little more than spectators, they have forgotten the exhortation, He that hath eyes to see, let him see!

Next, someone would have to make a similar film about

London, one about New York, about Berlin (East and West), about Rome and Peking: then one might have at least some idea of what is meant by "Soviet citizen," "Briton," "American," and so on. Idea for a Utopian movie: a million Soviet citizens strolling about in New York, a million Americans in Moscow, a million Germans in Peking. The only true, the only possible form of invasion, as well as the only possible kind of "understanding between nations," which ought one day to become an understanding between peoples.

Seen thus, this kind of picture book is certainly to be welcomed—as a means of opening eyes, correcting prejudices, and preparing us for future strolls in a country which to us is (and to which we are) still too alien. The survey of Soviet literature included in the book gives it a background that would be lacking in a mere series of photographs. Furthermore I am alway prepared to grant the Soviet Union and its peoples the handicap which they are consistently denied, although historically they are entitled to it: the extent of destruction, crime, and murder perpetrated on their soil between 1941 and 1945. This still-unevaluated handicap lifts to another level all that the Soviet Union has to show off, so that even its A's become more moving than sentimental. And if I wanted to make a movie showing only the faces and hands of Soviet people (I would probably have to forget about their legs: the subject of Clothing, Subsection Footwear, would require a whole sociology, philosophy, and theology of clothing that allowed for the East/West differential, so as to reduce to proper proportions the arrogance and snobbishness of Western audiences)—if I did want to make such a movie it would be only because I consider people and their faces to be the true sights worth looking at.

Given the same technical conditions, the second movie I would like to make would be about all the variations and stages of Moscow's spring thaw after a long hard winter; a film ranging between snow-white purity and that dirty, oily-yellow black into which something that may once have been snow piles up along the wide avenues leading out of Moscow. Aristocratic snow, proletarian snow, bourgeois snow, classless snow, holy snow, humiliated and insulted snow, snow on the streets and in the court-yards; a whole hierarchy of snow, pictured as it is left to lie in the relatively unimportant (in terms of traffic) side streets, trodden and driven into ice, while at the same time the great boulevards and "prospects" are kept clear of snow. Such a film, of course, would also have to show the solution to the fascinating technical problems posed by snow and ice in a city the size of Moscow: Where do we find the person responsible for ice and snow in Moscow —what is his name, what army of helpers does his bidding? Who has invented that equipment (slightly reminiscent of ships' propellers) with which snow is mechanically shifted onto conveyor belts and from conveyor belts onto trucks? Has he (if there must be decorations) ever been decorated? Does this prime bearer of responsibility stand, pajama-clad and with clouded brow, looking anxiously out at the night sky when he has just finished having the main streets cleared of snow and new snow is already falling? That snow-white, snowy innocence that probably draws a curse from his lips and makes him reach for the phone to mobilize the snow-removal trucks which, in threes and fours, in precisely staggered formation, liberate the great boulevards and "prospects" from this inconvenient innocence dropping from the sky?

The fascination of Moscow during the spring thaw is the simultaneous presence of various stages of winter: entire

mountain ranges of snow in back yards, like stockpiles
for a time of snow shortage, while on the streets it is
already spring. On shady streets women are hacking away
with crowbars at layers of ice eighteen inches thick, while
a few hundred yards farther on people are already sitting
about in the sunshine in the public squares; on those
streets you shiver, while a little farther on you take off
your coat. And finally the water: dripping from roofs,
flowing from sloping streets (following inexorable physical
laws) into lower ones, forming puddles, backing up at
blocked storm sewers; on the slightest unevenness of asphalt
or paving a little lake forms; from the massive roofs of
Moscow's Old Town women are pushing and shoveling
snow many feet deep, half of it turned to slush, down onto
the street, which has to be barricaded. Rivulets are formed,
their color and size depending on the gradient. The film
would conclude with the inevitable look into the storm
sewers where, now mixed with Moscow's street dust and
roof dirt, those gurgling masses of dirty water which once
were snow-white snow finally leave Moscow.

Measured by the standards of a realistic author, such
a film would consist of straight A's: an A for the chief or-
ganizer of the Moscow snow-removal commandos, A's
for the women shoveling snow off the roofs, for the men
guarding the barricades on the streets, protecting pedestrians from injury, and of course for the engineers who
designed and built the storm sewers and deliver up the
snow-become-water to its transitory fate. Such a film
would have to be in color and would, I fear, be regarded
as abstract, as nonrepresentational, although it would
contain no fiction of any kind, nothing but organized
material, what is commonly known as "reality." Maybe
such a film, which contained nothing invented, which
would be merely composed, would help correct some

foolish prejudices about art. Besides, it seems to me that the snow of Russia, the snow of Moscow, the snow of the Soviet Union, deserves a monument. The long hard winter may be regarded as a curse by many inhabitants of Soviet Russia, but twice it was a downright blessing—in 1812 and again in 1941. Finally—for materialistic rather than metaphysical reasons—such a film must pay tribute to the heavens that allow snow to fall whenever it becomes "historically" necessary. And both films, I believe, would be moving rather than sentimental.

Lastly, a few words about the authors and artists who insist on looking into the sewers as well: we are so ready to suspect them of wishing only to see the dirt, the slums, the crippled, the less desirable; the fact is that for them, strange authors that they are, something else is "representative," that intangible something we call Life and that means something different to each of us, just as reality means something different to each of us. Those authors, that special breed, who—actually as well as symbolically— insist on looking into the sewers, are the only true realists, even when they want to turn the materials of snow and Moscow into abstract films; city snow is destined to become water and dirty, a blessing for those who would rather not live in eternal, pure snow; wherever eternal, pure snow lies, life can only be lived under artificial conditions.

1 Belser Verlag, Stuttgart, 1970.

The search for a new realism as it is taking shape in the Federal Republic of Germany around "Group 61," around the periodical *Kürbiskern,* and around various small publishing houses and the "Cologne School" is no fluke; our literature has yet to discover the working world, let alone the world of the workers. Our war literature did at least depict the worker in a state of alienation: as a soldier. The difficulty inherent in an approach by our literature to the world of the worker has been demonstrated by the shameful debate over Max von der Grün, who suddenly found himself between the two blocs that evince an *interest* in depictions of the working world: between unions and industry; and we might take as a third bloc those who would rather see their own world depicted as alienated, or, one might say, *exalted:* those who live within it.

For decades we in the West (among whom I include myself) have treated socialist realism with gentle irony. Retribution has already set in, it will continue. The demand now shown in this country for authors, stage directors, and graphic artists from Poland, Czechoslovakia,

Yugoslavia, and the Soviet Union seems to prove that socialist realism—even if only as a hated dogmatic antithesis—has neither incapacitated nor emasculated those authors who have lived under its sway. Today the only remaining objectionable aspect of socialist realism seems to be the doctrinaire optimism forced upon it, an optimism corresponding more than loosely, almost literally, to that cry for a "sound" world that still reverberates in our own ears. And yet this cry for a sound world, for Christian art and literature, is merely a new form of the yearning for the Greek *deus ex machina* who solves all problems effortlessly and automatically. In made-to-measure Christian literature (that of Claudel, for example), grace assumed the role of this *deus ex machina*, usually to embarrassing effect, as embarrassing as the mandatory final optimism in the socialist realism of official imprimatur. The West, which continues unswervingly to declare itself "Christian," will not only experience its own bankruptcy but soon (and this is more important) be obliged to acknowledge it. Less than half a generation has passed since it left behind the age of its trusty Christian literature, and an age may very soon dawn that sees an attempt to appropriate Günter Grass, perhaps, as a great exponent of "the Western world."

Trends in art and literature may well reverse themselves: the Western world will tire of its "formalistic" games and seek a new realism. Pop, Op, and Happenings are way-stations in which the entire Western aesthetic, still dreaming of the Greek ideal, is turned upside down, and that is a good thing: to "disintegrate" is the first duty of artists and writers. The Eastern world will have to experience the whole gamut of "formalistic" games, it will be spared nothing (an artist or writer who is spared something or who spares himself something is neither artist nor writer), and in the end it will return to its great, its wonderfully discursive realistic tradition. Here as there, there will continue to be much infighting. In his heart of hearts every statesman yearns for the "sound" literature that confirms his policies, whether it be Christian, Occidental, grace-laden, or socialist realism, which is welcome to remain critical as long as it ends on an upbeat.

Solzhenitsyn's *Cancer Ward* may one day be seen as a link between the old and a renewed socialist realism, a model for the largely pathetic attempts at a new realism in the West. The objection of a number of Western European (and soon no doubt Eastern European) authors to the continued survival of the novel, arises merely from a misconception of their own position and potential: that they write poems in prose, a magnificently concise poetry of situation.

In reading *Cancer Ward* it must never be forgotten that the novel is placed in the year 1955, two years after Stalin's death, when the period of rehabilitation, the time of great hopes, was beginning. The two contrasting main protagonists are Rusanov and Kostoglotov. The first is by nature and character an opportunistic official, a specialist in questionnaires and interrogation, also an informer, a privileged person who suddenly—in an emergency, since time is short and Moscow is far away—finds himself placed in an ordinary proletarian cancer hospital. The deprivations he laments? His own private toilet: "If only I could use a private toilet! Oh how I suffer! The kind of toilet they have here! No partitions! It's all in the open." And as an author's comment on these lamentations, Solzhenitsyn's note in brackets: ["Using a public bath or toilet inevitably undermines the authority of an official. At his office

Rusanov, instead of using the common lavatory, went to another floor."] This man, who is suffering from a cancerous growth while at the same time being *himself* a cancerous growth in society, wails even louder, the gist of his lamentations being:

> During that wonderful, high-principled time, the years 1937 and 1938, the social atmosphere was becoming noticeably purer: it was easier to breathe. All liars, slanderers, overzealous enthusiasts of self-criticism or supersmart intellectuals had disappeared, shut up, lay low, while men of principle, reliable and utterly devoted, Rusanov's friends and Rusanov himself, walked proudly, their heads held high.

It can be no coincidence that at the end of Part I of the novel Rusanov's daughter Alla, a budding author who one suspects will be successful, says:

> "If an author has mistaken ideas or the wrong attitude, his sincerity merely increases the harmfulness of the book: sincerity is *harmful!* Subjective sincerity may prove detrimental to a truthful presentation of life. Can you follow such dialectics?"

These remarks are addressed to Dyoma, the patient in the next bed to her father, who has been humbled to the status of a proletarian patient. And it is to this fresh, vigorous, confident young Alla that Solzhenitsyn, ironically enough, gives the final word of Part I of the novel. To her father, tormented as he is by his malignant tumor and his malignant nightmares, worried by the possible return from the camps of those he has denounced, she says (and this is the very last sentence of Part I), "Don't worry about *a thing! Everything, everything's* going to be just fine."

Strangely enough, Kostoglotov, exiled in perpetuity to Ush-Terek, a miserable little place at the back of beyond, enjoys recalling his exile, his doctor friends the Kadmins, their dogs and cats; he meditates on the relativity of luxury and consumption (something probably worthy of meditation). Kostoglotov's return is probably being awaited by some other "Rusanov" who denounced him in the first place in order to keep the world "sound."

The cast of the novel is a large one: doctors (male and female), nurses, cleaning women, visitors. It is surprising how much the novel tells us about the conscientiousness of medical care in the Soviet Union—and in 1955 at that. It is a book full of bitterness but also of gaiety, and there is one thing I fail to understand: that it cannot or may not be published in the Soviet Union. To acknowledge that cancer really does exist on this earth should no longer pose a problem for even the most ardent advocates of a "better future"; and to acknowledge the existence of cancerous growths in society who are not writers but "Rusanovs" could have only a liberating effect on socialist realism and render its literature as "competitive" as Solzhenitsyn's novel. In its innumerable conversations the novel also reveals the immense thirst for knowledge of the Soviet citizen, who reads voraciously and is talkative to the point of garrulity. Isn't it true that one of the weapons against cancer is disintegration?

[1] As appears in the German version, *Krebsstation*. The quotations in this essay were translated into English by Professor Bogdan Czaykowski from Russian-language editions of Solzhenitsyn's book.

A series of questions was submitted by Manès Sperber[1] to several German authors, among them Heinrich Böll. It was left to each author to ignore certain questions, or to group several questions under one answer, or to deal with them from other points of view, as if they had been quite differently formulated.

DOSTOEVSKI—
TODAY?

(1972)

I

Q. 1—When did you first hear the name Dostoevski? When did you first actually pick up one of his books? Which one?

A. 1—It must have been 1934 or 1935. In those years there was a very well-attended series of lectures sponsored by the Society of Catholic Academics in Cologne, for which high-school and university students were offered tickets at greatly reduced prices. I probably heard the name Dostoevski during lectures on Solovyev and Berdyaev. Or I could have first heard the name from Reinhold von Walther, who was then living in Cologne as a Russian-language lecturer and translator. In this series there were also a few lectures on Eastern liturgy, given by a Catholic priest by the name of Tyciak. There was also at that time a movie called *The Brothers Karamazov*, which I didn't see myself but which my oldest brother told me about. Anna Sten played the role of Grushenka. I can't remember which of these was the first occasion I heard Dostoevski's name. The first of his books that I bought was in 1935, second-hand for a few cents. It was *Crime and Punishment.*

Q. 2—Can you recall what impressed you most deeply at that first reading? And what do you consider today to be remarkable about that same work, in terms of literature or otherwise? How much of it do you still remember?

A. 2—Raskolnikov himself did *not* make the strongest impression on me; he seemed to me like an idea, highly abstract, like a necessary construct required to provide a background for all the other characters—and even his deed, the murder, seemed to me unreal although it was planned and carried out with the utmost degree of criminal sophistication and for a while could be kept secret. On the other hand, everything else in *Crime and Punishment* seemed very real, probably because it enabled me to identify the Marmeladov milieu, which I very soon rediscovered transformed into the milieu of the Micawbers in Dickens: a decaying petty bourgeoisie with that specific hysteria which is a kind of self-protection. The most impressive characters were Sonya, Svidrigailov, Razumichin, Raskolnikov's sister, the examining judge—and the nameless petty-bourgeois type who occasionally accosts Raskolnikov on the street. I should add that I have since reread *Crime and Punishment* several times and that my first impression is now, of course, mixed with later ones.

Q. 3—When you first read this book you were no doubt familiar with other works, particularly by German writers. Did you find any similarity in content or form between Dostoevski and other authors? Or did he seem to you unique?

A. 3—I didn't know many other authors, not even German ones. I knew Wilhelm Raabe, Theodor Storm, a bit of Goethe. They all seemed to me rather insipid compared with Dostoevski. The first German authors who seemed to me—this was one or two years later—on a level with him were Kleist and Hölderlin. I knew the Grimm brothers' fairy tales, some of which, of course, have demonic dimensions. When I read Dostoevski for the first time he seemed to me unique as a writer. I then bought his collected works from a cheap junk catalogue, a sort of pirate edition with no date or place of publication or translator's name and very poorly printed: that was in the days when our chief reading in German in school was *Mein Kampf*—accompanied, incidentally, by highly ironic comments from our German teacher.

Q. 4—When you first started to write, did you feel influenced in any way by Dostoevski—perhaps in the choice of subject, of form, in any particular treatment of main or secondary characters?

A. 4—It was soon after that, in 1937 or 1938, that I myself started to write. The material for my first stories sprang from the familiar milieu of the steadily declining petty bourgeoisie, which in self-protection indulged in irony, hysteria, and bohemian poses. My father was operating a sculptors' and carpenters' workshop in a typical nineteenth-century tenement with courtyard and rear buildings—the Marmeladovs and Raskolnikov could have lived there, gloomy and run-down as it all was. There is no doubt that my first attempts at writing were influenced by Dostoevski —but there was also another influence at work, a completely opposite one. At about the same time we discovered G. K. Chesterton—his witty Catholic elegance was so totally different; then again almost simultaneously we discovered Bernanos, Bloy, and Mauriac; the "inside" tip-off in terms of contemporary German literature was Ernst Jünger's *Marmorklippen*. All these authors were heatedly discussed not only among my family but also in Dr. Robert Grosche's study—Dr. Grosche being a priest who had been banished from Cologne and was in turn one of the discoverers and translators of Claudel.

With all these remarks, the historical background must not be forgotten: by now we were eighteen, nineteen, twenty, and of one thing we were sure—there was going to be a war, and we would be caught up in it. The Brownshirts were marching in the streets. Under those circumstances many authors paled, and we were left with Dostoevski, Bernanos, and Bloy.

Q. 5—Many years have passed since you first read Dostoevski. You must be familiar with his entire oeuvre. Many of his books will have retained a permanent presence for you: which are they? And why those particularly?

A. 5—*The Possessed* and *The Idiot*. *The Possessed*, if only because I have never been able to forget the description of the murder of Shatov since I read it in 1938—but also because, after my experience of more than thirty years of history, it has become both a classic and prophetic model of the blind, abstract fanaticism of political groups and trends. It is an accurate prediction of what we now call Stalinism. *The Idiot*, because of the two "rivals," Myshkin and Rogoshin, and also because of Katharina Ivanova, the object of this "rivalry." These three figures made me realize that the opposite of "healthy" is not "sick," but "suffering." I read *The Idiot* at a time when a political ideology of health was being propagated in Germany in every possible variation. Ever since then, the "healthy person," a person who does not suffer, has seemed to me to be the worst kind of monster—just like the "healthy instincts of a people," and "healthy art."

Q. 6—Many literary critics and essayists have insisted that Tolstoi and Dostoevski must be regarded prototypically as different if not contradictory. In that case: which of the two do you feel closer to? And why?

A. 6—Certainly the two are prototypically different and contradictory, and yet there can be no doubt that both were Russians, wrote in Russian, expressed "Russianness." I see them as complementary: Dostoevski was what Tolstoi always wished to be—close to the people—assuming here the Russian concept of "people." Dostoevski came from the people, lived with the people, the people were, in the very broadest and only possible sense, his "material." Tolstoi sought the people whom Dostoevski took for granted. Since I don't *have* to choose between them—both being available—I find it hard to imagine which one I would choose in such a hypothetical choice. Perhaps right now I would choose Dostoevski—at another time maybe Tolstoi. It seems to me that a person has alternately his Dostoevski period and his Tolstoi period.

II

Q. 1—Your own work reflects our age with its troubles and dangerous contradictions, with its tendencies toward faith, its doubts, and its aggressive lack of faith. In your opinion, is Dostoevski one of those writers who has dealt in depth with the fundamental problems of humanity, that is to say, present and maybe future ones too? Or do you believe that in feeling and judgment he was too closely associated with time, people, and country?

Q. 2—If you feel that Dostoevski has dealt with the essential problems, wouldn't you conclude, in view of the uniqueness of his creations, that he is timeless just *because* he was so deeply involved in his own time, and that his humanity was universal just *because* he was never able to divert his gaze from Russian humanity?

A. *1 and 2*—Just because he was so deeply involved in time, people, and country, Dostoevski is timeless, in other words constantly present. Perhaps this quality becomes especially apparent at this moment in history because Dostoevski was one of the first writers—if not the first—to accept the *big city* and its inhabitants, its proletariat, its petty bourgeoisie and officialdom as worthy objects of literature. His "poor people," his "insulted and injured," inhabit the big cities of our day in many social and national variations, and it is fairly safe to say that the fate of mankind will be decided in our super-cities. For Dickens the big city was still, despite all the misery he depicted, a romantic entity—Dostoevski was the first to describe the loneliness and alienation experienced by dwellers in the big cities; perhaps he could do this so convincingly because he lacked any kind of ideology toward rusticity or Nature. Poverty, miserable living conditions, usury, lack of social responsibility are, in their most blatant form, big-city problems—similarly the minority problem becomes more blatant in tenements and slums than it can ever be in the country. That which in the fifties and sixties of the last century was a novelty, almost sensational—"the big city in the modern novel"—has since become highly topical.

Q. 5—Dostoevski adopted the strongest possible stance against the revolutionaries, against atheism, against Western civilization. He was attacked from all sides as a reactionary, indeed as a minion of the Tsars. How would you judge his political pilgrimage today?

A. 5—I regard many of Dostoevski's political utterances as psychologically conditioned and relative. His attacks on atheism and revolution may have originated from his fear of himself. If we take his oeuvre as a whole, with all its characters, problems, and situations, it suggests an inner cosmos that must have frightened him and awakened in him a longing for the faith and order he never found within himself. To this extent many things may have been a reaction to the chaos within him, which he could keep in order and under control in his *novels* but which must have scared and driven him when he was not writing. In order to judge his attitude toward Czarism I would have to know what I cannot know: how he would have looked upon a czar like Nicholas II, an incredible, absurd, and tragic figure in Russian history. His anti-Westernism, as I see it, goes hand in hand with his anti-atheism. He must have sensed that the great godlessness would come out of the West, a godlessness hiding behind "Christian" governments, churches, a Christian industrial society, even behind Christian parties, a godlessness lacking that power with which Sonya Marmeladova is endowed: humility, of which Dostoevski says that it is "the most terrible force to be found on earth." If we simplify the "West" of Europe, which means including Germany both West and East, we can see it, through the eyes of Eastern Europe, very much as a "Christian world" that never seemed humble but always humiliating.

I regard Dostoevski's political pilgrimage—that which we might call reactionary or "Czarist minion" about him— as fear of himself. He had a criminal imagination and power of destruction that functioned with incredible precision: remember that he took his entire cast of characters from within himself. He must have been very lonely, frighteningly lonely and alone with this cast, which explains his search for order.

Q. 6—Dostoevski's hostility toward the West has also been expressed in his descriptions of his travels. No philistine could have written with less insight about Florence, Paris, and London. Moreover, he detested the Catholics, the Poles, French, Jews, etc. Do you think that, in assessing Dostoevski, one must take this strangely narrow-minded stance into consideration? Or may one ignore it?

A. 6—I don't feel that his acounts of his travels brand him as a philistine. He had no eye and no feeling for architectural showpieces, not even in his own country. He had hardly a good word to say for such an immensely beautiful and remarkable city as St. Petersburg—where he spent many years and which is the locale of many of his novels and stories—nor did he ever describe a single one of its attractions; all he does is mention them, list them, without ever describing let alone doing justice to them. The cheapest guidebook does better justice to the sights of St. Petersburg than does Dostoevski. The surprising thing is that he was trained as a draftsman and must have made architectural drawings and studied architecture. Yet not a word about the architecture of St. Petersburg. Nor did he have any feeling for social showpieces—generals, high officials and such appear in his works merely as supporting characters, usually ridiculous ones at that, likable only when they have come down in the world. In the same way, he was only interested in architecture when it was dilapidated. The great sights of Western Europe seemed to him arrogant, at times even a personal affront, as if they had been designed to give him an inferiority complex. The only work of art he respected, indeed revered, and for the sake of which he spent a long time in Dresden, was the Sistine Madonna—paradoxically enough, a work painted entirely according to the rational canon. My own explanation for his aversion to Western architecture, his indifference to all these treasures—with which his education must have made him familiar—is his sense of being a foreigner, of being under continual stress. He was nearly always on the run, you remember, and feeling constantly humiliated, whether by humble landlady or hotel doorman. My explanation for his occasional outbursts against Catholics, Poles, Frenchmen, Jews, and also Germans—Englishmen too, I expect—is his dread of humiliation: he probably suspected superiority in all these groups, and when he was not writing he must have been completely defenseless. Wounded, vulnerable, and ill, as we know. I don't see this as being narrow-minded, or as something to be ignored. He drew his own limits—confined himself, would not permit all those things to penetrate him.

III

Q. 1—It has been said that Dostoevski was first and foremost a religious writer. How would you define his particular religiousness? What does it mean to you? What might be the relationship between Dostoevski and those theologians who proclaim that "God is dead"?

Q. 2—It is possible that Dostoevski's particular kind of faith may have contributed to his habitual tendency, if not compulsion, to think up extreme situations from which his heroes try to extricate themselves by extreme deeds. There is hardly a single work in which the action is not marked by abysmal hatred, uncontrollably passionate love, violence, mayhem, and murder. How do you explain this extremism? What does it mean to you as a reader? And what as an author?

Q. 3—In Dostoevski, guilt lurks in every corner, but atonement can be sensed not far away and often determines the further development of the principal characters. Thus atonement and remorse are basic motives of this writer. This can be interpreted in psychological and biographical terms and/or regarded as a crystallization of fundamental religious ideas. What do you consider to be the determining factor here?

Q. 4—Dostoevski believed that the shibboleth problem of his time was godlessness, that the triumph of godlessness would provoke a disaster—which, incidentally, bears an astounding resemblance to the totalitarian destruction of human beings and their limitless humiliation in our time. Do you also believe that godlessness was the most important question—that it has remained so?

A. 1–4—It is not up to any of us to question Dostoevski's professed Christianity, yet we can reproach the author with his religiousness or dispute it. In his novels he expresses everything from the most profound faith to total nihilism. Both are represented *convincingly*—for instance, in Ivan Karamazov and Sonya Marmeladova—and both in many variations. As a Christian and as a writer, he never took refuge in a pretended order, he exposed himself and his characters to fear, absurdity, alienation, not in a geographical sense but in a metaphysical one, a sense in which even the Son of Man remained alienated. The world "rejected" him: that applies equally to Camus's stranger, or to Kafka.

Many of Dostoevski's characters are "strangers" or at least, in the final analysis, "estranged"—like the worldly Mitya Karamazov who, although innocent, was condemned. As long as human beings are "strangers," "estranged," or alienated (also in the Marxist sense), the Son of Man has not yet become Man: or, put theologically, not yet or not again arisen—in other words, "dead."

Most of the theologians who proclaim today that "God is dead" are merely stating that God (God-become-Man) has remained a "stranger." That wouldn't surprise Dostoevski, since it comes from Western Europe (as opposed to Eastern, where God is coming alive again), for in his eyes the "western God" was already dead. Myshkin's alienation, even that of Rogoshin—who seems so crude yet in fact is enormously sensitive—Katharina's alienation from both and from herself: that is religious writing, in the only possible sense. It is the destruction of iconology, of the canon of the "sound world" and the "sacred." Behind these many depictions of alienation there is the yearning for brotherhood, for redemption. The development of Socialism and Communism in all their facets seems to prove that this yearning is impossible without God, the Son of Man become Man, no longer a stranger. It is no accident, certainly not a fad, that in the Soviet Union God seems to be "coming back"—He will be a brotherly God, humanized by the crimes and errors of dogmatized Socialism, a God without ecclesiasticism, without authority. In this way the Soviet Union, after a long Tolstoi period, may be about to enter upon a Dostoevski period—not, of course, in terms of the ruling powers.

This potential Dostoevski period would probably be as extreme as he was himself, only in reverse: powerless, apolitical, without hatred or murder—a "passion for God" directed solely toward mankind. It would fail to understand the "God is dead" theology of Western Europe, being ignorant of the context, also of the fact that our "God is dead" theology must be seen historically in the particular, extreme-Christian, extreme-capitalist, and extreme-godless trends of Western Europe. This new Russian "passion for God" would be far more likely to find allies in the United States. It is related to, perhaps even originates from, the vast mass of monstrous suffering—to this extent I regard it as Dostoevskian, because for him suffering was only reality, because he foresaw the suffering. A Dostoevski any further projected, further developed, would result only in an extreme: extreme humanity as the conqueror of alienation, the conqueror of domination. Godlessness as propagated in the Soviet Union was merely a consequence of the domination of the Russian Orthodox Church in its ecclesiasticism, in the domination of the "vicars of God," of the "proclaimers of God," for whom guilt and atonement were principles of hegemony like *divide et impera*. (The almost total extinction of the practice of confession in the Roman Catholic Church indicates that this principle of hegemony is no longer effective in it either.)

Hence the shibboleth for West as well as East might well be "godlessness," not the godlessness feared by Dostoevski but possibly one concealed in his work—particularly in *The Grand Inquisitor;* for men must become "godless" when they feel the atheism of the "Christian" hegemony, which is never humble, merely humiliating. Probably many people—atheists and "atheists"—sensed the humility in Pope John, that most terrible force to be found on earth—and people even sensed this at third or fourth hand via television, press photos, etc. Maybe he was the first Pope of the "godless," one who would no longer tolerate any form of humiliation: neither of the Jews, nor of the Protestants, nor of the godless.

Q. 5—As we know, it was Dostoevski's project—which he kept undertaking and invariably regarded as a failure—to write the great novel of the repentant sinner who becomes both sage and saint. Staretz Sossima was just such a saint, the sinner Stavrogin was meant to be one. Perhaps Dostoevski, had he lived longer, would have finally achieved this goal. Do you believe that nowadays a theme of this kind would even be "viable" for literary purposes? That in terms of literature the saint can be made a convincing figure? That it might be possible to identify a modern revolutionary, for example, with a Dostoevski saint?

A. 5—I believe that Dostoevski has succeeded—although personally he may not have acknowledged it—in writing this great "novel of a saint" in *The Idiot*. Myshkin is the most humble of all Dostoevski figures, and at the same time endowed with the utmost sensitivity and insight; rather than "full of understanding" he is full of insight. His epilepsy (a condition from which Dostoevski also suffered) gave Myshkin insight into the background to crime, compassion, sin, guilt, insight into something as intangible as innocence. Myshkin is the boldest attempt in literature to give concrete form to the Son of Man as the fellow-sufferer. Myshkin is full of a sense of reality and yet unworldly. He is anything but a stranger, he is poor and rich, he is loved and ridiculed, he is tormented, threatened, misunderstood.

As for "saint" and "sinner," I regard them as entirely "viable" for literature. But these concepts, as well as their iconological background, would have to be discussed at length. Our entire culture, so it seems to me, was largely determined by iconography and iconology. Hero is merely another word for saint; our traditional iconography and iconology have their origin in myths and legends, the Christian "lives of the saints" were merely variations of myths; the rediscovery of antiquity and of heathenism— from an art-historical and literary point of view—is merely a reversion to older iconolatries. I fancy that Vincent van Gogh was the first painter to destroy the canons; perhaps Dostoevski was on a similar path. Meanwhile, even the "non-hero" of modern literature has already become a hero again because he lives off the negative cliché and, what's more, feels quite comfortable. With the exception of Myshkin, Dostoevski's heroes and saints are still too strongly motivated by idealism. The materialized and materialistic hero—the Son of Man is always concretely material—has not yet been found; he would have to be neither iconological nor anti-iconological but self-evident —there are heroes and saints of such material and materialized self-evidence in the works of J. D. Salinger— offhand I cannot think of anyone else. If "material" as an adjective is no longer equatable only with soulful or "soulless," heroes and saints once again become entirely "viable."

IV

Q. 1—Some say that Dostoevski was a master psychologist who modeled his characters with the utmost psychological perspicacity and depicted them as the disturbingly complex creatures they are. Do you agree with this? If so: to what extent is the contemporary novel *in this sense* psychological? Or is it instead anti- or apsychological, since it often ignores all but certain aspects, sometimes even fragments, of its characters? And would this mean that Dostoevski must be banished to the dumping ground of anachronisms?

Q. 2—Others are of the opinion that it is quite mistaken to interpret Dostoevski's characters psychologically and that they should be regarded within the context of a mythology. To put it more plainly: the main characters are neither types nor persons conceived as having an individual psychology, but rather extreme concretizations of an *imago;* not individuals but outright human beings as reflected in a broken mirror whose splinters have not yet fallen apart. If this be the case, would you agree that Dostoevski was one of the first to create that type of hero who is virtually indispensable to the philosophical as well as to the essential or existential novel, but certainly not to the realistic or naturalistic novel?

Q. 3—In the philosophical novel, the hero's passion is normally directed not toward the beloved person, nor toward power or money, but toward an idea. Can Dostoevski's novels be called philosophical in this sense? Isn't this contradicted by the fact that money and greed play so great a part in so many of his works? We have only to think of *The Gambler* on the one hand and *A Raw Youth* on the other. In both cases, however, greed is highly problematic; yet almost every one of his novels contains a character obsessed with greed. Raskolnikov kills not from greed but to escape the humiliation of poverty and to find a path to freedom. Smerdyakov kills to escape humiliation; others dream of doing it. Would you then say that the claim of idea-oriented passion remains valid?

A. 1–3—Since psychology as a whole was not developed to its full impact until after Dostoevski, I feel that the word "psychological" evokes too many scientific associations which could lead to misunderstandings. I imagine that the classic separation of body and soul also harbors a *divide et impera,* like that implemented by traditional aesthetics in the classic separation of "form and content." In the Christian tradition of Western Europe, people of all denominations have been conditioned to "save their souls," to keep them "pure," constantly to "purify" them, and so on. It is this tradition that makes any discussion of the soul so embarrassing; for in the final analysis I see all that massive advertising for soaps and detergents, in which (at least in this country) the "conscience" is constantly being appealed to, as the ultimate destination of this tradition of purification of the soul. I don't know enough about the Russian Orthodox tradition to be able to say whether or not it attaches the same importance to the "pure soul." In washday advertising—in all advertising, in fact—I see psychology being corrupted: either being exploited or, contrary to its intention, proving exploitable. No doubt pharmaceutically-minded cynics would wish to prescribe a powerful tranquilizer or an analysis for those hyper-emotional and hysterical women, Marmeladova and Katharina Ivanova. This is precisely the analysis undertaken by Dostoevski the writer because he is so thoroughly familiar with the souls of the people he has created, as well as with their bodies. In my opinion, every author lies hidden in all his characters, they are the sum of his soul and his body, a sum that cannot be added or divided, since no one—not even the author—knows the mathematical factors involved. The sum total of Dostoevski's characters represents his cosmos, in which he is familiar with, among other things, their souls. So I don't see Questions 1 and 2 as alternatives, since I recognize no contradiction between "psychology" and "mythology."

In fact I see a relationship between Dostoevski's unclassifiable religiousness, his "psychology," and "mythology." It goes without saying that he anticipated both existentialism and the absurd, the whole alienation of mankind, its agony and its passions—one of which is money, a "matter-non-matter" as rational as it is irrational. Money is as abstract as it is real; it is dirty, clean, and divine. It is nothing if you can get nothing for it, and it is everything that you can get for it. Present ideas about money are too bourgeois: we don't mention money, but we have it, and we earn as much of it as possible—it is despised as being dirty, yet it is worshiped. In Dostoevski I discover a new, truly proletarian conception of money. For him it plays almost the same role as Moby Dick, the white whale, did for Melville: Dostoevski and most of his characters are forever running after it and never have it. Political economists always believe, and always assume in their predictions, that money is something calculable. There are few things—actually none—that are *only* rational. This is a root error of the classic godless figure of the nineteenth century and of the godlessness of capitalism: that they turn money into something unreal, hidden in accounts rather than transformed into "bread and wine." There is hardly a letter or diary entry of Dostoevski's that does not mention money—not one hero in his novels who is not concerned with money, most of them being either extremely poor or extremely rich; and that is no coincidence. I fancy that Dostoevski, in describing himself as a proletarian writer, actually envisioned a money proletariat; money was part of his religiousness. I don't believe that greed is the right word; rather—and to our surprise— might we apply what young Marx wrote about money— and a further unexpectedly relevant author, Leon Bloy, who looked for the metaphysics of the proletarian relationship to money and to the godless who administer and render it abstract. Money, too, harbors a *divide et impera*, the separation of form and content, a bourgeois aestheticism that resulted in the worst forms of humiliation, and that has even permeated the strike-disagreements of our own day. It is still considered uncouth and vulgar to mention money—let alone in public. Dostoevski talks about it openly and publicly—I fancy it was for him a part of God-become-Man. Consequently I don't regard the passion for money on the part of many of his heroes—or his own personal passion for money—as an idea, as a philosophy. There may be philosophies of money that I don't know about. There is certainly no theology of money, probably because theology has so far been a "masters' theology," and masters need not talk about money, even when they have none. They can even afford to be poor, to remain pure. The pose of purity and cleanliness as demonstrated in the liturgical washing of hands is the classic pose of nonsolidarity, for all men must get "dirty" by handling money except for those who wash their hands in innocence.

Q. 4—What work written now, in the late afternoon of our century, could pass as a Dostoevski novel? By you, for example?

A. 4—This novel could only be written in Russia, in the Soviet Union, by a person who has experienced not covert but overt godlessness, who could feel compassion for the godless without accusing them. It would have to be a novel in which no one is humiliated, hence a novel without satire, irony, or hatred.

Q. 5—To which of Dostoevski's characters do you feel so close that you could depict that person's brother or sister in one of your novels—appropriately transformed as a contemporary?

A. 5—There are several. Myshkin, in *The Idiot,* and Rogoshin—and of course Shatov and Kirillov in *The Possessed,* also Katharina Ivanova. At the moment I would feel closest to Lizaveta, the feebleminded sister of the woman pawnbroker murdered by Raskolnikov, because in today's discussions about abortion, about birth control, I sometimes—not always—rediscover fascist ideas of euthanasia, of which Lizaveta would most certainly have been a victim. The destruction or prevention of "unworthy life" is one of the great humiliations of our age.

Q. 6—Raskolnikov, Myshkin, Dolgoruki, Stavrogin, Ivan and Alyosha Karamazov—how, what, would each of these be today? This foolish question is aimed at the claim that every one of them exists today, is living among us, but has assumed completely different forms of expression and appearance, in life and in literature. Which forms?

A. 6—Of course they all exist. Alyosha Karamazov has changed his sex, he is a young girl in a Moscow suburb who feels compassion for her philistine surroundings while at the same time feeling solidarity with them; she even has dark, sparkling eyes that one might think were fanatical if one didn't take a closer look and discover that she also has wit, even humor. She has lost her job as a teacher because she has not only displayed her religious feelings too openly but has even tried to pass them on. She reads a lot of Florensky, also the Bible: in spite of her philistine surroundings she does not feel alienated, she has friends. I don't know what will become of her; she ekes out a living by giving lessons and doing short translations, she doesn't despise money yet is by no means materialistic, nor is she idealistic. I have no fear for her because she has none herself. Perhaps it is Stavrogin who sometimes pays her a secret visit, just as a certain Nicodemus secretly visited Someone else. Stavrogin is a fairly senior member of the Faculty of Philosophy and is also a candidate for the Academy of Sciences; he earns a good salary but is too shy ever to bring the young girl anything: tea, chocolate, flowers, maybe some cigarettes. He takes her for an idealist, he is smart and sometimes laughs wickedly—but he isn't smart enough to know that she would accept a gift from him because she really is hard up and a small package of tea would be welcome. She would not consider that humiliating. Sometimes Ivan Karamazov also comes to see her, when her friends meet at her place. He has studied mathematics, lost an arm in World War II, was arrested at the end of the war because he criticized as being unsocialist the manner in which Germany was occupied, conquered, and the people humiliated: he spent ten years in a prison camp but did not resume his studies after his rehabilitation—he has a small pension, is modest in his requirements, also taciturn, and now and again he makes a bit on the side as a reader at a music publisher's. Some people believe he is an informer; his smile is somewhat pained whenever anyone reads aloud from the Bible.

[1] *Wir und Dostojewskij: Eine Debatte mit Heinrich Böll, Siegfried Lenz, André Malraux, Hans Erich Nossack, geführt von Manès Sperber.* Hoffman und Campe Verlag, Hamburg, 1972.

About the Author

Heinrich Böll, winner of the Nobel Prize for literature in 1972, is one of the most prolific, and most popular, of postwar German writers. Since 1947 he has been widely acclaimed for his novels and short stories, which have focused principally on the Second World War, its aftermath, and the havoc it wreaked on the people of Germany; his fiction constitutes a "working-through," not merely a remembering, of this horrendous Nazi experience. A master storyteller, Mr. Böll is in the first rank of contemporary European writers. Among his many books previously published in this country are: *Billiards at Half-past Nine* (1962); *The Clown* (1965); *Absent Without Leave* (1965); *End of a Mission* (1968); *Group Portrait with Lady* (1973); *The Lost Honor of Katharina Blum* (1975); and *The Bread of Those Early Years* (1976).

Heinrich Böll is a past President of the International P.E.N. and in that capacity has been active on behalf of writers throughout the world. He and his wife live in Cologne but spend much of their time at their farmhouse in a tiny hamlet in the foothills of the Eifel range.